# CELESTIAL

S.E. ANDERSON

CELESTIAL




First published in 2018 by Bolide Publishing Limited

http://bolidepublishing.com

ISBN 978-1-9999529-9-0

*To Alix, To Cora, To Val,*
*My ground control, cheerleaders, friends.*

TITLES BY S.E. ANDERSON:

*Starstruck Saga*

Starstruck

Alienation

Traveler

*Novellas*

Miss Planet Earth

The Horrible Habits of Humans (Pew! Pew! - Bite My
Shiny Metal Pew!)

Miss Planet Earth and the Amulet of Beb-Sheb-Na
(Pew! Pew! Volume 4: Bad versus Worse)

Dark Star (From the Stars, Torment Publishing)

# CONTENTS

# CELESTIAL

BOOK 4 OF THE STARSTRUCK SAGA

# CHAPTER ONE

## *SALLY WEBBER AND THE TEMPLE OF DEATH*

The day I ran out of Prozac, I landed in the Temple of Death, which is the worst possible way to start an adventure. Then again, I wasn't looking for adventure; I was looking for home and the temple got in the way. Buildings like that crave attention.

It started off as all good adventures do: with a sense of excitement and endless possibilities. Zander and Blayde, two immortals I somehow got to call my friends, Nim the boy we had partially kidnapped and partially rescued from a literal bubble society, and me—all four of us holding hands on the ship we had just saved, ready to be whisked away to another world, with me silently hoping it would be Earth. I was prepared for the interstellar atom shredder that was Zander's jump, a method of crossing space in the blink of an eye, though your eyes can't blink when they're particles on a cosmic wind.

The second my being was opened to the immensity of the universe, I was filled with a sense of meaninglessness. It was so powerful it made me want to shrivel up and out of existence. I felt empty. I felt lost. And yet—through all this—I felt like I was part of something bigger, something I could not yet comprehend.

Nothing compared to the first jump—the feeling of bliss that had come from being dragged through the rips in the universe, becoming one with everything around me—nor the pain of having it taken away again. Every jump since was easier, a smaller taste of those feelings, as I learned not to give myself up so entirely or so easily.

But none of those jumps had a temple in the way. Out of nowhere there was a shove, and just like that I was lying on cold stone, my head spinning.

I had never felt something physical in the space between the stars. I had never experienced anything other than the whole 'not being me' part. And how had I run out of breath when I hadn't stopped breathing?

I groaned and pushed myself up to sit. The world around me was dark, the air smelling heavily of mildew and mold. I clutched my chest, willing the pressure to dissipate, but the tightness grew.

"Arms ... fingers ... head, toes, shoulders, and shit, everything's here," I said as soon as my mouth allowed it. My body trembled from the shock and the pain. I had to calm down. I had to get my body straight.

And there was no answer.

My eyesight took an eternity to return. Fingers of

nothingness pressed against my eyelids. It was so dark I couldn't see my hands in front of my face. I couldn't see anything. I couldn't hear anything. Or maybe the room was windowless, lightless, everything-else-less.

I wondered, for a second, if I was still floating in the in-between space of the universe, if this was what death was like. The idea of being dead scared me a whole lot less than the thought of being alone.

I forced myself to my feet, my muscles screaming as if I had just run a marathon. Before I could even take a step, my stomach decided it was time to announce itself and I threw up.

Dang. I thought I had gotten the hang of jumping without retching. It's never a good way to start the day.

"Hello?" No answer. "Zander? Blayde?" Still nothing. "Nim?"

Nothing. Nada. Zilch.

I pushed my hair from my clammy face. First things first, I needed light. Then I needed to find my friends—assuming they were nearby.

I shuddered at the thought of where else they could be. Halfway across the galaxy, perhaps, with no way of reaching me.

My trusty iPod was in my pocket, and I pulled it out, turning on the flashlight and scanning my surroundings. The chamber was about the same size as my living room back on Earth, though entirely empty. Every wall was carved stone, and the air inside was stale but damp, with a definite salty smell and a hint of rotting fish. Lichen grew on the walls, adding a nice touch of green to the place. That explained the smell but nothing else.

The ceiling was too high for my light to reach, so either it was way up there or my iPod sucked.

This wasn't a cave; it was man-made. Or intelligently made. I wasn't too sure on the nomenclature.

Panic rose in my chest, and I focused on breathing, forcing it back down. An attack right now wouldn't help in the slightest. My control over my panic attacks was tentative but growing stronger. I was confident I could keep it at bay until I found Blayde and my meds.

"Is there anybody out there?"

I hadn't expected a response, and I didn't get one. My voice barely bounced off the walls; the chamber was that tight. I flashed the beam of light across the walls, desperate for a door. The room seemed smaller, closing in on me, suffocating me.

I had to get out. Now.

A new kind of fear filled me. One that threw me back to the look on Zander's face after I had run him over all those years ago. To the terror of being abandoned in a place he did not know, alone, with no idea where his sister was. This chamber could have been anywhere in the universe for all I knew, and I was alone.

And then my beam landed on something that made every drop of blood in my veins retreat. Because there on the wall, in nice bold, excited letters, were three words I never thought I would see on the wall of a mysterious stone chamber.

*Welcome, Sally Webber.*

"Sally? Are you in here?"

Zander's voice shattered my thoughts. Relief coursed through my bones, and I rushed forward. He had been holding my hand when we jumped, leading me through space until the terrifying shove had ripped us apart.

"Zander?" I sputtered, stretching out my hands.

"Sal! Hold on! I'll get you out."

The stones before me quivered and then slid away. The door had been hidden in the features of the wall. Now that it was in motion, it was so evident that I could have smacked myself for not seeing it.

And there he was: my immortal friend, complete with gravity-defying hair slick with dust and sweat, his skin tinted blue in the light of my flashlight. I flew at him, desperate for his reassurance.

"Zander," I said again, giddy with relief. I breathed in deeply, filling my lungs with mildewy air. "What happened?"

"I don't know." He touched his hand lightly to my cheek before pulling away again. Three words I hadn't expected to hear. "I haven't found Blayde yet, or Nimien."

"But what happened?" I repeated. "The jump? That . . . push."

"Let's find Blayde."

My heart dropped. Zander rarely avoided a question, not without a witty remark to distract me. He wasn't even trying to cover up his terror; something had gone terribly wrong.

The outside of the chamber looked the same as the inside: more stone, more lichen, no light. How Zander had navigated his way through without a torch was beyond me. He picked a direction seemingly at random, and I followed him, keeping my little iPod light on. This would kill what was left of my battery, and there probably wasn't an Apple charger for another thousand light years.

"What is this place?" I didn't know why I was whispering, but something about the cold halls clenched my vocal cords.

"It feels ancient," he replied, running his hand along the moss, "like a temple or something."

"Or a labyrinth. We're lost like rats in a maze."

"But rats like solving mazes."

"They do?"

"Why else do they make humans build them?"

I had no reply to that, or for anything else for that matter. But before I could even sputter out a reply, Zander threw out his arm to stop me.

"Did you hear that?" he whispered. I shook my head; his hearing was better than mine, anyway. "This way."

A few minutes later, I heard it too: a faint rustling and maybe footsteps. The soft fall of light feet against stone. And then the soft steps weren't so soft and weren't so quiet. Blayde appeared out of nowhere, her rainbow hair disheveled in the gloom, my duffel bag slung over her shoulder.

"Zander."

"Blayde."

"Heya, Blayde."

"Sally."

"Have you seen Nim?" asked Zander, giving no sign of being happy to see her. She shook her head.

"I haven't even found a way out. What *was* that, Zander?"

"I thought you might know."

"I don't." Short, direct, to the point. There was a sudden animosity between them or maybe a shared terror. It was hard to imagine something that could scare two immortals.

The three of us set off in silence, hunting for the last member of our party: Nimien, the boy we rescued from a life of indentured servitude to the Alliance, only to drop him in a mysterious maze, a labyrinth of twists and turns that led nowhere. Not a great way to make him trust us.

As we talked, we found a torch on a peg against the wall, and Blayde lit it with her laser pointer, giving us a better touch of light than my phone. I had been the only one of us three to appear in a chamber—Zander and Blayde had found themselves in a corridor, with Zander narrowly avoiding a booby trap; a large log sailed right for him when he appeared.

I whispered about my welcoming sign. They said nothing, but the air around us got colder.

We turned a corner, and there he was. Nimien was slouched against a wall, his back to us, his weight on his shoulder. The first time I jumped, I had fainted, though that was before I woke up and threw up on Zander's shoes, of course. Jumping was a shock to one's system, as I could attest to. Maybe Nim was going through the same thing. If being shoved during a jump had felt so awful to me, I couldn't imagine what it might have done to the kid on his first intergalactic time-space warping experience.

"Nimien!" I shouted, rushing to his side. He slouched forward, collapsing on the stone floor. Before I could reach him, Zander had jumped to his side, his face turning ashen.

"Did he faint?" asked Blayde, but as he fell back in Zander's arms, we knew the answer. I was afraid to move any closer, but I had to know.

Nimien lay motionless, his Alliance uniform stained in a thick, dark liquid. No noise escaped his mouth, not a whine or groan from those bloody lips. There were hardly any lips left; most of the skin on his face had torn away like it was nothing but cloth.

Not to mention the rest of his body. I never thought skin could tear so easily and thoroughly. His body lay in shreds. What had once been a brilliant young man with a genius mind was now a bloody mess. I turned to Blayde, her face as unchanging as the stone walls of the room.

Blayde crouched beside the two men, saying nothing more. She didn't look sad. She didn't look angry. She looked tired.

"What ..." I couldn't finish my sentence. My stomach lurched, and I leaned over as if to retch, but my stomach was empty.

That was when I saw the booby trap on the side of the wall: a gate of spikes that had swung back on its hinges and was dripping in red.

"Is he ..."

"He's still breathing," said Zander, his ear close to Nim's mouth, "but I don't know for how long."

Tears welled in my eyes. Useless. I was so useless. All I had wanted was to save Nimien from a life of servitude. Was that too much to ask? Was Nim destined to be ripped from his home, saved from the Alliance's child-hire program, only to be torn to shreds before he had a chance to see the universe?

Jumping was not an exact science, but there had been no faults with it in the few trips I had taken with the siblings. Well, except maybe with the fact that they had gotten me lost in the middle of nowhere in space, with no way to get home, and quite possibly years ahead of my life back on Earth.

Maybe I put a little too much trust in them.

Zander was my friend, though, and as such, I seemed to make excuses for him at every turn. But the truth was, if Nim died, he would take it personally. I had to save Nim. I was the one who had insisted he came with us.

I crouched by Nim's side, knowing my stomach was empty enough to handle seeing him like this. He wasn't dead, but he was close to it. His chest was heaving, but he was breathing all the same.

The tattered skin was too far gone, though.

"We have to do something." I wanted to put my hands on Nim and comfort him, but I was afraid it would cause him more pain.

"We can save him," said Zander, slowly, not taking his eyes off Nim.

"Absolutely not." Blayde glared at him. "It's too dangerous, we still don't know if—"

"I did this," Zander snapped. "Me. I convinced you he would be safe, and I jumped us to this… place. I have to save him."

"But we don't know the long-term effects." Blayde reached for his arm. He pulled it away quickly. "Zander, we can't do this. It isn't safe."

"We have to."

He looked up at me, as if asking for permission. I shuddered. I hadn't been following their conversation, not as closely as I should have been. My mind zoned out as soon as the possibility of Nim being saved was put on the table.

"Do what you have to, Zander," I said, "Please. Save Nim. He has to live."

He nodded slowly, once, twice. His eyes returned to Blayde, and she shook her head.

"He's in my care," he said. "It's my decision."

"Then he's your responsibility. Whatever happens, you will be held accountable."

"Of course." Zander looked down at Nim, delicately placing the skin where it should be. Nim didn't react. I don't think he even knew we were there.

"But ... what are you going to do?" I asked, my voice coming out in a faint squeak.

"I'm going to donate some blood."

What was I even supposed to understand about that? Was it supposed to somehow reassure me? Was he really saying what I thought he was saying? I wanted to call out and tell him no, that it was wrong, that Blayde was right; they didn't know what it could do to a person.

But this was Nim. He *had* to live. The universe was screaming it at me from every direction, as if it needed the boy alive at all costs. Though maybe it was the guilt gnawing at my stomach.

"What can I do to help?" I asked.

Blayde rifled through the duffel bag, and to my surprise, she pulled out a tiny first aid kit that definitely wasn't mine. From inside, she retrieved a bright yellow syringe, handing it to me. I hesitated, my hand hovering over the device, fingers trembling at the knowledge of what was to come.

Zander nodded. With one hand cradled under Nim's head, he outstretched the other arm, holding it out so I could pull his blood from the bulging vein. I looked down at the syringe, the arm, and my friend Nim dying on the floor.

"Remember, you're not going to hurt me," said Zander, his voice low and casual despite how serious the situation was.

"I know." I stuck the needle into his arm and drew out the warm crimson liquid, trying to keep my trembling hands steady.

He took the syringe from me then, his hand touching mine for an instant, filling them with warmth the same way that door had. He looked up at his sister. "I know you don't approve, but please. Take his feet. I'll owe you one."

She said nothing, but crouched down and clasped Nim's calves, holding them in a vice-like grip.

"Sally, you hold his head steady," he said. "Don't let him move."

I clutched Nim's head, my hands clammy against his bald scalp. Tiny hairs were growing there now, prickling my palms.

Zander drove the syringe into Nim's chest, but it was too late. He was dead. And it was my fault.

The three of us knew it was over, but no one dared say a word. My hands trembled as they clasped Nim's head. His skin was so pale, even under the torchlight. Nimien had stopped breathing, and by the look of it, he wasn't going to start again.

"Nim?" I stammered, brushing the sweat from his brow.

I knew he couldn't answer, but I wanted to hear his voice again. I wanted to hear the excitement he had been bubbling with when we promised to take him away from that ship. The same excitement I'd had when I was invited to see the universe.

But I would never hear it again.

Nimien was dead. Until, out of nowhere, his back arched.

# CHAPTER TWO

## *MORTALITY SUCKS, AND NOW WE ARE HERE*

Nimen's mouth flew open, and he gasped for air. My hands tightened around his head, the sweaty skin sticky against my palms. My eyes flashed to Zander, but he said nothing, entirely focused on the boy, holding him tight.

Nim was breathing. Where one second he had been dead, he was now shaking, snapping, breaking. I bit down on my lower lip to keep myself from screaming.

*Live, live, please let him live!*

"Hold his head!"

I clutched my hands tighter around Nim's scalp, not sure where the voice was coming from. His back arched again and then fell, hitting the stone floor with a heavy thump. He began to shake, foam building at the corner of his mouth, his body electric.

Zander forced Nim's hands down, but even without the flailing it was damn near impossible to watch. Nim was choking again, the foam flying, his head trying to wrench from my hands. It took all my strength to keep the skull in place and from slamming against the hard granite floor.

The muscles first, then the skin on his body, were beginning to stitch together. His face smoothed out, the skin spreading like spilled milk to cover the gashes in his cheeks. His torso went from having large red cuts to light pink stripes to just being skin again, as perfect as the day he was born. The hair on his once-bald head began to grow hair, pushing through my fingers until they were deep in a lush thicket of sticky, dark hair.

It lasted mere seconds, but it felt like a lifetime. His muscles gave, and the body relaxed in a jolt. As suddenly as it had stated, the ordeal was over, and it left Nimien still on the cold, hard ground with an expression of calm and serene sleep.

I removed my hands from his scalp, which was now so thick with sweat it was as if it had been held under a faucet. I wiped the foam from his mouth with the edge of my bloody Alliance uniform, feeling the hot breath escape his lips.

Nim was breathing. He was alive.

Zander and Blayde removed their hands with the same reverence as attendants leaving their king. Neither of them said anything. Like me, they were waiting for Nim to be in the clear.

His eyes fluttered open as delicately as butterfly's wings. He stared up at the ceiling, his breaths heavy. The pounding of his heart in his chest reverberated around and through us, echoing off the walls of the maze.

He rolled to his side and purged his stomach of its contents, most of which were a crimson red. It was only then that he turned his head to look at me, his eyes wide and bright, a beautiful brown so vivid I scrambled back in shock.

I had seen those eyes before.

Now I was the one shaking. Zander put a hand on his shoulder, which made Nim cringe. But the moment was gone, and my heart began to still.

"You're all right, Nimien," he said, calmly. "Your skin will be tender for a few days, but only because it's new. Now, follow my finger with your eyes ... please, Nimien. We need to make sure your brain isn't damaged."

Nim did as he was asked, staring intently at Zander's finger as he paraded it back and forth in front of his line of vision. Zander nodded slowly to himself.

"Good, the kid's alive," said Blayde, standing up and brushing the dust off her knees. "So now can we get cleaned up? Do some recon?"

"The 'kid' just came back from the dead, Blayde. Chill, please," said Zander as he helped Nim to sit up then eventually stand. Nim teetered a little uneasily on his nearly regrown legs, but otherwise he stood fine.

"What ..." Nim asked Zander, gripping onto him for support. He looked back at me, and his piercing brown eyes met mine. In an instant, I felt like I had recognized an old friend again, someone I had known and somehow lost, but I was shaking too much to say anything. Then, he looked away, and the familiarity vanished once again.

I guess my eyes were playing tricks on me. After all, I was scared and emotional, projecting. His eyes were his eyes and no one else's.

"Something pushed us in the jump," said Zander, calmly, though I could see his hands shaking in the gloom of the torchlight. "We ended up in this ... place."

"And then you triggered this bad boy," said Blayde, patting the bloody gate of spikes appreciatively. "Only booby trap in this whole place, and you get hit by it. Now that's what I call tough luck."

Zander shot her a look. "We're sorry this happened, but we did everything we could to help you."

"You tried to help me," Nim repeated. "How? What exactly did you do?"

I didn't know how to answer, and neither did Zander. Luckily, neither of us had to. Blayde, the eternal bearer of bad news, flew into the conversation with her magical words of wisdom.

"Oh, we jammed some of Zander's magic blood into you, though we have no idea what it'll do. Glad you're alive, kiddo."

"What? Please, don't call me that." Nim shuddered.

"Hey, we saved your life," she said. "I think that gives me a pass. Now, let's get going before anything else tries to kill the mortals."

"We're not going anywhere with Nim like this," said Zander.

"Like what? At peak health? High on immortality juice?"

"You're immortal?" asked Nim, looking up from his hands. He ran his fingers through his newly grown hair, pulling at the roots, his gaze sliding past the duo to land on me.

"They're immortal," I said, thrusting my index at the siblings, "and they're space travelers. I thought we covered this in orientation. I'm just here for the ride."

"Oh." He pulled away from Zander, standing alone now, and I realized that the hair wasn't the only thing that had changed in him. It was subtle but he looked stronger, sturdier. Ready to take on the world and anything it threw at him. He was even standing taller, almost as tall as Zander, and he radiated an air of confidence. It like he was emitting an aura that wanted to draw you in. I guess it was a byproduct of surviving death.

"I'm not jumping again," said Zander. "I need to rest. We all do. Let's ask the locals for some food, maybe a place to sleep, then be on our way. Okay?"

"If there are any locals. Hey, you owe me big time for this," said Blayde. "Veesh, it's as if you built a little army of mortals just so you could team up against me." She turned away, hiding her pout.

"We should ... I don't know, leave?" Nim turned to Zander. "The temple at least, I mean. I have a bad feeling about this. Something feels familiar. But nothing out here could be familiar to me, so I would take that as a bad sign."

"I don't want to jump anywhere until we're sure you're all right, Nimien."

"Well, time's a-wastin'," said Blayde, rubbing her hands together. "Let's go figure a way out of this stupid labyrinth."

"Wait, we're just going to walk out there?" asked

Nim, his eyes opening wide. "Without knowing what we're walking into?"

"He's right," said Zander. "Look what happened a few minutes ago. We should proceed with caution."

"And this is why I didn't want you to bring the humans, Zander!" Blayde said, crossing her arms over her chest. "We can't have any fun with these two getting in danger every five seconds."

"That's enough, Blayde. Come on, they don't want to be here any more than you want them here. You lead if you're so worried."

"Right, and you can pick up the rear. We'll keep the mortals from *mortal* danger. Is that all right with you, your royal highness?"

"That sounds fine," Zander replied coolly. "Thank you."

She harrumphed and spun on her heels, taking off down the dark corridor without a sound using the torch to light her way. Nimien didn't hesitate and followed like a bewildered puppy.

I said nothing, just turned my iPod light back on. As exciting as it was to follow the siblings around and join in with their adventures, they were life-threatening, as Nim's accident had just proved. I could die from pretty much anything, at any time, without ever going home. And while I had come face to face with death a few times in the past few days, I hadn't actually died.

As for Nim, while he was probably glad not to be working for the Alliance right now, he had been ripped from his home and wiped from the memory of his entire civilization. There was no home for him to go back to, and yet I was sure he would rather be there.

Even so, he was walking so tall, so confidently. The image of him bleeding out on the floor was still fresh in my mind, superimposing itself over my vision. But he was alive. And it was a miracle.

His head jerked every time he looked around, like a stiff puppet following along. A small curl of hair on his forehead shifted from side to side as he walked, like a comic book Clark Kent. He pushed it away.

"You know staring is rude in pretty much every culture, right?"

The voice in my ear was so close I could feel the breath raise the hairs on my neck. Zander had spoken in such a quiet voice, I doubted even Blayde could pick it up. We walked faster to catch up with the other two.

"How is this even possible?" I asked as Blayde led Nim down the corridor, checking around for traps. "How can he be alive? Nim was dead. I saw it."

"He wasn't dead *yet*. That made all the difference."

"You're not answering anything here."

"Let's just say I'm a universal donor and leave it at that."

He sped up again, not as worried about my wellbeing and mortal danger as he had sounded when he'd argued with Blayde. I couldn't tell if he was joking, but the tone was jovial; he wasn't trying to push me away or stop me from prying.

So, pry I would. "You're afraid, aren't you?"

"What makes you think that? And afraid of what, for that matter?"

"You've never done that before, have you? Brought a man back from the brink of death. You didn't turn him into a vampire, did you?"

"What is this with you and vampires?"

"Safe point of reference. And don't change the subject. If you need to talk, you know I'm here, right?"

"Thanks, Sally." He reached down to take my hand. I had forgotten how soft his skin was, pure baby new skin devoid of any scars and calluses he should have had from his line of work.

"So, you think this is Earth?" he asked, pulling his hand away.

"I doubt it. I've never heard of any temple mazes before, outside of Indiana Jones movies, that is. I think need my meds." The thought occurred to me as I forced the anxiety back down into my gut. I had been getting rather good at controlling my attacks, keeping them at bay—at least until I had time to process the anxiety and panic in a healthy way, which was a massive break-through for me. A combination of proper medication and an opportunity to confront my fears, perhaps. Extreme exposure therapy?

But when I pulled the tiny orange bottle out of the bag, I realized, to my heartbreak and dismay, that it was empty.

How had I not noticed? Somewhere between running for my life and falling out of the edge of space, it must have slipped my mind. My heart plunged into my stomach as I realized all my amazing progress was about to go down the drain. Not to mention I would have to go through withdrawal again. The last time I had gone through that I thought I was going to die.

"Everything all right?" asked Zander.

All I could do was nod. Twenty-four hours had passed since my last dose, and already, I could feel a trickle of electricity at the back of my brain, the feeling of being zapped by a small current. The withdrawal had begun.

The breeze sweeping through the hallway hit Blayde's torch, and the flame died out. We all froze, the surprise of it taking us off guard.

"We're getting close," said Blayde, relighting the torch and studying the new direction of the flame. "The exit must be near."

I experienced a sudden urge to walk forward, like I was caught in a trance. My feet ached as they took steps on their own, pulling me toward the torchlight. I wasn't the only one: All four of us stepped forward, curiosity piqued, caution already thrown to the wind. A surprisingly hot wind.

"Anybody else starting to get a little ... sticky?" asked Nim, wiping the sweat from his brow with the back of his hand.

But it was a dead end.

"Well, it's been a fun ride," said Blayde, "but I guess we don't deserve a way out of here."

"Why is Sally's name carved in the stone?" asked Nim.

I followed where his finger was pointing, and my heart dropped. Just like in the first chamber, a message was scrawled on the wall, left, apparently, for me. *This way out, Sally Webber.*

"Spooky," Zander agreed, gazing down at me, and I shuddered, saying nothing.

Out of instinct I didn't know I had, and still in the same trance-like state as before, I ran my hand down the cold wall, feeling tears of heat trickling down my face as I did. Only, there was a portion of the wall that wasn't cool. The heat came as a shock, and I yanked my hand away. Where my hand had been, a light glowed blue then faded away.

A light. Coming from inside the stone.

I put my hand back on the spot again. The heat grew, warming my palm, and the light spread from my hand and up the wall until an entire doorframe was surrounded with a soft blue glow.

*Speak, friend, and enter,* I thought wryly. But no words appeared. Instead, the thick slab of stone disappeared without a sound, and before I had time to think about how this was acting exactly like an Alliance doorway, I was hit by the smell of rotten eggs.

I had assumed it was coming from one of us, gross and tired from our experience on the *Traveler*, but as my eyes grew accustomed to the brightness, I saw the world in front of me wavering. The heat from something far below made the air outside shimmer, which would have been worrying in and of itself even if there weren't flecks of sparks and ash rising too.

"Place your bets now, people," said Blayde, dashing through the exit before any of us could stop her. She stopped, turned, and flashed us a sly grin. "Too late. I'm going to tell you. We're on top of a fucking volcano. Now, who guessed volcano?"

A volcano was probably the furthest thing from my mind. But now I was standing above the crater of boiling, bubbling lava and wishing I had a really good pair of shoes. Also, checking to see if Gollum had followed us here, as I certainly didn't want to get in a fight.

But well, yup, that's a volcano all right.

The smell of sulfur was overwhelming, and I threw my arm over my nose. The air seemed like it was on fire. With my eyes tearing up from the heat and the fumes, I turned back to the trio. Blayde didn't seem shocked about any of this. Per usual, she took everything in stride, as if it were an everyday occurrence to appear in a sealed room above a volcano. She looked gleeful as she stared into the pit.

"Right, well, this is pretty awesome," she said, indicating the lava. Her face lit up red from the heat. "Haven't been in a volcano in ages. So, Sally?"

"Um, what?" I snapped my gaze from the bubbling pit below.

"Is this Earth? Can we leave you here?"

"Earth or not, I would just love it if you left me on the side of a volcano," I replied, my sentence punctuated with a cough.

"But is it an *Earth* volcano?"

"How should I know? I've never been inside a volcano before!"

"Dammit, Sally, didn't you do anything interesting before meeting us?" she scoffed, glaring at me. Two of her favorite pastimes—dismissing and judging others—wrapped into one. "Can't recognize her own volcanoes. I guess that means we keep going. I want to find a civilization that has invented the steam bath."

"If there are people around," Zander muttered, not to anyone in particular and certainly not to his sister, "then it would be logical that they live near this place. The ground is more fertile, and if they are able to avoid the eruptions ..."

The only person who wasn't digesting this information with any kind of calm was Nim, who appeared to be having a minor anxiety attack. His mouth kept opening and closing, like he wanted to say something but couldn't find the words, while at the same time doing a great impression of a fish out of water. His hands had gone up to his scalp, clutching at the short tendrils of hair there, grabbing at the new growth. A new habit was already forming to calm his ever-growing nerves.

"Should we be ... doing something?" I asked, edging closer to Nim. "I mean, we can't stay here, right? It's not safe."

"Party pooper," said Blayde, who shrugged and made her way away from the edge of the crater. There was already ash on the bottom of her new dress. "Suit yourself. Let's get out of here and get some food. You doing all right there, kiddo?"

"Don't ..." the boy rasped, clutching a large rock for support, "don't call me that."

It was then that we heard the scream.

# CHAPTER THREE

## *CYBORG CYCLOPS FIGHT CLUB*

My head spun around so fast I probably gave myself whiplash. The scream had been shrill and terrified, the cry of someone fighting for their life. I saw her quickly, the only spot of white in the dark span of black rock; across the crater, the girl was wrestling a golden-clad man on a raised platform. A man who appeared to be trying to push her into the pit.

"Don't go anywhere," said Blayde before disappearing entirely. The sight of her vanishing into thin air was something I would never get used to. Seeing her reappear the same instant on the other side of the volcano was like something out of a science fiction novel.

"But... active volcano, much?" I shouted after her, but my voice was drowned out by a geyser of gas in the fiery pit below.

"You two should probably stay out of the way," said Zander, eyeing the situation from afar, obviously itching to go. His hands were jittery at his sides. "Blayde and I can handle this."

"I want to help!" Not that I was any good in a fight. I just didn't like the idea of being abandoned outside a mysterious temple with lava all around.

"By the time you get there, the situation will already be over," he promised. "Relax. Blayde and I have got this. Take Nimien and get a safe distance from this place. We'll meet up with you soon."

And then, he was gone. Of course. I should have been used to this by now.

"Oh, come on! You can't seriously be doing this again! How many times has that been a good idea?"

But it was too late. Zander had left me in favor of a good fight, and I would have to wait for him to find me. Again.

You've been with me so far, right? I told you about all the crap that went down when I got lost on Da-Duhui and when I walked away from the bridge for *one freaking second* back on the *Traveler*. So you know how trouble tends to find me when there's no one around to dampen it. And then my panic would find me, too, and we'd all have a happy party and a spiral of terror, but that was neither here nor there. Every fiber of my body told me to get out of this volcano, and that was exactly what I was going to do.

It was also telling me I was running on empty and about to crash. The slow tingles running up my arms were becoming harder to ignore, but there was nothing

I could do about them.

"Come on, Nim, let's blast this joint," I said, indicating the path before us in a feeble attempt to distract myself. It was gravelly and steep, but it was *there*, and we weren't going to lose anything by getting out of this heat. "It's too hot to think."

"Um-hum," he replied, his eyes transfixed by the fight on the platform. Zander and Blayde were battling a hoard of leopard-print-wearing men with spears, but they were hard to make out from this distance. Best guess was always that they were being badasses. They certainly didn't need me getting in their way.

No matter how much I suddenly wanted to.

Shit. Today's dose of withdrawal side effects would include a manic swing, not the depression I was expecting. This was going to be a thrill ride no one was ever going to forget.

"Do Zander and Blayde always get this kind of greeting?" asked Nim, somewhere between excited and sour.

"I wouldn't know," I answered, starting up the path. "We've never been in a place like this before. I mean, we've been in weird, dangerous places, but not in a volcano. Talk about being in the hot seat."

"Should we do something?"

"If Zander said to stay out of it, best we stay out of it." It was my turn to be sour, though—apparently, I had been given babysitter duty.

Well, that *had* been part of the agreement since the beginning. I just didn't think they'd take me up on it so soon. I had promised to keep Nim safe—a small price to pay to keep him free of the Alliance. I understood now what Zander meant by promises being hard to keep out here.

The path was steep and led up and around the crater, dangerously close to a hundred-foot drop into the boiling lava. My jittery legs wanted to run, but Nim's were newly minted and not the best for this kind of sport. I avoided looking down as I walked, just as Nim avoided making conversation. By the time we had reached the lip of the crater, we were both sweaty and covered in ash.

The outside world was beyond beautiful. Rich green grasses led down to a sapphire sea, a small coastal village along its edge, a luscious jungle to our right. It looked like paradise, or Hawaii, or maybe that island from *Lost*. Please, don't let there be any smoke monsters.

"Where... where are we?" asked Nim, squinting into the distance.

"Anywhere."

The two of us found the path down the mountain and found a grassy knoll to wait on, a place that would make us easy to spot, once the immortals had finished their badassery. It was quiet outside, the breeze gentle and delicate on our sticky skin. I put down my duffel bag, the only items from Earth I had by my side.

"Ha, look, they're already done," said Nim, pointing toward the volcano. I followed his gaze. The figure was hard to make out, and I squinted, straining my eyes.

"I don't think that's them. He looks a little big to be Zander."

"He's walking right toward us, though."

"Then let's hope he's friendly."

"Should we run?"

I waved my hands at the empty expanse. We were in the middle of nowhere. Running wouldn't get us anything but attention. I stood up straight and adjusted my now-bloodied Alliance uniform, almost absent-mindedly.

"I don't think there's any point," I said. "He obviously knows we're here."

I tried to make out the details of his body to see who, or what, we were dealing with. He seemed much bigger than the average human, and bulkier too. In the light of the midday sun, he looked a little bronze, and his skin shone like it was metal.

Or maybe it was metal. The closer he got, the more I realized it was an it and not a he. The man was not a man at all, but a machine, tall and looming and definitely bronzed.

And it was speeding up.

"Delay that last remark," I said. "I think maybe we should run."

"Seconded!" sputtered Nim, who turned and took off running faster than I thought possible.

The metal man began running, too.

I grabbed my bag and sprinted down the hill away from the creature, my hands pumping at my sides as my terror grew. Shit. Shit, shit, shit. Just my luck that we'd be on a planet with volcanoes and giant robots! Would I ever just get a pristine island paradise?

Nope. Probably not. I guess I had bad karma.

I tore down the hill, racing as fast as I could, barely stopping myself from tripping over my own feet. Nim had a head start on me, and the distance between us was growing. He was a fast runner. I, on the other hand, was the girl who ran nothing but Netflix marathons—but you already know that. Hashtag: Relatable. My heart pounded as I forced myself to run faster, the air burning my lungs as I inhaled. I was more out of shape than a toddler's playdough.

With one quick scoop, the creature knocked my legs out from under me. It tossed me into the air and caught me again, bringing me up to his eye level, staring at me with the intense, empty gaze of a machine.

And I do say eye level, since there was only one eye. Say hello to the cyborg Cyclops. Or the Cyclops cyborg.

"Put me down!" I ordered, swinging my fist at it, which resulted in sending a shooting pain through my hand when it collided with unflinching bronze. "Ouch! Shit!"

The Cyclops squinted as if it were scanning me. I struggled in its grasp.

"Remain still," it ordered. "Your termination will be completed more swiftly. This is for your own comfort and safety."

"Screw that. You're not terminating me any time soon!"

There was a scream—not mine—as loud as thunder, a war cry that pierced the peaceful air and rattled my ears. Then, with a heavy, hollow *clunk*, a vibration swept through the cyborg, enough to rattle me like a rag doll.

Nim was at the creature's feet, hammering at its leg with an enormous stick. He was slamming it into the metal over and over again, wielding it like a baseball bat, fueled by fury and rage.

"Get back, Nim. You'll get hurt!"

"I'm not letting it take you!" he shouted as the creature dropped its second hand to scoop him up, too.

Great. Now we were both trapped. Fantastic.

"Please remain still," said the creature. "Your termination will be swift and pleasant."

"How about *no* termination?" I spat.

"That is not an option."

"Any discussion on the table?"

"That is not an option."

"Fine, screw you then," I snapped, swinging my fist forward to punch it right in the eye.

The cyborg Cyclops let out a mechanical whirr, dropping Nim and me from its grasp. I fell hard on the ground and struggled to my feet, throwing my hands forward in a poor imitation of a fight stance.

"Run, Nim! I'll hold it off!"

If Nim argued, I didn't hear it. The adrenaline coursing through my veins made it sound like my heart was beating in my ears, blocking out any other sound there was. The cyborg made a blind grab at me, catching me with its arm and winding me as it spun me around. I dug my arms into the metal plates at its elbow, holding on for dear life.

When had I gotten so brave? Surviving my encounter with Doesso must have infused every fiber of my being with confidence I didn't know I had. Or maybe there was some instinct kicking in to protect Nim, but either way, I wasn't going to stop fighting this beast.

Maybe it was my brain struggling to dish out the right chemicals at the right moment. Who knows.

Now I wished I had spent more than a lazy half hour at the gym after New Year's. My biceps burned as

I tried to hoist myself up, but its arm was swinging around wildly and I couldn't get anywhere. I kicked, hitting the giant in the ribs with enough strength to make it take a step back.

The arm stopped for a second, and with incredible effort I hoisted myself onto its shoulder. Both robot arms tried to pull me off, but something was getting in the creature's way, distracting it and forcing it to try to be in two places at once.

*"Calm is advisable when facing your inevitable end,"* the cyborg intoned. *"Your extermination will be more tolerable if you process your emotions beforehand. If you do not have a licensed therapist, one will be assigned to you. However as one is not currently available, I must act as one. Now, tell me how you feel about your father."*

It was a cyborg, and I had seen enough sci-fi films to know that robots needed a power source to work. I just needed to find it, disconnect it, and stop the creature before it could harm Nim or me. Or anybody else, for that matter.

But I was ill-equipped for this kind of thing.

If I were Blayde, I would have my laser ready to rip into the wires of this creature's head. If I were Zander, I'd find a way to trip it up, put it at its mercy. I didn't have the gadgets, I didn't have the strength, but I did have small fingers and a lack of rationality. Not to mention a manic moment setting in.

I made a fist, took a deep breath, and aimed my bunched-up fist at the metal plate above its earhole. The plate gave away, showing an intricate set of gears and metal spokes.

What the heck? This thing wasn't running on wires

and circuit boards, but thinking and processing through *gears*? What was this, a steampunk island getaway? Was that a thing?

Grabbing the creature's thick bronze eyebrow, I pulled myself up to stand on its shoulder, balancing against its angered reeling, and kicked.

But before I could do any damage, the giant plucked me from its shoulder, as effortless as if I were a piece of fluff on the collar of a coat. I was forced to watch as the creature opened its mouth, opening it wider and wider and wider, wider than any mouth should ever go...

I shoved my feet out as it dropped me, my shoes slamming into the rows of metallic teeth, wedging it open and stopping my fall. The jolt that ran up my legs and into my hips was agony, but the monster had it worse. While I struggled to stay upright, my legs pushed into a split, steam spilled out of the seams in the monster.

It was trying to close its mouth, but I was too stuck in place for either of us to go anywhere. The steam spewed now, getting thicker by the second; my thighs screamed. And then, with one sharp jolt, it slung forward. I was thrown twenty feet into the air, coming down hard on my back just in time to see the light in the Cyclops's eye go out.

"*Please... terminate... expense reports,*" it said, then froze and fell, face first, on the green grass, its teeth biting into the earth.

I had taken down the Cyclops. Say hello to the new Ulysses!

"Sally!" shouted Nim, dropping his stick and dashing toward me. Apparently, he hadn't run like I had told him to. Again.

"Oh god, Nim, are you all right?" I asked, checking him for scrapes and bruises. But he was fine. There wasn't a scratch on him.

"I should be asking you!" His expression was somewhere between shock and awe. "You... you killed it!"

"It would have killed us if I hadn't." I forced myself back on my feet. I hissed as I stretched my legs. The fall had hurt like a real mother. Not to mention the burning in my thighs. I was going to have cramps tomorrow.

"The prophecy has been... fulfilled!" The voice rose through the air like a song on a breeze. I lifted my hands to my eyes, wiping out the dirt, blinking in the light. Was I imagining things?

No, I was not. I couldn't be imagining the entire army of people before me. People dressed in bright-colored clothes, warm togas, and sandals. And the cheering, there was so much cheering.

My head spinning, I turned to face them. At the head of the pack were two men and three women, all dressed in bright colorful togas sporting what appeared to be entire birds on their heads. The feathers had been wrapped in their hair so intricately it looked like seagulls had perched there, but only for a moment, and were about to take flight. They wore large gold bracelets up their arms, men and women alike, bringing out the brightness of their olive skin.

"Behold!" the woman dressed in blue said, marching toward us. "The goddess Selena has heard our cries and come to rescue us from damnation!"

She bowed low, the feathers of her head-bird

brushing my skin. I took a step back, trying to take it all in.

"You're making a mistake." I put my hand gently on her shoulder. "I'm just Sally. I..."

And then I saw it. How I hadn't earlier, I had no idea; maybe because I was fighting a giant Cyclops. It was only natural that I hadn't noticed how close I had gotten to the little town. To their temple. To their shrine.

My shrine because, lo and behold, there sat a bronze statue of me wearing my Alliance uniform, ten meters tall, hands extending in peace to the people of this world.

"Oh." I stared in wide-eyed terror at the monstrosity.

"Oh?" said Nim, looking back and forth between the statue and me.

I turned back to the crowd. They were no longer standing. Every single one of them were bowing, their faces kissing the dirt at my feet, eyes turned away.

Well, except for Zander and Blayde. They stood at the edge of the crowd with a scared young woman, who dropped to her knees the second I made eye contact.

Blayde dropped her face into her hands, which was exactly how I felt right now.

# CHAPTER FOUR

## *I GET MY OWN GOSPEL, MINUS THE SONGS*

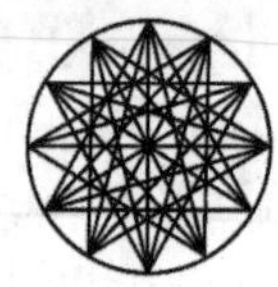

So, on Thursday I became a goddess, which made a lot of things better and many more things worse.

And apparently, a goddess didn't have a lot of personal space because it went from silent bowing to excited "hoisting of this stranger over our shoulders" very, very quickly. Before I had any idea what was happening, I was high above the crowd and being marched into the small coastal town.

Going with the flow was going to have to do.

The parade grew with every house we passed. Soon, hundreds, if not a small thousand, were in the procession. And they were cheering, whooping, all excited and full of glee. How were they so human? Every single one of them looked ripped out of the pages of a history book, ancient Greeks on parade.

They took me to their temple—my temple—the temple of the woman who looked like me but definitely could not be me. The thing was monstrous, imposing like the parthenon, all white marble columns and heavy bronze fixtures. And in front of it all, their statue to me.

She looked much more imposing from down here. What had seemed like gentle, open palms of peace now more closely resembled hands ready to strike, to smite. I shuddered at the sight. She reminded me of my reflection before I had my morning coffee.

The large wooden doors were thrown open for us, leading into the dark temple beyond, the space open and wide and lit only by large candles and a thin shaft of sunlight filtering in through the smallest of openings above. Other than that, it was dark and surpassingly cold. The few people who had been inside when I entered turned to stare at me in shock before being ushered out. I heard the large doors slam shut behind me, and realized that I was now terribly alone.

Which was when they tossed me into a holy dunk tank.

One second, I was on their shoulders; the next, I was entirely submerged in water, a deep pool from which I couldn't make up from down. I struggled in the icy water—my system shocked and panicked—and clawed my way to the surface where I could finally gasp for air. Cold water had flown in through my nose and caused my brain to freeze, and I sputtered the water out, struggling to breathe.

Not very godlike.

And they were waiting for me, those bird-people, with their feathered hats and animal skins and colored tunics held down with gold. They said nothing as I pulled my bruised body from the pool and forced myself to my feet. No one came to help. Not even with a goddamn towel.

Was I supposed to say something? I probably should. Wait, shouldn't I deny all of this? I mean, I wasn't a goddess. It would be immoral to have them think otherwise.

And yet... the statue.

I didn't know what they wanted from me, but I sure knew what I wanted from them.

"Where are my friends?" My voice cracked from the cold. The sound made them jump, as if they hadn't expected me to speak.

No one dared to answer. This was going to get old fast.

"Oh, Great Goddess Selena," said the woman in charge, "they do not have the rank! Their sacrifice will please the rest of the gods."

"Sacrifice?" Shit! This was more serious than I thought! Nim was only just recovering from his last death. So I did what I was getting slowly better at doing: I played along, feeling grimy the entire way. I marched toward the stranger, my bare feet numb in the freezing water, my hair dripping ice cold drops with every step. My movements rippled through the basin.

"They are more highly ranked than any of you." I kept my chin held high. "They are my trusted traveling companions, journeying with me through the heavens themselves, and you're going to treat them like lowly mortals? Sacrifice my help? No. Have I been too hasty, thinking you were worthy? Stop this now and bring them to me."

By the looks on their faces, I struck a chord. But what did they expect, calling a deity down to the earth? That she would do whatever they wanted? They couldn't go killing people they had just met; that was poor form.

I wasn't this goddess Selena they were waiting for; I wasn't a goddess at all. But if I wanted my friends to get home safely, I sure was going to have to put on an act. And if I wanted to know who had built an effigy of me, I was going to have to do better than that.

I was going to have to play Goddess.

"Let them through to me." I stared all of them down with the best look of disdain I could muster. Murder was on my lips, and it tasted sour.

But whatever tone I had used was working, and the large doors opened. The bird-people parted, and Nim was ushered forward. He looked groggy and confused, his eyes blinking in the dim light of the hall. He must have been terrified. And no wonder. Yesterday, he had been in a bland, utopian society. This was not the best way to introduce him to the real world.

However real this mess of a universe actually was.

Zander and Blayde followed and, along with them, the young woman we had seen fighting for her life in the volcano. She wore white robes, though they had gone gray with the volcanic soot. Her skin was a smidge darker than the rest of the crowd's, her hair a gorgeous, curly black and cropped to her shoulders, surrounding her like a dark halo. She looked terrified at the sight of me, at being in this temple. Unlike Blayde, who was apparently bored. Blayde gave everyone the look I had been trying so very hard to convey, though with all the power that I failed to muster.

The relief I felt was overwhelming, and I wanted to get up and rush to them, but, hey, I knew better than that and I managed to keep my cool. I avoided looking at my friends for too long, instead focusing on the man who seemed to speak for them all.

"Now, will someone explain to me why I am wet?" I asked, putting my hands on my hips to look more impressive. It felt good to take on this role, almost like I was born for it. Or maybe that was my messed-up brain chemistry speaking.

"Oh Great Goddess Selena, it is—"

"And stop starting every sentence with *Oh Great Goddess*. I know who I am. I don't have to be reminded of my name every five seconds. Just talk to me. Tossing people into fountains isn't something that's smiled upon. Hmm?"

"No, oh great... Selena."

"Better."

"It was part of the ritual of cleansing," he said, biting down on his lip so that a little bead of blood appeared around his teeth. "Would you want us to... forgo the rituals?"

"If they involve any more spontaneous tossing, that would be great, yes. Right now, I'm interested in why you have summoned me into human form? I like being left alone." I forced my face into a stiff look of disdain. "I hope for your sake that you have a meaningful reason to call me forth."

"For the prophecy, oh Selena," said the woman from before, "of course."

"Which one?" I couldn't have been more catty looking unless I had been an actual cat. I wanted to pick up my fingers and inspect my nails, taking a page from the Mean Girls book. "There are quite a few written about me. Which one are you referring to?"

The people were getting antsy. I could understand why; they probably wanted their goddess to be a little ... different. Which was reasonable, seeing that I wasn't actually her.

"Oh, Great Goddess ..." A man stepped forward, and my eyes rolled despite themselves. This time, though, I said nothing. My brain grew fuzzy from me standing in ten inches of cold water.

"I'm getting quite impatient—and you wouldn't like me when I'm impatient."

"We should show her," said the yellow woman once more. "Then she will understand."

She stepped forward into the candlelight, and I watched her without saying a word, taking in her graying hair and the dark marks that circled her wrists. Two young women in simple gray robes made their way to her, a small chest shared between them. They gave it to the woman in yellow before retreating into the darkness again.

"The one where ..." she said, opening the chest and offering the scroll contained within. "The one where you protect us from the Sky People."

I shook my head. I was much too wet to touch such a delicate thing. She nodded, understanding, and rolled out the scroll on the altar behind her. The woman's team lent a hand until the entire stone slab was taken up by the thing. It was a monstrous piece of paper, old beyond years, worn from so many hands having touched it, but oh so beautiful. The artistry was refined and detailed with colors and words written in dark ink all around, like the text in a comic book, a language my translator had no trouble interpreting.

But I didn't read. I saw only the first figure—the first picture—and my eyes stopped there.

I mean, come on, when you see a picture of yourself in a centuries-old alien prophecy, it makes the statue outside seem like nothing at all.

The feathered people watched me warily. I dampened my gaze, like I was bored with the papyrus, while inside my stomach was a tempest. I ran my eyes over the scroll, trying to interpret what fate somehow had planned for me. There was mini-me fighting a Cyclops, just as I had done. Then she was fighting a woman with hair like Blayde's but whose face was closer to a demon's, contorted and evil with sharp, pointy teeth. I had apparently stabbed her with a knife, and the blood was gushing like in a Tarantino movie.

"It told us we would know you by your strength," said the woman quickly, "and it was right. The second we saw you fighting one of the gatekeepers... we knew it was you, Selena, that you had come for us."

Another one, a little further down, involved me speaking with—was that a dinosaur? It sure looked like one, dwarfing me in size, cruel and dangerous and glowing green. My arms were outstretched, like I was arguing or maybe pleading with it.

I spotted my traveling companions in the mix as well, never at the forefront as I was, but present all the same. Zander with a sword. Blayde floating around on a cloud for some reason. And Nim, glowing like a god himself, holding children by the hand.

The last one, the most confusing of all, depicted me riding a bomb. Nothing fancy, just sitting astride a giant metal bullet like I was about to blast through everyone on Mario Kart. A little unsettling to say the least.

That could have been a spaceship. I squinted, looking closer, but that was when the woman on the far left reached forward to roll out the scroll some more.

It had not been the last image.

Oh, how I wish it had been. Because before me was my face, engulfed in flames, laughing as I burned.

As we all burned.

I looked away. This was more than unsettling; it was absolutely terrifying. The bodies of my friends were riddled with arrows, and we covered the earth with our blood. Yet our expressions were tranquil and content, as if we had wanted to be there.

Like we had wanted to die this way. Like we had wanted to die.

My mouth was dry and I licked my lips, trying to stop them from stinging.

"I... I see." I forced the words from my mouth. "How do you interpret the scroll yourself?"

"It will all become clear as the river of time continues its flow," said the yellow woman then sighed. I expected her to keep talking, but she stopped short, averting her gaze once more.

It was surreal, having these strangers revere me. To

think they saw me as a goddess. I had stopped denying it to save my own skin, but it wasn't too difficult to keep them on the hook, to keep them believing I was exactly who they thought I was.

What I was.

Finally, I turned to my companions. Zander played the part incredibly well, standing tall in the corner, almost blending in with the guards. He or Blayde should be the ones pretending to be deities, certainly not me.

Their lives were in my hands. One false step, and it was over. Well, not too much of an issue when it came to the siblings; their lives never ended, after all, though the prophecy might hint otherwise. I preferred not to test it. Especially for Nim's sake. He had done enough dying for today.

Unlike the others, his life was *literally* in my hands. He was my responsibility since I had wanted him to come along. Just as I was Zander's. Blayde washed her hands of us mere mortals she despised. Now I knew how Zander felt.

"Tell me more of these Sky People," I commanded, returning my eyes to their leader. The man was getting used to my impetuous words and didn't seem the least bit phased. An improvement.

"They come," he said, his jaw clenching. His face was tense, every muscle like stone. "They come. They take. They destroy. They fly away with our children, leaving fire in their wake."

"You're saying they've been here before?"

"Many times." He nodded. "They have come thrice in recorded history, but we have proof they came before that as well. Every five thousand years, to the day, they come and take our children away and burn the surface of our world to ashes."

I shuddered. This was serious. First, the walls with my name on them; then, the prophecy with my face; and now, an actual alien threat. As terrifying as this thought was, I knew we were here for a reason.

Suck it, destiny.

Blayde coughed. It was the moment of truth. I knew we had to help these people. Heck, the universe seemed to think so. So, for once in my life, pushed on by an irregular brain and a need to do right by the universe, I nodded solemnly at the man before me.

"I will need to see these records," I said, putting that confident mask right back on. "If you have called us forth to protect you from these Sky People, then I shall see what can be done. These monsters must have a weakness, which we will exploit."

I didn't want to make promises I couldn't keep, but then again, I wanted to give these people what they wanted to hear to keep us on their good side. I wasn't interested in knowing how they dealt with their false prophets.

"When do you expect these Sky People to return?" I asked.

"In two days, we predict."

My jaw forced its way open. I snapped it shut before it could fall to the floor. These were not the words you wanted to hear.

There wasn't any time for any training montage.

It suddenly hit me what I was agreeing to. That I was promising—by my presence alone—to deliver them from these Sky People and to save their planet.

To save their children.

It was one thing to fight a Cyclops and win. I could barely keep Nim safe; how was I supposed to protect an entire civilization?

"We will need the help and cooperation of your people to succeed." I swallowed hard. "While in my mortal form, I cannot perform the miracles you know me for. My physical body is more fragile than my celestial one."

A few of the men looked taken aback at this, but their leader, the woman in yellow, was unflinching.

"We will cater to your every need during your earthly stay," she said. "It is a great honor and privilege having you come to us in our time of need. Our prayers have been answered! Our sacrifices have not been in vain!"

I wasn't so sure about that. "What shall we call you, she who speaks for this world?"

"Ancha," she said, with a sly smile that could have been pride. "I am the High Priestess of our city, Aquetzalli. May I introduce you to our wise men and women, who have a deep knowledge of the things to come? They are strong, spiritual, and will assist you with anything you need."

"Thank you." I nodded in what could have been construed as a little bow. I hoped that any faux pas on my part would have been ignored seeing as how they thought I was a god of theirs. Would they dare judge me?

"These are my celestial cohorts," I said, indicating my friends, "Zander, Blayde, and Nimien. And"—I looked to the women for indication, but she said nothing. Zander was the one to mouth her name at me—"and... *Gassy?* As my half-mortal attendants and friends, I would prefer you treat them with the same respect and attention you have given me. They will speak for me and act on my behalf."

"Of course," said Ancha, bowing to them as the strange woman glared at me. Her name was probably not Gassy.

Ancha's people did the same, giving each of my companions the reverence they deserved. I nodded my approval. Dang, this was weird.

Before I could say anything else, the men started leaving, dragging Zander and Nim behind them. Before I could protest, the doors slammed shut, drowning the room in darkness.

Only it wasn't dark. With the men gone, the women in their fancy bird clothes and the women in the simple white shifts all worked on bringing the place to life. As they touched the walls, stones began to glow with a soft blue light, the same light I had seen inside the pyramid. Over two dozen women were here, including Ancha and her younger peers, the women in purple and red. They had enough gold here to spare in this small room, yet Ancha was the only one in white wearing any at all.

Ancha was incredibly beautiful. Her soft brown eyes demanded attention, lighting up the room. When she stood, I could see her long black hair extended past her hips and down to her knees, straight and glossy like it had come right off a shampoo commercial. Marcy would be jealous.

I didn't know how to respond to all this bowing. "Please, none of that for me." I stepped forward, casting my eyes toward the door. "I'm getting tired of all this ceremony."

Ancha seemed shocked by my candor, her jaw dropped slightly, though her mouth didn't stay open for very long.

"We welcome you, Selena, with a gift, if you choose to accept it."

I glanced at Blayde for advice, who nodded almost imperceptibly with a little flick of her eyebrows. I nodded in response. The girl—Gassy, though that was definitely not her name—trembled behind Blayde, saying nothing.

"I will accept it," I said. "We will accept it."

I wasn't quite sure what I had just agreed to, but I certainly didn't think it would have anything to do with being stripped naked in front of every woman in town.

# CHAPTER FIVE

## *LET'S ALL TAKE A SPA DAY IN THE MIDDLE OF THIS*

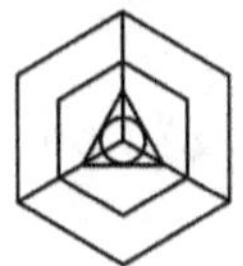

The men's mysterious behavior made sense the second the gushing women pushed me through to the next room. This was not just a temple; it was a bathhouse built on top of hot springs that probably meant a whole lot to these people. This was the kind of spa people on Earth would pay thousands to spend a day in.

We walked past the basins, taking steps down into the lower levels of the temple. I was sure we'd find ghosts, or at least some terrifying catacombs. Instead, we were led into a glowing stone room with stone seating carved directly into the walls.

The door was closed, and Blayde and I were left alone inside—along with Gassy. Blayde was on me in an instant.

"What the flying *fuck* have you gotten us into now?" she snapped, giving me a rough shove. Her fingertips jabbed my clavicle, hard enough to form a bruise. "We leave you alone for five minutes, and you go and establish yourself as the deity of some weird civilization? No offense, Angee."

"I am not offended," the girl more aptly named Angee stammered, throwing up her hands in confusion and distress. "The people of Aquetzalli are not my brethren. Why in Selena's name are you berating your mistress?"

"Because she's not my mistress," said Blayde. "I'm hers. Well, it's more likely she's my brother's, but he won't admit to anything. Anyway, Sally, spill. The fuck have you done?"

"I didn't do anything." I put my hands on my hips. "A Cyclops attacked. I fought it, and then there was a crowd, and I ..."

I stumbled back, falling on the stone and sending ice cold sparks up my back. The rest of my skin sweated like a pig, droplets forming all the way down my arms.

"The statue and everything was already here?" Blayde paused. "Wait, I phrased that wrong. It's not something they could just knock up. You know what I mean."

"It was here and so was the *prophecy* that *foretold* them of my arrival," I said. "Apparently, I'm a goddess... but I'm not. I mean, I don't even need to ask, I know I'm not. I'm..."

Angee let out a small squeak. "You're not Selena?"

"Oh hell," I stammered. "I am. I mean—"

"Oh, right, introductions. Sally, Angee. Angee, Sally.

She's the chick the prophecy foretold," said Blayde, "though she's not exactly a goddess, all right? Same Selena. Different delivery system."

"And who's Angee exactly?" I asked.

"Oh, Angee was being sacrificed by the neighboring city to call you forth. They really wanted to get your attention, Sal."

"Don't call me that."

"Why not?" She shrugged. "Zander does."

"You're not Zander."

"You're not Selena ..." Angee stumbled backward onto the bench, her hands trembling as she wiped sweat from her brow. My skin was itching with perspiration. Small sparks danced up my fingers and arms, reminding me my meds were nowhere near.

"She is," said Blayde, "and what the hell is that sound? Are they trying to gas us?"

"It's a spa, Blayde." I crossed my arms over my sticky chest. "We're in a steam bath, which I think I remember you asking for specifically."

"Oh." She sat on one of the benches then turned, lying down flat along the expanse, allowing the cold stone to touch every inch of her back.

"Yeah, purification ritual and all. Since I'm supposedly a goddess."

Not to mention the heat was making my mood swing the other way. I was burned out from the show I had just given, and darkness was descending on my mind, along with stronger pinpricks of electricity burning through my skin. I simultaneously wanted to dance, scream, and sleep.

"This definitely is not Earth," I said, awkwardly

lowering my voice. Not that Angee was listening to us. She was too far in her own thoughts to pick up on what we were saying. " If it were, it would have been far in the past. You don't travel through time, do you?"

"Not backward. But are you really ready to stay and help these people?"

"I want to, but I'm not sure how long I can keep up the pretense." I lowered my voice, glancing at the strange girl in the corner. "Or how comfortable I am pretending to be their goddess. Doesn't playing a celestial being go against the codes of ethics?"

"Didn't look that way to me." Blayde grinned, and for a second, I thought that just maybe she was paying me a compliment. "No white savior complex that I can spot."

"White savior ... wait, they have that on other planets?"

"I have no idea what that translator of yours is telling you, but if I'm saying it, then yeah."

"I'm just afraid I might be breaking some law of the universe," I said, trying to ignore her gaze "I feel ... dirty."

"Well, let's just check the list, shall we?" And out of nowhere—I might need to remind you at this point that she was not wearing a stitch of clothing—she brandished her journal. I cannot for the life of me begin to guess where it was hiding. Blayde must have had a pocket universe at her beck and call—if that even was a thing. If so, I needed to get my hands on one.

She flipped the pages until she reached the one she was looking for, clearing her throat before she spoke. Oh, so it *was* a literal checklist.

"We set these rules up when we started traveling," she explained, "so as to not get too deeply into trouble when things like this happened. It's gotten us far from messes before they've really started. Anyway, Impersonating Deities 101. Number one: Are you trying to say you're better than God? He really hates that. "

"What? No? Wait. Is there a God? Like ... the actual one?"

"That's ... complicated," she said. "Definitely too much for us to talk about today. Let me just say I have met gods, and they're not as cool as they sound. But there could be more to them and higher up. Anyway, one of them gets really pissed when you impersonate him, but he doesn't go by Selena, so I think you're in the clear.

"Number two: Are you just doing this to... never mind; that's for Zander. Number three: Do you intend to lead these people without question for your own personal gain?"

"No. It's just to get them out of this *people of the sky* mess. Does that make it okay?"

"In my book it does," she said, "but the list isn't over yet. Item four: Are you posing for sculptures, paintings, or photographs?"

"Definitely not, but they already have a statue of me, not to mention those pictures, which is weird, right?"

"Yup. Moving on, though. Item five: Using your established persona and power, will you attempt to create your own utopian society and manipulate your people into—and I will bother Zander about this one later. So, Sally, I take it we don't have to worry. Congratulations! Since this is not for your personal gain, it seems you've passed the test. You're a goddess now. How does it feel?"

"Pretty lousy," I said, shuddering.

"Well, impersonate this goddess all you want, she doesn't really exist anyway. You're doing them a favor."

Which is not what you say in front of the girl who was about to be thrown into a volcano to call you into existence.

Angee burst into tears, a small sob at first we hadn't heard over our conversation, though one that had slowly grown louder and louder until she finally snapped. Her face was red and puffy, but not from the steam of the room. She must have been crying for quite a while as he had argued in our little corner. She was probably no older than sixteen, poor girl, just full-on wailing into her hands.

"Hey, hey, it's okay," I said, scrambling over to her. It was only when I reached her that it occurred me she might not appreciate a hug from a nude woman impersonating her goddess.

"Angee," I said softly, shooting a glare at Blayde, "it's going to be all right, okay?"

She shoved me away, slapping me hard. Her handprint blossomed red on my arm.

"Imposter! I should tell. I should shout and let everyone know that you—"

"And what would that accomplish?" asked Blayde. "If your prophecies are correct, the Sky People are going to be here soon. You don't have much choice. Are you willing to throw out help over a technicality?"

"A technicality?" Angee spat out. "If they knew the truth, they would put you to death. I would, too."

"Even over a thousand-year-old prophecy?" said Blayde. "The kind that, I don't know, tends to get a little misinterpreted over the millennia? Does it say anywhere that Selena here is supposed to be a goddess, or do you just worship her because she was promised to come?" Angee said nothing. "Think about it: Nowhere in those prophecies did I see the need to throw a young virgin into a volcano to bring Selena forth. That was your elders. I personally don't believe in virgin sacrifice; it encourages young people to rush into things so they can stop being considered for murder. They were willing to kill you to bring Sally here. You need us."

"Wait a moment," I stammered. "What about Nimien?"

"What about him?"

"He's going to be in danger if we stay, isn't he? And I mean"—I glanced over at Angee—"he just went through a lot."

"Oh, relax, will you?" Blayde sat up and flashed the coy little smile that made my blood run cold. "You're not his mother. You seem to have got this under control, and I'd bet the kid has already learned the language."

"Come on," I scoffed, "he's smart, but he's not *that* good."

"He's a super genius. He's just hiding it. Trust me, I know the type. I give you two a hard time, but it's nothing personal. So, no, I think we're well equipped to handle this situation. We should stay."

Blayde stood just as the doors opened. Thank God—whichever one was listening. A brisk breeze flooded the room, hitting my soaked skin and sending shivers up my spine. It was magic.

Blayde flashed me a look. It was decided, I guessed. We were staying to help. Which meant that I would continue to play the part of the Great Goddess Selena, however long it took.

We were given simple, elegant drapes to wear. Mine was a deep purple, light on my skin. Blayde was growing impatient, her fingers drumming against her silk-clad hip as we followed Ancha out the back of the temple into a pleasant courtyard in silence. I guess it wasn't really part of the plan, talking to the goddess's attendants.

We made our way to what looked like a stone pagoda, high above the cliffs that kept the temple away from the sea. Wide, arching columns held up a small cupola, and beneath it, above the crashing waves, was a set of fancy patio furniture. Gulls cried overhead, and the sweet smell of ocean salt brushed my nostrils. The breeze was gentle against my exfoliated skin, soft and oddly warm.

My heart leapt as I saw them sitting under the pagoda, sipping from chalices. Zander and Nim both looked uninjured and surprisingly clean. Neither looked like they had stepped out of a volcano. It was more like they had stepped from the pages of a J.Crew catalogue—one where everyone wore tunics and togas.

"Your attendants have been cared for," said Ancha, directing this at me and bowing. "As they can profess. A last feast will be held in your honor. We must remove ourselves to prepare for it. Please, make yourselves comfortable. If you need anything, you need only ask." She indicated the pillows, smiling. "We did not know if you needed sleep in your mortal form, but we prepared for every eventuality. We hope we prepared for *every* eventuality. If you require company in your bed, that can be arranged as well."

"I'm... I'm good. Thanks, Ancha," I said, feeling the heat rise to my face. "You have done well."

Now she was the one to blush. And with that, she slipped away, leaving the five of us alone and confused.

"What happened in there?" asked Zander the second she was out of earshot. He stepped forward, almost urgently, stopping before he got too close. I gave him an awkward smile.

"Steam bath," said Blayde. "Apparently, and I'm not sure if you've heard this yet, but Sally is a goddess now. Neat."

"Way neat," Nim agreed, grinning widely.

"Dealing with the language all right, Nim?" I asked.

He nodded. "Enough to know how much of a mess we're in, yup."

"Aww, they didn't bring us any nibbles," said Blayde, throwing herself on a pile of plush pillows strewn on the floor. "You should make a fuss, Sally."

"Sure," I said, rolling my eyes as I took a seat around the stone table. The bench was cold through the thin silk. "Make them hate the goddess they called forth. Didn't we just have a conversation about not abusing my role?"

"They did ask for our help," she said, "and we're going to need theirs to get through this. You do understand that, right?"

"If you remember correctly, it's one of the things I asked for back in the... whatever that was."

"Right, good on you."

"We should get Angee back home," said Zander as he made his way to her. Angee pushed herself as far away from us as she could. "Are you doing all right?"

"I don't think you understand." She glared at him. "I can't go home. Not now, not ever. They were ready to throw me into a volcano to draw Selena forth. There is no way their sacrifice can walk back into town as if nothing happened."

"So, tell them Selena's here," said Blayde, without opening her eyes, "and that your sacrifice was not in vain or something."

"This is not Selena."

Blayde shrugged. "Whatever."

"Why don't you stay here, then?" asked Zander. "These people seem nice."

"Nice?" Angee scoffed, crossing her arms in front of her chest. "These people are brutes. We hate the Aquetzallians. We've been at war with them for centuries! The only thing I have going for me right now is they think I'm with you."

"And our real problem," said Blayde, "the thing no one is bringing up right now? The elephant in the room? Sally's a goddess from ancient prophecies. We need to know what we do next."

She hopped to her feet and dug a piece of charcoal from her mystery spot before drawing a straight line down the middle of the table.

"Right, so here are the things we know," she said, writing the heading on the left, "and the things we need to figure out."

"Wait, we're actually going to do this?" Nim asked as he sat at the table with us. "Isn't it incredibly dangerous? Not to mention wrong?"

"You don't have a counter on your neck anymore, Nimien," said Blayde, referring to his life back in the snow globe of a city. "You get to decide for yourself."

"Well, I think it's not safe." He crossed his arms across his chest.

"Let's vote then. All in favor of staying and helping?" Blayde threw her hand up in the air. Mine followed.

I glanced at Zander, expecting him join us, but he looked nervous. He stared intently at Blayde's charcoal, frowning as he avoided my eyes and ran a hand through his thick hair.

"I agree with Nim. It's not safe," he said, doing that thing with his eyebrows I could never understand. His gaze darted in my direction, and I realized he was talking about me. "Sal's not their goddess. We should get out of here before all hell breaks loose."

"What?" I stammered. "You think we should go? You're the one who always wants to stay and help! You can't possibly think we should abandon these people when they're about to be incinerated!"

"I'm not going to let you or Nim get turned into human toast," he argued. "We're supposed to be finding Earth. We're supposed to get you home safely, to fix my mistake, not put you in more danger."

"I think Sally's the one who gets the vote here," piped up Blayde from her pillows. "She's the one they're counting on. What do you think, Sally? You want to stay here and be the hero, or should we leave and let your people die?"

"Blayde," Zander growled.

"I say we're staying," I said. "I mean, destiny wants

me here for a reason, right? Zander, you keep saying it's the universe throwing weird shit in my path. Maybe it was leading to this— here, now. You saw the writing on that temple wall. You saw the statue. Maybe the universe wants me to help these people."

Zander's frown deepened. "Then the universe has a strange way of asking for help."

"I'm all for helping. If we can do anything, then let's do it."

Zander glanced at Blayde, and he lifted his hand.

"And all against?"

Nim's hand shot into the air. Blayde shrugged.

"All right, we're staying. Nim, you can hang out in this super comfy pagoda until this passes if it bothers you. Try and avoid dying again."

"I'm not the one I'm worried about," he muttered.

"Anyway, what do we know?"

We filled out the stone chart with what we knew. There were people who came every five thousand years and kidnapped the children. Why? That was for the unknowable side. We knew these people had the power to lay waste to the land and burn it to the ground but not why. Another question we had no answer to.

"Aliens," Zander asserted. "It has to be."

"All signs point to them," said Blayde, "though it doesn't match the M.O. of any group I know. What do they want with the children?"

"Maybe they're part of the group you told me about, back on the *Traveler*," I said. "Slave owners looking for manual labor."

"Possibly," said Blayde, adding *slave trade?* to the unknown column. "But there are easier ways of getting children off planets without having to roast the place."

All the while we discussed, Nim sat huddled on the pile of pillows looking wide-eyed at the sea. The poor kid was probably overwhelmed. Maybe it would have been better if we'd left him with the Alliance. At least then he wouldn't have to deal with this insanity. But he would have traded one form of mind control for another. At least with us, he had a choice.

Angee sat across from him, staring at Nim and avoiding the rest of us as much as she could. I didn't blame her.

"We also have the problem of being present in artwork here," added Zander. "What's that all about?"

"Maybe destiny does exist?" I asked. Blayde smiled, a muscle drawing the corner of her left lip up oh-so-gently.

"Or maybe we've been tricked," she said, "and this is a trap."

"Weird trap," said Zander. "What do they hope to accomplish?"

"No idea," said Blayde, adding the word *TRAP?* in all caps across from the question. "But these documents are old, which means whoever wanted us here could travel through time."

"Is that even possible?" I asked.

"Yes, and quite easily," said Zander. "I was once at this party held by seven-dimensional beings, and they were always going back and forth to get the best drinks. Heck, there was this juice that lets you see five seconds forward and five seconds back all at once, which—one planetary collision is bad, two is worse, but fourteen? Yes. There are species out there that can travel backward, forward, sideways—and imagine seventeen other directions too—anyway they want. Time is nothing for them."

"So, have you pissed off any higher dimensional beings, then?"

"You mean recently?" Blayde laughed. "I don't think so. Zander?"

"I haven't," he agreed, "but it's possible we will, in their reference frame. Time travelers make a real mess of things."

Blayde added that to the column, too. Looking at the chart in front of us, I was beginning to worry things were less clear than when we'd started.

"So..." She turned away from the table, her smile gone. "We know they've been expecting us. Either the somehow-conscious universe or a time traveler planned for us to be here. And those Sky People are coming around, threatening everyone. What do we do?"

"We save them," said Zander. "Trap or no trap, these people need us."

"Glad to see you're on board now, Zan." Blayde gave him a quick wink. "We have to give them a plan, so what do we do?"

"We negotiate with the Sky People," he suggested. "With our translators and special skills, we could find out what they want from these people and get them to leave them alone."

"You sure?" I said. "Maybe it won't be that easy."

"If they're going for this planet because it's easy pickings, they'll turn around when they know it's protected," he said. "And if we have to fight, we will."

"I'm not so sure about that," I said with a shudder.

"Well, it's the start of something," said Blayde. "Sally, you keep the people calm and reassured. Zander, you show the strength. I'll do research and try to contact these Sky People. And Nimien... Nimien can nap for all I care."

Nimien said nothing. A quick glance behind me showed that he had fallen asleep on a pile of golden pillows. Good for him.

"Everyone good with that?" asked Blayde.

"Yup," I replied. Zander nodded.

"And what about me?" asked Angee, glaring at us. "I'm your *attendant*, after all. Shouldn't I be ... attending?"

"If that's what you want," said Blayde. "It's not much, but it's a start."

I yawned. I felt exhausted. I hadn't slept since the hotel under the ice, and since then I had been in a spaceship crash, discovered an alien city, kidnapped a kid, thrown out of an airlock. Oh, and stopped a coup. It had been a long day, to say the least.

As if my body was finally accepting my exhaustion, it let out a second yawn, a yawn so strong it hurt the edges of my jaw. I clutched my hands to my face.

"And let's avoid planet-lag as best as we can," said Blayde. "Take a nap. We have to be perfectly divine beings at this feast of theirs, so sleep might be in our best interest. In *all* of our best interests."

She stood, tossing herself onto a gigantic pillow monstrosity.

"Oh, come on," I snapped, marching over to her. "That's mine. I'm the goddess here."

"You're the goddess to them," she said, jutting her chin toward the temple. "To me, you're just our tagalong Earthling. Sleep where you want, but I'm not moving."

Zander hit the pillows snoring. I glared at Blayde and did the same. The cushions were so plush I didn't really mind.

But it was the principle of it all. I was the goddess; I deserved a real bed.

# CHAPTER SIX

## *EVERYBODY PARTIES LIKE IT'S XIXLXIX*

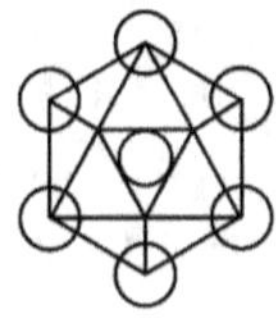

I awoke to a sharp poke on my shoulder.

"Oy," I grumbled, reaching for the hand. "Sleeping."

"We have a feast to attend," said a voice, and I bolt upright, suddenly remembering where I was and what I was supposed to be doing—impersonating a goddess of all things. And sleep drool wasn't very godly. I wiped the side of my lip and looked up.

The poker had been Angee, who sat staring at the temple. By the look of it, we wouldn't be alone for long. I stood up, catching glints of setting sunlight on the golden headpieces coming our way—an entire procession led by the head priestess and the holy women, flanked on either side by large, burly men in varying degrees of fractional nudity.

"Oh, Great Selena," said Ancha as she descended upon us, dressed to the nines in a shimmering version of the simple robes she had been wearing earlier, sans bird, "the time for feasting has arrived. Your presence would be most welcome."

"Of course." I grinned before realizing that Selena would probably be a little more dignified. I ironed away my smile. "A banquet in my honor would be quite fitting."

Too much? Too little? I didn't know, and Ancha gave no indication either way. She bowed again, turning to lead us away.

"Shall we go?" Zander asked politely, holding up an elbow for me to clasp. I looked at him sideways. "We need to time this just right ..." He held up a hand, urging us to stay still, and we waited as the sun inched lower on the horizon, the hills tuning a marmalade orange, the sky a salmon pink.

"Good a time as any," I said, my heart racing. "Okay, team, we stay for the ceremony, have a few drinks, then we come back here. Nothing more, all right?"

They nodded, but I was sure they weren't as confident as their posture showed. This would be the show of my life, even crazier than my fifth-grade talent show where Marcy and I created a musical rendition of *Macbeth*. Hopefully, this would be more fun.

Not that my mind was on fun right now. The tingling was back and with it, surges of half-eaten emotions. Darkness and gloom slipped over my eyes only for my back-brain to poke in with the cheery thought that I was succeeding at something. The feeling of being a complete failure while simultaneously being at the top of my game was overwhelming, but I had to smile through it.

Ancha was wise. Scheduling this show right after I had been washed would ensure I wouldn't look like a random woman they pulled off the streets to lie to them.

Ha, little did they know, right?

I took a step forward, and, out of nowhere, two of Ancha's entourage grabbed me. Before I could do anything, I was hoisted onto a chair that they lifted onto their shoulders, golden chains jingling as it hit the men's skin.

I kept my calm—but just barely.

"What is this?" I snapped, a perfect imitation of Mrs. Price, my former boss—the one *before* the man who tried to kill me. "You dare to touch your goddess without consent? I should strike you down where you stand!"

The men said nothing. If anything, it was as if they could not hear me at all. Ancha turned to glance at me, avoiding my eyes in that odd, practiced way she did.

"Apologies, our great Selena," she said. "The guardians are not known for their grace or poise. They do not speak as a rule. It is how they function."

One of the holy women gave them a sign, and as one, they moved together, each step in time with the last. It was as if they were one person, one functioning unit, a machine.

They carried my chaise out to the plaza, the one with the awkward statue of yours truly, where hundreds of people were gathered, torches in hand. It was still a little light out for us to need them, so I assumed they were largely ceremonial. They said nothing as I came into view, and for a second I thought this might have been a funeral dirge.

And they were staring at me.

I had no fear of public speaking until then. I had been fine for twenty-odd years until that moment, when a city of people who thought I was a goddess expected some great speech from me.

I gulped. Audibly. Loud enough for Zander to shoot me a troubled, sideways gaze.

I needed to say something.

Should I ... should I stand?

I waved a hand, emulating Queen Elizabeth. That got no response.

"Greetings," I said, forcing my voice to remain unwavering, "people of Aquetzalli. I, Selena, have heard your cries. And I have come to help you in your time of need."

This seemed to go over well—but still no reaction from the crowd.

"I thought this was supposed to be a party?" I asked Ancha. "Why's everyone so glum?"

"They're waiting for your show of power," she said, taken aback. "They're waiting for you to take one of them with holy sky fire."

"What? I'm not going to do that. We need everyone we can get for this Sky People problem. I'm not going to kill able-bodied people, or anyone for that matter. From now on, I want a stop to all sacrifices. We're done with that, you got it?"

And then there was the cheer. Amazingly enough, but not at all surprising, when you take away the ritualistic murder, people tend to like you more.

"Right," I said, smiling as I faced the crowd, "we have a lot of work to do in the morning. But for now, let the festivities begin!"

The crowd went wild. Wild! Dancing and cheering and hooting and partying. The guards carried my chaise through the town, and people flocked to our side, the streets thick with people ready for a divine feast. As was I. I was ravenous at this point.

All along the beach, enormous bonfires had been erected and were lit as the procession walked by. My chaise was taken to the sea, and I stepped out barefoot onto the soft sand, taking my place on the straw mat next to Ancha. She said nothing as I sat, but I could feel her shift away from me.

The sun was finally sinking into the ocean, and darkness deepened quickly. I crossed my legs and looked straight ahead. The heat tickled my skin, and I melted into it.

There were baskets upon baskets of food. Grilled fish, straight from the sea. Loaves of bread, buns, and rolls. Something that tasted an awful lot of like honey drizzled on dry black crackers. A fragrant white paste served on leaves the size of my face. The flavors were so alien, yet so familiar. I tried to look classy as I ate, the way I would imagine a goddess should eat, but I was so hungry and there's not much grace to be found without utensils.

I glanced over at my friends, who had their own mat all to themselves. I wished I could be with them; at least it would be less awkward. I wished one of them had been the fated Selena, as I was definitely not up to the task. Keeping up the pretense was strangely draining, and I could feel my body slow. I kept my eyes on the newly arriving dancers, breathing deep to keep the stress at bay.

They were dancing around the bonfires—slow, rhythmic dances to the drums—and it felt oddly stiff and ceremonial. The kind of party you might find back on Earth, maybe the equivalent of a gala. Everyone was poised and focused, complete with mysterious canapés.

But then they sent the kids to bed, pulled out the wine, and things started to feel like a party.

Once the food was gone, people got up to dance. They attached ribbons and bells to their legs, and out of nowhere they were suddenly creating endearing rhythms. The drums sped up, and a sudden choreography fell upon the crowd. The dances were intricate, the footsteps rehearsed to perfection. More instruments, mostly percussions, were added to the mix, and together the sound of a town celebrating rose to the heavens.

One of the serving men filled my clay cup with the wine, and I took it, thanking him. One whiff of the stuff was enough to curl the hairs inside my nostrils. This was not a drink for savoring; it was one for celebrating. I took a swig, and it was like taking a blow to the head. This wasn't wine. Of course it wasn't. I was on an alien planet, and I hadn't seen a sign of grapes anywhere. The drink—if I had to call it anything, it would be punch— was thick and fruity, spiced generously, and burned on its way down like liquid fire, even as it made my mind explode.

I loved it. How could I not? It shut up the anxieties that had been screaming at each other, turned my mind away from the panic, from the withdrawal. I had always wanted a switch that could turn it all off, and here, on an alien planet, I had found it.

I was on my feet now. When I had gotten up, I didn't know. I was leaning over to Zander, whispering in his ear that we needed to keep Nim away from the stuff, and he was telling me it was too late. Nim's smile stretched wide like a laundry line.

Angee was giving him the Bambi eyes, and he was following her into a dance, the two of them swaying to the music at the foot of the bonfire. And I was smiling, too, happy the boy was letting loose. After living in his world for so long, I didn't know if he'd ever be able to.

I took a second drink of the punch, ready for it this time and welcoming the sweetness. I was buzzed, and I loved it. I looked over at Angee and Nim and realized I totally shipped them.

"I do, too!" said Zander, grinning sheepishly.

"You do what?"

"Ship them!" he said. "Like Harry and Hermione! I ship them."

"I said that aloud?" I realized that I must have if he was answering. "Hold on, you finished the *Harry Potter* books?"

"Nah," he said, sadly. "Just started *Order of the Phoenix* when ... you know."

"When you blew up my workplace and showed me my boss was an alien?"

"Yeah, that! You want to dance?"

I took another swig of punch, putting down the clay cup before joining him at the bonfire. The music had switched up at some point, becoming more rhythmic, almost like a hip-hop beat. I let Zander lead, my head spinning inside and out as he swung me around. It was only during the third dip in two minutes that I made the connection.

"You okay?"

"I'm fine," I replied with a nod. The world was spinning, and I loved it.

"Homesick?" he asked, slowing his movements to simple swaying.

"Always."

"After this is done, we're going on a vacation."

"I thought this was supposed to be a vacation?"

"The first trip was," he said, trying to play it off as cheerful but shame crept into his tone. "The rest is just... aftermath."

He let out a heavy sigh, turning his eyes heavenward. The stars were bright, even with the bonfires on the beach, and the moon was just beginning to rise out of the water. "Don't you ever... just feel how amazing it is to be out of your own galaxy? To meet other cultures and just... feel so... so gifted with all this? We're the only people in the universe to have seen Earth, the *Traveler*, the legendary city of Da-Duhui, and this place—all in one week."

"Yeah, it's... amazing. All the stories I can tell... but to whom? No one will believe me."

"Marcy would love to hear them." He took another swig from the cup. "This punch is freaking amazing. Oh, and Dany?"

"If I ever see them again."

"Do you doubt me that much? I promised I'd get you home, and I will." He smiled, though the confidence wasn't convincing. "You know me."

"I don't," I said, realizing I had no control over my words whatsoever. Stupid subconscious was taking charge. "You're not the same person who lived with me two years ago."

"How so?"

"When you lived with me," I blabbered, "you needed to be taught everything. You couldn't work a shower, you got yourself in trouble with coffee, you got nervous about going to work. You were rash, headless. You took a bath in a freaking pond, for goodness sake! But out here, you're, well, you're different. The only time I ever saw you like you are now was when you had to deal with the people who wanted us dead. You come up with plans, think them through, and bring them to completion. You save lives just like that. You've gone from goofy to heroic."

He shrugged, but I could see him thinking that over. "I guess I'm better at this."

"I'm sorry. I didn't mean to be rude."

"No, no, you're right. Those two months on Earth, when I didn't have to think about life-threatening plots, when I didn't have to leave after a few days, when I didn't have to worry about anything interstellar... it was great. It took me awhile to focus on mundane activities and not feel like I had to devote half my concentration on everything that happened around me. But then I'm out here, and it's just my nature."

"Are you the same man I met all those years ago?" I asked.

"Are you the same woman?" he asked. "Two years have passed since we first met, at least for you. Since then, you've had to lie to your friends for me, you've had to trick your boss, survive an explosion—"

"With your help," I urged, trying not to dwell on that last bit.

"No," he said, shaking his head. "You survived flesh-eating parasites, tricked alien mafia, not to mention infiltrated a palace, and fought your way through a hoard possessed by a robotic entity. In twenty-four hours."

"Again, with your help," I muttered.

"You figured out the plot to the sabotage on the *Traveler*," he added, "and you survived being thrown out of an airlock!"

"Not alone!"

"No, all by yourself." I tried to interrupt, but he continued. "And now you're impersonating a deity so you can save an unknown civilization from their prophesied demise."

"But I couldn't have done this without you ... or Blayde. And ... I'm scared."

"You?"

"What?" I laughed nervously at his reaction. "I'm not immortal. I could drop dead from an alien disease, get murdered, whatever, all without my parents having any idea where I am."

His gaze said not to remind him of that. "I already told you, that's not going to happen."

"I'll hold you to that."

He finished his punch, jumping away and back so quickly I wouldn't have noticed he was gone if I hadn't seen him turn slightly transparent for a second or notice his glass disappear. "You know, Sal, you're braver than you give yourself credit for." I blushed slightly. "No, I mean it."

"Are you drunk?"

"No, I don't get drunk. Liver cleans up fast."

"Except when it comes to coffee?"

"The caffeine lies in it for a while. Alcohol, though, doesn't." He smiled. "You asked me if I was the same person you met two years ago." He took a step forward, offering a hand. "I can still dance."

I took his hand slowly, following him to the dance floor again. "Last time, on Earth, you freaked a few people out."

"Well, I'm not on Earth anymore, am I? Plus, we have some good music this time, and it's not the early evening at a bar. No, this is a party with other people dancing along with us."

"You're still going to stick out like… an alien at a party."

"I always do."

Suddenly, we were dancing again, his steps in time with the music yet more intricate than anything anyone else was doing. This time I wasn't surprised, but I was still amazed at how fast he would pick up their paces, replicating every step and creating something more elaborate, more visually stunning than the others around us. We were floating, flying, swirling, and swooping.

"How did you learn to dance so well?" I asked him.

"I have no idea. Another question for when we get answers."

"Maybe you should look up the best dancers in the universe and figure out which one of them was a regenerative space jumper."

"You might have a solid lead there."

"You sure you're not drunk?" I asked him again, trying to meet his gaze. He couldn't hold my eyes.

"Bitch, I might be." He laughed. "Is that a thing? Someone yelled it at me on Earth when I asked them if they were into accounting, and I *still* don't know what it means. Also, I'm reacting to something in this punch, but I'll get over it."

"Don't."

"Don't what?"

"Don't get over it." I laughed, planting a sloppy kiss on his cheek. "I like you like this."

His face turned a violent shade of red.

"Oh, what's that?" he said, cupping a hand to his ear. "I think I heard someone call my name. Sally, you should dance with Blayde."

And he trotted off, or ran off, a tornado at his heels.

I tried not to be offended by his reaction. It's not like the kiss meant anything. It probably surprised him as much as it surprised me. Tipsy Sally was flirty with anyone. It was nothing personal.

Even if it was, I didn't have the brainpower to think about that right now.

"So, we doing this?"

I turned around drowsily, and there was Blayde, hands outstretched. She glowed like an ember under the orange light, her skin shimmering as her sweat reflected the flames. Her strong, muscular arms were waiting for me to grasp them.

"Doing what?" I asked.

"Dancing." She took my hands. In an instant, we

were swinging around on the sand, her elegant body moving against mine in ways I didn't think were legal back on Earth. At least, not in public.

I leaned in. She was a deft lead. Not that I'd say it to her face, though I think she knew. I didn't exactly make it a secret I was into girls like her. And she wasn't exactly staying away from me. I could feel her tight body through the thin fabric of our tunics, inviting me to dance.

This punch was really glorious.

Should a goddess be acting like this? Probably not. But I couldn't stop myself anymore. I didn't want to. I wasn't even going to try. I was having too much fun.

Her hands were wrapped into my hair, and I was giggling like the loser of a tickle fight. She was breathing that sweet punch breath on my face.

And then she collapsed on me, snoring.

Because, of course, she did.

"What happened to her?" asked Nim, handing me a new cup in exchange for Blayde. He helped me lay her down as I held his drink.

"Zander and Blayde don't get intoxicated like the rest of us," I said, handing him back the now-empty cup. "They get hit hard then pass out as it flushes out of their system. Happened to Zander back when he was my roommate."

"You lived with Zander?"

"For a little bit, when he was stuck on Earth. Can you help me with her?"

We rolled her onto one of the straw mats, laying her out peacefully like she had just left her vessel for a quick break. If anyone asked, that was the official story:

a quick trip back to the heavens to tell the other celestial beings how rad this party was.

I was a very tipsy goddess; my excuses might not have been the best. Not that anyone dared ask.

"Can I dance with you, Sally?" asked Nim when we had finally dealt with Blayde.

"Sure, why not," I said. "What happened to Angee?"

"She got tired of the glares. The others don't seem to like her people."

"Is she okay?"

"I think so." He shrugged "She didn't want me to come with."

"Ah. Okay, let's dance."

Nim didn't know anything more about dancing than I did, so there was a lot of awkward clubbing moves I had picked up over the years. A lot of hip juggles and hopping, which was making my head spin.

"More punch?" asked Nim as one song shifted into another.

"You should probably stop." I smiled. "Have you had alcohol before tonight?"

"Nope." He grinned. "It's been banned on my planet since the colony was planted. But I'm fine, you see? I'm not drunk."

"Yeah, but we don't know what's in the drink," I said. "We don't know if your body can handle it. Zander and Blayde are having an interesting time, to say the least."

I glanced at Blayde, still snoring on her mat, and scanned the crowd for Zander. He was doing magic tricks, pulling shells out of people's ears as they clapped for him. He was making all his own sound effects, and

I could hear them from here.

"You don't seem to mind."

"I'm ..." I licked my lips. They were getting pretty dry under the heat, and I needed another glass of punch to help keep hydrated. That's how it works, right? "I'm a responsible adult. And you're my responsi ... responsah ... responsibility."

"Wow, third time's the charm." He laughed. "You don't have to worry about me, Sally. You don't ever have to worry ..."

And then he was learning in. He was going for it. His soft, brown eyes shimmered and closed, and with a gasp I sidestepped him, avoiding the oncoming lunge of the pubescent heartthrob.

He stumbled, opening his eyes to glare at me. I opened my mouth to tell him he wasn't thinking straight, that it was the punch and I was doing the same thing, but a cry of panic took the words right out of my mouth.

"Raid!" came the cry, loud and terrified. "Atlans! Atlans!"

# CHAPTER SEVEN

## *THE BATTLE OF DRUNKEN BEACH*

"Atlans?" I asked, but no one answered. They were too busy running for shelter as a barrage of spears flew through the air. So, I did what I did best—I ran. Though with my head spinning from the punch, finding a straight line was damn near impossible.

"Nim!" I tried to find him, but he had disappeared in the confusion. "Nim, where are you?"

I turned my head around, scanning the beach for him. And, to my surprise, I found not one but two Nimiens. He and his identical twin brother were running my way, their hands waving frantically.

"Where's Blayde?" the two of them asked at once.

"Um, um, she's here!" I pointed at the mat where

we had left her, but of course, she was gone.

Right then, a spear landed in the dirt only a yard away from me. Purple sparks of electricity flared up the handle, sending a bolt deep into the earth. The sand sizzled as it turned to glass.

"Ok, lesson learned," I said, though the words came out in a mush. "Don't get hit with a spear."

"Sally, we need to get out of here!" Nim and his brother grabbed my arm and gave it a sharp tug, pulling me out of my trance.

"But we need to find Blayde."

"There's no time. We have to get off the beach!"

As if to amplify his point, a second cascade of spears ripped through the air. One landed in the sea behind us, dead fish bobbing up to the surface in the wake of its shock. Another hit the bonfire with such force that some logs flew out, sending sparks spewing into the air.

The edge of my tunic caught fire, and I watched as the pretty flames moved up the fabric. Nim gave me a sharp shove into the sea, where I toppled over, dousing them just as quickly.

"Thanks, brah." I grinned. I was soaked through but barely caring.

"Sally," he snapped, apparently all trace of tipsiness gone. His twin brother faded away as the cold water helped my mind clear, if only momentarily. "We need to go, now!"

He grabbed my hand and dragged me forward with surprising strength. I had no choice but to follow, clutching the edge of my charred tunic and racing after him.

People were in a panic, running away from the beach with only one goal: survival. I kept a hand on my head, as if that was going to help, while my other hand dug into Nim's sturdy palm. He wove in between the terrified people, trying to get away from the bonfires, the beach, and the invaders.

"Blayde!" I shouted, spotting her in the crowd. She had taken a spear straight to the gut and was lying underfoot as the panicked masses trampled over her. I tried to let go of Nim's hand, but his grip was tight, almost painful.

"Leggo!" I begged. "We need to get her!"

"No time! She'll slow us down!"

"Nim," I stammered. "I think she'll stay dead with that spear like that! I don't know what'll happen to her if we leave her."

His hand relaxed, and I took my opportunity to pull away from his clasp and run toward Blayde. The spear was in deep, and she was most definitely dead, that lazy bum.

I grabbed the spear with both hands and gave it a sharp tug. It didn't move. It was embedded in the sand, having gone straight through Blayde's stomach. Her guts were spilling out in a small pool of blood.

*Ew, gross.* I turned my head and threw up my dinner, though the punch probably had something to do with that. Everything was spinning. Whatever clarity the water had given me, it was fading away already.

*Sorry, Blayde.* I jammed my foot on her pelvis, grabbed the spear, and tugged. The hip snapped, but the spear came out with a rewarding squelching sound. I toppled backward, spear in hand. Kick ass.

I bent over to scoop her arm over my shoulder, and stood up, using the spear as a prop. Nim grabbed her other side, and together we staggered forward, our limp—and currently resuscitating—friend between us. Her skin was slowly knitting itself back together over her guts.

The barrage of spears had ended. Now the Atlan soldiers were coming right for us, picking through the people left on the beach. Nim and I ran, trying to get away from their reach as they took on people who posed more of a threat.

But together, the three of us were weak and easy pickings. A soldier reared before us, appeared seemingly out of nowhere, brandishing a large curved sword. He was dressed in thick metal armor, oddly reminiscent of the warriors of Troy. He didn't seem to know who to go for first: Nim, the young warrior-looking man; me, the drunk girl with a deadly spear; or Blayde, the... corpse.

He probably wasn't going to go for Blayde.

"Hi-ya!" I shouted, dropping Blayde without a second thought, brandishing the spear. My mind was a fog, and my body was the soup.

*Wait. What?*

I swung the spear at the stranger, and he avoided it easily. After all, he was a trained soldier, and I was a drunk, goddess-impersonating, former personal assistant. Probably handling the spear backward, too, to top things off.

Not to mention Nim's twin was back. I was just getting better at focusing on what mattered.

And what mattered here was getting Blayde—and Nim—off the battlefield..

That, and hoping that Zander had made it to safety.

I swung again. The soldier parried, shoving my weapon away. I stumbled, trying to re-adjust my footing, and fell forward, dropping the flat part of my spear against his armor.

Which, apparently, was just what the spear needed to activate the electrical mechanism. Sparks flew from the golden tip, right into the enemy's armor, and he jolted. He fell over, gasping, shocked.

"Sweet! I am the storm goddess! Goddess of the sparks!"

"Shut up and grab Blayde!" shouted Nim, and I snapped out of it long enough to sling Blayde's arm back over my shoulder. Dragging one foot in front of the other, we took off into the night.

We had to get off this beach. My head spun as I ran, thoughts still murky from the punch. One thing was clear: We had to escape. Get out first, find Zander later.

But I was their goddess. I was supposed to stop bad things from happening. I had to save them, these people, my people. And right now, I was failing.

My foot hit cobblestone. We had reached the street, the fires behind us. I spun around, searching, but the beach looked clear. If anyone had been left behind, they weren't moving now.

I shuddered.

"Sally," snapped Nim. "A little help here?"

We ran, or tried to. Blayde was heavy, but between us, she was manageable. I didn't know how long it would take for her to come back from death, but I sure hoped she would wake up soon. It was hard work carrying her and the heavy golden spear.

The fighting hadn't been limited to the beach, though. Here, soldiers fought the people of Aquetzalli, who had picked up arms as well. While the intruders were outnumbered, the locals were outmatched. These Atlans had brought their tech.

And their Cyclops friends.

"We have to get out of here!" I said to Nim, as we dodged down a side street. Not that either of us knew our way around this city.

"No duh." He hoisted Blayde higher on his shoulder. "Not dying would be nice. I've already done that today."

I would have laughed if the statement wasn't so weird.

The alley brought us back to one of the main avenues, and we hid in the shadows before deciding which way to go. One way would lead us out of Aquetzalli; the other, right back to the sea, right back to the beach. Though, right now, both directions were waving at me.

"Which way?" asked Nim.

"Right!" I shouted and yanked my two companions along with me.

"That's left!" he replied, but no matter. So long as we were moving again.

And then, four Cyclopes blocked our way.

Oops.

"You shall never take us aliiiive!" I cried, jumping forward and slashing the spear at the leg of one of the Cyclops. It went right through. "Shit, they're holograms!"

"No, Sally, it's behind you!" shouted Nim, just in

time for a thwack to come from behind and send me sailing. I shouted out, dropping the spear as I flew through the air, my head coming down on the cobbled street with a loud thwack.

Something in my nose snapped. If I hadn't wanted to throw up before, I sure did now. I was dizzy, either from alcohol or maybe a concussion, a ringing in my ears that screamed into my mind.

I put my hands down on the pavement, trying to push myself up, but there was no strength there. And what with the world spinning around me, I wasn't quite sure which way was up anymore.

"Get up, Sally Webber," shouted a voice from behind me. "Get up now or never get up again!"

I forced myself up, panting, turning to see Blayde clutching the discarded spear in her hand. She twirled it expertly like a baton, ready to leap, to fly.

She looked glorious. Her silk tunic was torn and bloody, sand coating the sweat on her head, but she looked more like the goddess I was supposed to be than I ever would. Her colorful hair billowed in an imagined breeze as she crouched on her bare feet.

"Now get behind me!" she shouted. I happily obliged. She sprang at the Cyclops, stabbing the spear right into its eye, the sparks shooting from the impact. It froze and toppled over.

The woman casually marched forward, ripped the spear from the creature's eye, and then spun it so the sharp tip pointed toward the ground. Thick black oil oozed off the blade.

"Shall we get going?" she asked, then turned around and retched.

"Blayde?"

She grinned. "Thank heavens for muscle memory." She giggled. "I haven't felt like this in two centuries!"

Oh fuck. Even after coming back from the dead, she was still drunk as a skunk. The only person in our trio capable of getting us out of this alive, and she was teetering on the spinning pavement.

"Don't just stand there!" said Nim, surprisingly level-headed. "Are we running?"

"Yes, running." Blayde shot forward, but the path she made wasn't straight. Not even close. I took off after her, though I had no doubt my own path wasn't any better than hers.

There was shouting and fighting all around us. While Nim and I were trying to outrun it, Blayde seemed instead to want to get in the fun. She laughed as she threw herself into the fighting, knocking over soldiers left and right, bringing the Cyclopes to their knees.

"Catch!" she shouted, tossing a sword at me. I caught it by the hilt—coolest moment in my twenty-odd years of life.

"What ammi supposed todo with dis?" I asked, my words unusually nasal. Ah, the nose. Still broken.

"Hands, fingers, knees, feet, ass," Blayde listed, slapping an enemy soldier in the latter before she knocked him out with the hilt of her spear. "Aim to maim!"

"Fuh no!" I shouted back.

"Do you want to survive or not?" She turned to glare at me—well, not me, but the air slightly to the right of my shoulder.

"How are the Cyclopes controlled?" asked Nim, running forward and just barely avoiding one of them falling on top of him. "How do they know not to attack their own troops?"

"Programming?" I swished the sword in front of me in warning to the enemy: I would be fighting back. Not that I knew how to.

"Yes, but how are they capable of processing ..." He grinned, and turned around, racing back down the street.

"Nim!" I shouted. But he wasn't listening, and now he was hidden by the fight.

And a Cyclops was on me, again.

"Hey, One Eye!" I shouted. "Why don' you pih on someone your own thise?"

The creature ignored me, just like his brothers had. I forced my eyes to concentrate, so I could make sense of the cyborg, rather than focus on his three brothers.

I dropped and rolled between his legs, hopping to my feet and stabbing my sword into the hinge in his back before he could turn around. Score for Sally! Only now, the sword was stuck, and it hadn't done anything more than annoy the creature. I kicked his ass as hard as I could, hoping to topple him over, but he was heavy and firmly balanced. That was a definite fail.

"Sally, put this on, now!" shouted a voice. Something small and gold sailed through the air, hitting me smack in the temple, and I toppled over. I looked up to see the Cyclops staring down at me, his one eye fixed on my face, his hand raised to smash...

And he turned around and left.

I sat up quickly, my hands slimy with sweat. I felt

my heart beating insanely fast as I realized how close I had been to death itself, to dying on this alien world.

On my lap was a golden armband, looped around and looking a little like a snake. Before I could do anything else, Nim snatched it off my dress, reached for my hand, and slipped it up as high as it could go. He gave it a tight squeeze to hold it in place.

"And now, you're not the enemy anymore," he sniggered, pointing to an identical band on his own arm. "Come on."

He helped me to my feet, and I staggered on exhausted legs. Before I could thank him for saving my life, he raced forward, dragging me with him so fast he almost pulled my arm out of my socket.

Blayde was back among us now, her golden armband firmly in place. She also had two spears, a helmet, and leather sandals, and she looked like the warrior princess of my fantasies. She flew through the air like a valkyrie.

"Almost there," she said, and turned around to retch, breaking me out of my short reverie. She wiped the puke from her lips with a strong swoop of her arm. "Just up that hill."

I took off after her, panting as I breathed through my mouth; my nose hurt too much to be of much use. My bare feet pounded the bloodied ground, trying not to slip, as I followed my friends out of the city.

The grass was soft on my feet but damn cold. We didn't stop running, taking off across the plane as fast as we could, not looking back. Behind me, I heard the screams of the people left in Aquetzalli.

My people.

I fell forward on the grass, exhausted. Bad idea. My nose hit the ground, and pain reared from the contact. I forced myself to turn over while tears flowed from my face like a torrent, soaking down my sweaty face and onto my soiled gown.

"We have to go back," I whined. My hands held my nose in place as I sobbed. My body felt like jelly.

"And what?" said Blayde, stumbling on the grass. "Get the two of you mortals killed? No, thank you. Sally, sit up."

My body moved without my control. Somehow, I had pushed myself up into a sitting position, but I couldn't see much through the veil of tears. My tolerance for alcohol had dropped in the past few years since I stopped drinking, and the punch was strong to begin with; add that to my ever-growing list of reasons I needed to be sad, and you can see why those tears absolutely did not want to stop.

Then Blayde added to that list by snapping my nose back into place.

I let out a scream.

"Don't touch it!" she said, patting me on the head like a good doggy. "You don't want it to come back crooked, do you?"

And with that, she fell onto the grass and started snoring.

"What the hell just happened?" asked Nim, his hands grabbing at his skull like the thing was about to explode.

"She's still drunk," I said through the sobs, trying to keep my hands anywhere except my face, but the pain was stabbing and I knew there was blood on my lip. "I think. I don't know what happens to her when she's like this."

"Where's Zander?"

"How the fuck should I know?" I snapped. "Ugh. Sorry. Sorry. I don't know what to do, Nim."

"I'm going to try and find Zander," said Nim, patting me on the shoulder. "With the cuff on, I should be okay. You stay here and watch Blayde?"

It wasn't really a question, but I nodded anyway. I didn't watch him leave. Instead, I stared at the city. Hot tears ran down my cheek.

"I was supposed to be their goddess," I muttered, "and I'm sitting on a hillside, watching them die."

"A fitting end for an imposter."

I flew to my feet faster than I believed possible, spinning around to see Angee standing in the moonlight dressed in a pure white silk jumpsuit. A circlet of gold surrounded her head, and it twinkled as she sneered at me.

"Angee?" I stammered. The world just wouldn't stop spinning.

"Hey, Selena, or should I say, *Sally*. Nice to see you abandon your people so easily in their time of need."

"What do you want, Angee?"

"Easy. I want you, or should I say *we* want you."

She snapped her fingers high above her head, and the world shimmered around us. It was like a veil lifted from the emptiness. A dozen or so soldiers materialized around us, surrounding Blayde and me.

"Well done, child," said a woman in full golden armor, a blue cape fluttering from her shoulders. "You have deemed yourself quite a worthy asset."

"The goddess commands it," said Angee, bowing into clasped hands.

"So, you're the one they call Selena," said the stranger, turning to stare me down. "Strange. You do look like the etchings, though I expected something ... more." She held out her sword, and for a second I thought she was going to slice me down where I stood, but she held it at my neck, the cold blade pressing on my chin.

"What, you think I need a shave?" I smirked. Where was that coming from? Go home, Sally. You're drunk.

I would if I could.

"The gods do not bleed," she said, sneering at me.

"They do when they're inhabiting a weak, mortal vessel," I said right back to her. "What? You really think any of you are worthy of gazing upon my holy form? Fat chance."

"She's quite full of herself," asserted Angee, "but trust me, she's an imposter from another world. I heard them say so. They're just as bad as the Sky People."

"That'll be for the council to decide," said the commander. "Take her to the chariot. We'll bring her back to the cells."

It was at that moment my body decided to just screw it. The alcohol gave my brain a sharp tug, and then I was falling, falling, the ground further away than it should have been.

I landed with a silent thud, but not before catching a recognizable sight in the sky. A great white orb with the face of a man clearly visible if you were squinting, which I was. Something that looked an awful lot like a moon.

Something that looked an awful lot like my moon.

# CHAPTER EIGHT

## GETTING KIDNAPPED AND OTHER WALKS OF SHAME

Hangovers are the worst. But even worse than the worst hangover? Waking up lying in a jail cell with a woman hanging by her ankles beside you while hungover.

"And here she is!" Blayde laughed. "The Great Goddess Selena in the flesh! The crowd goes wild! And they're screaming!"

"Oh, would you please stop?" I groaned. "My head is killing me."

Even in the first months after my brother John's death, when I had turned to the bottle rather than my therapist, I had never had a hangover quite like this. My head was throbbing stronger than it ever had before, my brain switching places with my heart. Every beat too loud for my ears, pushing against my cranium. Nausea trickled through my body, hitting my stomach in waves. I wanted to heave, but at the same time I just needed a nap. It was all very confusing, made worse by the room spinning and all.

"I'm sorry. Am I inconveniencing you in any way?" She raised an eyebrow. Or was it lowering, seeing as how she was upside down? "Have you never been drunk before?"

"Not like this, and not for a very long time," I replied, "Probably wasn't that godlike of me."

"No kidding."

"What do they think of me now?"

"Not much. They were all pretty drunk as well."

"Why are you here, Blayde?" I asked, sitting up on the granite slab I was given for a bed. The thing was insanely cold on my exposed skin, even through the silk of my tunic. The golden armband was now gone, leaving me at the mercy of their tech.

I threw up a hand to keep from retching as I moved. This would pass; this would pass. I just needed water and maybe an entire brunch. And something to jam into my mind to stop it from producing those black clouds all of a sudden. I was hitting a low: sugar low, hangover low, emotional low—I was crashing, and I was coming down hard.

Wasn't my nose supposed to be broken? My hand slid over the soft skin there, but the appendage was intact. Maybe I remembered wrong: I must have been pretty drunk to imagine that kind of pain, though.

"Same as you," she said. "Got kidnapped by invaders who thought I was your attendant. Goddess Selena, party of two!"

"So, go if you hate it here so much. Nothing's keeping you."

"A lot's keeping me." She shrugged. Again, all this was upside down, mind you. "Mostly a mortal trying to pass for a celestial being."

Ah, she was here for me. I mean, that made sense. A woman with her abilities could leave at any time. The only thing keeping her behind bars was my hungover self and her warped sense of responsibility.

I tried not to draw any attention to that, throwing my legs over the edge of the granite slab. I cringed as my feet hit the cold floor.

"You have a breakout planned? We have to get back to Aquetzalli."

"Hell no," she said. "We're still trying to get the Sky People to stop incinerating the planet, and I'd much rather have this army at my back than the super religious people on the other side of the spectrum. These guys have electricity, Sally!"

"And they tried throwing Angee into a volcano, might I remind you," I said, "and massacred a city of some really nice people we knew."

Ancha, was she all right? Had she survived? Or had she died because enemy soldiers were hunting me? I shivered, and it wasn't from the cold. The fog sitting in my mind got thicker and heavier. The knots in my stomach were getting tighter, forcing a sob through my lips that I passed off as a burp.

"Okay, so maybe not morally the best," she said, ignoring this, "but if the ends justify the means, and if we need to stick around so these clowns have a chance of defeating child-kidnapping aliens, I think we should take that chance. Not to mention they keep a rather nice prison. Most have something dripping somewhere, don't you think? I haven't noticed any dripping here, so that's a nice change."

I stood up, groaning. I didn't like the idea of siding with these murderous assholes one bit, but she was right: They had way better tech. I seemed to be falling further and further down the ethical rabbit hole.

"A fat lot of help we'll do from inside a jail cell, all that aside."

"We'll be out soon." She smiled.

"So, explain why you're upside down, through all this?"

"Because I need the blood to flow to my head, sweetie." She flipped herself back around the right way, her feet landing lightly on the floor. The chain she had been hanging from was probably used as some kind of torture device on less lovable prisoners. I was quite glad Blayde wasn't shackled to them.

But when she landed, something wasn't right. She took a step forward and staggered, reaching for the chains to keep her steady. She turned back to look at me, her face still red, so red. All at once, it became clear.

"Blayde," I asked, licking my dry lips, "are you... are you hungover?"

"I'm a fucking immoral," she said, her gaze tightening on me. "I don't get hungover."

"You weren't supposed to get drunk, either."

She nodded, slowly. Only her head wasn't nodding. Her body was doing the moving, her head somehow staying quite still. I rolled my head backward and laughed.

"Shut up, Sally." She put a hand to her forehead, as if the pressure would help.

"Holy shit! You're worse off than I am." My laughter made my head spin. My mind might have been teetering on the sea of despair, but this sure was keeping me afloat. Even if it did make my ears ring.

"Shut up or I'm not springing you out of here, all right?"

I jammed my mouth shut and watched as she regained her balance, standing still and facing the bars of our cell. Her gaze extended beyond, into the hallway, hopefully plotting a jump to take us out of here. She took a series of long, deep breaths.

"You ... you sure you're up for jumping?" I had never seen her or Zander struggle like this before.

"Shut up, Sally."

The room resonated like a gong. One second she had been standing before me, and the next she collided with the cell's bars, sending them ringing as she toppled backward on the stone floor with a crash. The great and powerful Blayde had cut her jump half a yard too short.

I couldn't help it. I burst out laughing. Again.

"I'd like to see you do better," she spat, pulling herself off the ground and begrudgingly wiping the dust from her dress.

The spinning in my head was becoming too much, and I had to lie down again. The cold now felt good on my back, and having something stable to ground me as my world spun was a bit of a relief. The snaps of electricity were all over my legs now, and I struggled to ignore them.

"This isn't just a hangover for you, is it?"

I opened one of my eyes. Dammit. "What makes you say that?"

"You were acting strange before the alcohol," she said. "You look like you're in withdrawal. Does Zander know you're an addict?"

"I'm not an addict," I muttered.

"What?"

"I'm not an addict!" I spat, sitting up now, gripping the granite with both hands. "I just ... I ran out of my antidepressants, okay?"

"Oh." And, of all things, she sat beside me. Her voice was calm, all trace of accusation gone. "Why didn't you tell me?"

"No offense, but I didn't think you cared."

"I don't, but I can't keep you safe if you don't tell me what's going on."

"Ah. Thanks for being blunt."

"You think I'm uncaring, unfeeling," she continued, still sitting beside me but radiating no warmth, "but in truth, when you've lived as long as I have, you realize how little pleasantries matter."

"And you've lived how long, exactly?"

"Don't you know it's rude to ask a woman her age?"

"I thought you didn't care for pleasantries."

"I'm not even sure Zander knew of your condition before we left," she said, and the granite beneath her hand broke, crumbling in her hand. "You're putting yourself in more danger. You've betrayed his trust. You've betrayed mine."

"No!" I flew to my feet, relishing my turn to glare

at her. "You keep acting like I'm some kind of porcelain doll that can't take care of herself. You think being a mortal means that I'll inevitably die right here, right now. No more. I'm not fragile; I think I've proved that by now."

She watched me with keen eyes, saying nothing. Why was I waiting for her to speak? I hated myself for caring about what she thought of me.

"Why do I need to keep proving myself to you? I can handle myself," I said, at first for my benefit, but my voice grew louder and stronger. "I can handle the responsibility of caring for my own life, thank you very much. I've managed my condition for years. I fought for stability every single day the two of you were gone. I found a therapist who helped me. I found the medication that stabilizes me. *I* did, Blayde. I fought this battle, and I'm winning. My health, my life, is in nobody's hands but mine. So, respect that or don't. I have a short life, and I'm not going to waste my time worrying about what you think about me."

Blayde's eyes were wide now. Maybe it was the alcohol wearing off or maybe it was being stuck with me in a cold dark cell, I don't know, but at some point a smile appeared on her lips, and it hadn't stopped growing.

"I knew you had a backbone in you somewhere."

"Oh, come on. Don't tell me that this was all a game. Seriously, were you being cold to me all this time just so I would stand up to you?"

"Hell no. Who has time for mind tricks? I was hoping, though."

"Then ... shut up. Because I'm going to be fine."

"I know you are but so was Nim, and you watched him die, as did I.. You can't promise that's not going to happen to you. I let him die."

"You saved him," I added. "You brought him back."

"That's not going to work on old age, Sally," she said sternly. "Because face it, you might not die right now, but you will one day. It might be in ... I don't know, a hundred years? And on that day, Zander's heart is going to shatter into a million pieces. Trust me, I've seen it happen before. A hundred years might be a lifetime to you, but to us it's an afternoon. In the blink of an eye, you'll be gone and leave him broken in your wake."

I leaned against the cold wall behind me, closing my eyes for a second. I had been right: Blayde's coldness toward me was because of her brother. She didn't want us getting close. But it wasn't because she was jealous. It was because she knew how it would end. Even if I didn't want to admit it to myself.

"I'm looking out for the most important person in my life," Blayde said again, slowly. She stared at her feet, wrapped in those light leather sandals. "He's the only one like me in the universe and the only family I have ever known. I am an immortal lady; I am sullied knowledge. If you were in my shoes, you would do the same."

I let out a long breath. She was right. If John were still alive, I would do anything to keep him that way. I would do anything to bring him back. He was my brother, but he wasn't my only family. I could never imagine what it was like for her.

"I'm not pursuing Zander," I admitted, knots

forming my chest as I said those words. "Even if I wanted to, which I'm not saying I am. Wanting, that is. I know I can't. It's not healthy for either of us. I'm happy with us just being friends."

"Are you sure?"

I nodded. "Positive."

"I don't think that's going to be enough for him." She stood up, dropping the chunk of granite she had broken off, and it hit the ground with a *thunk*. "I'm sorry, Sally, but it might be too late. I think he may have fallen for you."

My head was spinning now and not just from the hangover, the withdrawal, or the exhaustion. Hearing her say those words opened a floodgate in my mind, and suddenly I was being dragged away by an overflow of emotions. If he did love me, if he loved me *back*. The things I had been trying to hold back, the feelings I had developed for Zander, feelings that could never reach the surface. Because if they did, it would break him.

Break the man I ... loved? I wasn't sure that was the word for what I felt for him, but I was feeling something. Something powerful. Something I had to ignore.

"When we reach Earth," Blayde said, pulling me out of the whirlpool of my thoughts, "you have to end it—and make it permanent. He can't ever come back. We might be immortal, but our hearts can break. And there's not going to be an antidepressant in the universe that will put us right."

I nodded, slowly. It would be the most painful thing I would ever have to do, but I would do it, for Zander. I knew depression. I knew what it felt like to have that unwanted roommate in my mind. I wouldn't wish it on my worst enemy, let alone imagine my best friend crumbling under its weight.

I could live without him in my universe, if the universe could still have his light.

"I'm sorry I've been so cold to you," she said, reaching out her hand. Somehow, I found myself taking it, accepting the warmth in the gesture. "I thought I could protect my brother that way. I forgot what it's like to talk to someone."

"And I'm sorry I didn't tell you about my ... condition. I wasn't going to let it get in the way of me living my life."

She shrugged.

"I probably didn't make it easy for you to open up to me."

I laughed. "Easy? You want to know how thick those walls are around you? Because I sure couldn't find my way through."

Not that I had been trying. She hadn't exactly given me a reason to. But opening up to her now felt like dropping anchor. There was nothing like having a friend you could confide in when the entire universe was out to get you—or force you to play a part.

"And you're not exactly the most stable person in the room, either," I said.

"Hey, my brain chemistry is perfect. What I chose to do with it is my problem. You going to be all right?"

I nodded. "I need to get my blood sugar up. That's the first step. It's not going to be easy impersonating a goddess while my anxiety if flaring."

"Fake it 'til you make it." She gave my hand a tight squeeze before letting it go. "I'll be right behind you, every step of the way. As a matter of fact, let me do the talking unless it's absolutely necessary. It gives for a good effect."

I nodded again. Whatever block had been between us was coming down. Now that we had started talking, I realized I didn't want it to stop: Blayde could actually be my friend.

"Don't think that because we have an understanding I'm going to go any easier on you," she said, her demeanor returning to the refrigerator. "I meant everything I said before and everything I will say now. I expect only the best from you."

"Agreed. So, what now?"

"Well, we need to get out of here, meet the head of state, get them to trust us, lend us their army to fight the Sky People, all while investigating what the Sky People want —oh, and we need to find Zander."

"Easy peasy. Where do we start?"

"First, we ask for the head honcho," she said, "and get out of here in a good, timely fashion."

"And how do we..." I started, only to be interrupted by her throwing her hands over my ears and screaming the word *ALARM* very loudly. Even through her cupped hands, the sound was enough to spin my head like a top.

"What the hell?" asked a deep voice, though I couldn't see who it was, what with my eyes trying to go all Ides of March on me. A prison guard.

"Yo, the goddess hath awakened," said Blayde, standing poised like only she could, even with her half-drunk sway. "Hath? Am I going too far, here?"

"So?" the guard asked, opening the door with a

touch of his hand, like we were inside the volcano maze all over again. The same technology: I suspected the Atlans must have been behind the place.

"So, if you don't want your entire planet incinerated, say, next week, I think you might want to put her in front of someone in charge. Chop chop."

"You do realize who the prisoner is here, right?"

Before he even had time to blink, Blayde lunged forward, grabbing the guard's head in both hands, throwing him to the ground as if he were nothing but a rag doll. She stood, her foot pressing gently on his windpipe, enough to make breathing difficult but not enough to suffocate. He wheezed, staring up at her in obvious awe.

"I'm not your prisoner," she said. "Or I am, but only as long as I see fit. Now, are you going to take us to your leader, or am I going to have to call your replacement instead? He'll probably be quite excited about his promotion."

"I'll ... I'll go," he said, his voice barely a whimper.

"Good man," she said, taking her foot off his neck.

"I thought she wasn't the real Selena, though," the guard said as he stood back up. He clearly didn't like being talked to in this way, but Blayde knew how to get what she wanted. The look she gave him made him shut his mouth pretty quick.

"It doesn't matter if I am Selena, does it?" I said, running a hand through my knotted hair. "I'm here to save you all, whether you like it or not."

Blayde gave me a curt nod, and I felt my chest warm. Now more than ever, Blayde was on my side. She had my back, and I had hers, for all the good that

that would do. I would have to play the part of the goddess if I wanted to save my friends and these people—or die trying.

# CHAPTER NINE

## MAKING FRIENDS IN HIGH PLACES, ON TOP OF PYRAMIDS AND SUCH

The prison was a simple layout with cells on either side of a long stone corridor. Sunlight streamed in from open skylights above, square gashes in the ceiling that let everything through, dirt and all. It didn't seem like a secure system, but then again, we were the only people in the jail. It was either a testament to their laws or to how poorly contracted this place was.

"Um, it's this way," said the guard, pointing down to our left. I blinked out the sunlight, trying to ignore the blaring headache with all my other aches and pains I had gotten from fighting for my life. I needed food *now*.

The guard led us to a dead end, then ran his hand over the stonework on the left wall, tracing intricate symbols with his index fingers. The wall faded out of existence, leaving us with a door out.

He led us out of the tunnel and into the sunlight. We were on the coast again, the prison right next to the ocean with its glorious sapphire waves lapping at the shore. I smelled the salt in the air as I listened to gulls chatting in the breeze. If it wasn't for the armored escort, I could almost imagine I was on a pleasant stroll along the coast.

The road wound toward a city, one with squat square houses, the roofs connected to each other with bridges and stairs that linked terraces and raised gardens. It led down the cliffside into a beach below, much more compact than Aquetzalli.

We didn't go into the city, though. We continued quite a distance down the road until the buildings behind were hidden by trees and space. We seemed to be moving toward a nice stone mountain, one with a comically pointy tip.

Only it wasn't a mountain. As we made our way closer, it became clear that it was an old stone pyramid, overgrown with greenery. It was the kind of pyramid that looked like stacked buildings, not a perfect triangle.

"Admiring the architecture?" spat the guard. "I don't have all day, you know."

We marched forward until we reached the pyramid, and then it was an upward kind of march. The stairs were steep and polished from use. This thing was old.

The guard didn't lead us to the very top. We stopped at the middle tier and were led inside, through another one of the appearing doors these people seemed to have everywhere. Fancy technology for an odd sort of people.

Inside, the room was large and covered in more gold than El Dorado. Banners and shields hung from the walls, basking the cathedral-like room in a warm, rich glow. At the center sat an empty dais and three empty chairs, or thrones I guess, completely unoccupied.

"So much for a welcome," said Blayde, shooting the guard a glare.

"What did you expect? Some kind of feast?" he said, rolling his eyes at her.

"Aquetzalli threw us a party." She scowled. "I take it your unprovoked attack on them was one-upmanship, so your feast has to be fan-fucking-tastic."

"What the heavens is this?"

The commander from last night approached from a side door, her golden armor gleaming in the sunlight, blue cape whipping behind her as she stormed into the chamber. Angee trotted along dutifully behind her, giving me a cheeky grin, the kind a younger sibling would throw if they had just tattled and you were about to be grounded.

In sunlight, this woman was even more imposing. A temporal mishmash, she wore Greek armor over bright Incan patterns, her dark hair in tight Viking braids. A pair of twin daggers hung at her hips, and there was no doubt in my mind that they could soar through Blayde and my hearts in an instant if we didn't keep on our toes.

"Um, the prisoners, ma'am, they..."

"What did they offer you?" she snapped. "Power?

Fortune? No, don't tell me. There's no excuse."

"Selena offered him his life," said Blayde. "A little too easy to take, if you ask me. Are you forgetting how powerful we are? All things aside, look, we just want a chat."

"This could have waited," said the commander.

"Not if you truly believe the Sky People are on their way," I said, stepping forward. Blayde wasn't going to need to cover my back twenty-four-seven. I was Selena, after all, and I had a planet to save. I had a destiny, and I needed some hash browns.

"Which they most certainly are," said the woman, "but you are of no help to us."

"Why did you raid Aquetzalli if you thought nothing would come of it? You wouldn't waste troops on an attack for effect."

"We wanted the goddess," she replied. "The attack was planned the second we heard word of your arrival in our enemy's village. And when Angee told us what you really were, we had to see for ourselves. The fact we took you so easily made one thing quite clear: You are the imposter you say she is."

"The fact you took me so easily proves that I wanted to come with you. Nothing else."

"I do not believe you," she said, her face growing cold. I had struck a nerve.

"Then we got off on the wrong foot." I took a step toward her. "Hi. Let me introduce myself. Selena, goddess of the moon, here to save the world from Sky People and incineration. And you are?"

"Chancellor Bismuth," she said, inclining her head. "Do not expect me to bow to you."

"That would be a waste of time," I replied, "seeing as how I don't care. I'm just here to save the world. I don't care so much for ceremony. Right. Let's get down to it. the Sky People are coming, and we can stop them."

Angee snorted from behind the chancellor's back. "They don't have the slightest clue how to do so," she told Bismuth. "Trust me. I was there with them while they were talking it over. They're from the same place the Sky People are, and they're liars, the lot of them."

"Last time I'm saving you from a fiery death," muttered Blayde. "You're not really the grateful type, are you?"

"Watch it!" said Chancellor Bismuth. "This child has been blessed by Selena. The true Selena. The flames took her attendants, but the volcano sent her back alive."

"Yes, the *volcano* did!" Blayde was practically stamping her foot. "Angee, come on. These people wanted to throw you into lava yesterday. You can't seriously want to give us up to *them*."

"You people are impersonating Selena," she scoffed, "a goddess I have pledged my life to serve. I can give you up to whomever I see fit."

"And the people of Aquetzalli?" I stammered. "That was a massacre. They died because of you. You betrayed them."

"They died because of *you*. Were you the true goddess, you would have saved them."

Ouch, that hurt. I snarled at her, baring my teeth in the most animalistic way I could. I could have bitten her neck off if I thought that would have helped me feel better. Not very godlike, but at this point, I didn't care. Angee had cost those people their lives, and I was going to make her pay for it.

I realized what was happening and tried to pull myself out of it. The pendulum was swinging back the other way, the sugar crash hitting rock bottom. I put my hands on my hips, knowing that was the best place for them right now. I was becoming unhinged. My moods were flipping this way and that like they hadn't done in months, and it took all my energy just to keep myself in check.

I was screwed. Doubly screwed. Triply screwed.

"Chancellor," I said, taking a step toward her. I held my head high and my back straight, breathing through my stomach. I needed to keep my mind clear and focused. "I might not be the goddess you expected, but I'm the one you have, right here, right now. You are a Wise Woman; you command armies, so you know that prophecies are subject to interpretation, to changes in perception. Ask yourself: How do I not fulfill them?"

She leaned back on her throne, tapping a long index finger on her bottom lip, contemplating this.

"It is true that I expected something ... more," she said. "The people of Aquetzalli have different interpretations of the ancient texts than we do. We were expecting a warrior, one that could lead us into battle against the people of the sky. But you look like a child."

Thanks for that. "I may appear young, but does that make me anything less? You trust Angee, and she's a teenager."

"She was raised in Selena's temple," the woman said sternly. "She grew up preparing to serve Selena her entire life. She is wise beyond her years."

"And you yourself told me you're an imposter,"

Angee added. She looked red in the face at this point, frustrated beyond belief. "You can't expect me to believe anything you say now."

"Look," I said, returning my attention to the chancellor, "I know you don't believe me. I don't need you to. I just need you to trust me. We want to save everyone, and we think we know a way how." That last part was a lie, but only until Blayde came up with a magnificent plan. Reuniting with Zander and Nim would have to wait. "Is there any way we can earn that trust?"

"You can't seriously be listening to this." Angee's mouth hung open as the chancellor considered this for a minute.

"Well, I don't see the harm," she said. "After all, we wanted to see you in action with our own eyes. So be it. My feline, Magnus, is missing. Bring him back, and I'll consider listening to what you have to say."

"Your ... cat?" I stammered. Had I heard that correctly? Was she giving me an easy way through this? "At a time like this, you're worried about your cat?"

"Yes." She nodded. "He ran through the forest of whispering trees, and none of my men are up to the challenge. Not that I'd want to risk any of them. So, bring me my cat, and I'll give you an audience. We'll listen to what you claim to offer."

I let out a breath. This was good, wasn't it? Finding a cat wasn't difficult. I mean, there wasn't Twitter on this planet to help me, but I was a cat person, so maybe this was the right challenge for me.

Although, whispering forest—I hoped that was a fanciful name and not an actual description. What the trees could be whispering about I wasn't quite sure. But if well-trained soldiers were scared of it, it might not be the place for a novice like me.

"Fine, I'll find your cat ... Magnus, is it?" I smiled. The woman didn't smile back.

"Ensure you return to us before the setting of the sun," she replied, as stone-faced as a statue, "and then I might consider what you have to say."

"Sunset?" I stammered. "But—"

"The Sky People are our biggest threat right now. I don't have any time to waste."

"So you'll send me to find your cat rather than listen to free advice that could save your people and your world. And you're saying we don't have time to waste?"

"I want proof that you're someone who can be trusted."

I scowled internally but forced my body to calm, breathing out the negative thoughts. Not that it was helping much against the rising anxiety; there wasn't much I could do about that. I would have to search for this cat with the feeling of a knife in my gut.

The breathing technique wasn't very successful. I felt adrift at sea without my medication to anchor me. If Blayde hadn't been with me in the cell this morning, I probably wouldn't be standing right now.

Some days, like the ones where you wake up hungover in a prison cell pretending to be someone you're not in order to save the people who killed those who believed in you, those days deserve a pass button.

Panic rose in my chest. I felt the urge to run, to find a calm dark corner in which to hide as the terror ran through me and threatened to stop my heart. But a moment of weakness here could kill more than my already guilty conscious could carry.

"Chancellor, we'll bring you back your cat. You have my word."

I asked for new clothes and food before we left, my voice calm and level while pointing out that traveling around covered in blood wasn't suitable for anyone, goddess and human alike. They led us to a small set of rooms no bigger than cells—probably an in-house jail—in which we could change. There, I crumpled on the floor and let the attack wash over me. I clenched my fists as I fought for breath. My heart raced with too much adrenaline pumping through it. I screamed and cried into my tattered silk tunic, muffling the sound with fabric coated in the blood of the people I had sworn to protect just moments before they were sliced down by the people I was pledging allegiance to now.

When my body gave the control back to me, I put on the linen tunic, wiped my tears on the silk, and tossed it in a corner. I rose up and left that Sally behind. I've got my ugly bracelets; now I'm ready. Sometimes, when you don't have enough spoons, you make do with a fork.

We were given horses to ride to the base of the pyramid, though I hadn't been on horseback since the ill-fated year when my mother had finally gotten her way against my dad and I was free of karate class. It took me just one session for me to realize I had made a huge mistake. My ass chafed from the awful saddles, and I hated every minute of putting my life in the hands of a giant animal with no regard to my safety. But I couldn't tell my parents that. I couldn't let Dad be right all along. I grinned and pretended to love it, even though Mom could tell something was up.

Eventually, this turned into her rewarding me with milkshakes after the class so that I'd come home from it happy. Happy enough to let Dad know she was right, and I could decide what I wanted for myself. So at least my memories of horseback riding were fond ones, though not because of the horses. Nasty, terrifyingly large beasts. Which were somehow apparently native to this small planet in the middle of nowhere.

There wasn't much of a saddle to speak of. This was going to be much worse than expected.

Blayde managed to climb onto her horse easily, and it looked content with her on its back. She patted the beast's shoulder playfully, and the horse somehow appreciated it.

"You can ride a horse?" I asked, amazed. It never struck me that she could.

"I can ride, drive, or pilot pretty much anything in the known universe. You name it," she replied. "Well, if they want to behave, of course."

I glanced up at the horse, but this thing was massive. Think climbing onto the roof of a jeep without anything to grasp onto.

I saw a tree stump, not too far off, that could do the trick. I just had to guide the horse there, nice and easy ... I walked in front of it, and it took a step toward me, its ears pointed forward, curious. I took another step back, and it followed, its nostrils flaring and trying to sniff at my clean linens.

"What the hell are you doing now?" asked Blayde.

"Horse whispering," I replied, the beast following

me closely. "Don't tell me you're not impressed."

"I won't tell you I'm impressed, either," she said, her glorious eyebrow lifting ever higher. "No. Sometimes, I know when to keep my mouth shut."

"Oh, you do, do you?"

The horse lined up with the stump. I stepped up and tried to give myself a boost over the creature's rump. No use. I was just an inch too short of reaching my leg all the way up.

"Need a hand?" asked Blayde.

"No, no, I've got this," I said, gripping the horse's coarse mane with my left hand. The horse took a step forward, and we were no longer aligned with the stump.

"You sure?" She was now right beside me, a troubled look on her face. "I would remind you that we do have time constraints."

My face went a vibrant shade of red. "I don't need your help, Blayde."

I didn't need a grown woman lifting me onto a horse like a child was what I really meant. This was embarrassing enough as it was. But she hopped off her horse, looping her fingers and creating a stirrup for me to place my foot on.

"You need to talk about something?"

I glanced back at the crass-mouthed guard, who stood at the base of the pyramid watching the three of us intently, judging. I didn't like these people.

"Maybe once this is over," I said. "Moral dilemmas are not my strong suit."

"When this is over, we're going to get you home," said Blayde. She counted to three and boosted me up as I swung my leg, miraculously placing me on top of the horse. I took the leather reins and admired my newfound position of height.

Cool, albeit uncomfortable. Maybe I needed to ride side saddle.

Blayde hoisted herself back onto her horse, which had patiently waited for her the whole time, with the poise of a natural cowgirl. With a tap to the horse's shoulder she was off, trotting down the road beyond the pyramid. Boy, I sure hoped she knew where she was going. I mean, it wouldn't be too difficult to find a forest of actual whispering trees, would it?

# CHAPTER TEN

## FORESTS THAT WHISPER THINGS ARE CREEPY ON TWO LEVELS

As it turned out, we really didn't have far to go. We followed the road for what felt like an hour—longer, if you believe what my ass was screaming—until it veered dramatically to the west, seemingly to avoid a densely populated and very dark forest.

"I take it this is the place." Blayde waved a hand at the thicket of trees. "Shall we?"

"Don't mind if I do," I replied, somewhat nervously. Well, incredibly nervously. So far, I wasn't picking up on any whispers, but, boy, that place was dark. Even looking through the trunks didn't get you very far. This place was old, and there was a certain aura around it that made my spine tingle.

We led the horses in slowly, and they didn't seem too bothered by the place. Heck, I wasn't bothered by the place—and still no whispering anywhere.

That was, until, my face brushed against a branch.

"Oh, yes, just like that ..." said a voice.

I almost fell off my horse. "Did you hear that?"

"Yup," said Blayde. "Who's there?"

Silence.

"Way creepy," I said. This time the shiver ran through my entire body. The knots in my gut grew. "Is that the point of this place? That it's just really unsettling?"

"Maybe," she said. "I had a good talk with some people before we left, and they said the forest turned people mad. Voices with no words, muttering and uttering from nowhere in particular ..."

"No words? Well, I'm pretty sure that tree just came on to me pretty hard. I'd rather have just had the wordless muttering, thank you very much."

"Yeah, breathe it in, birch," said a voice, wafting dreamily through the air. "Let me pollinate your face!"

"Eww!" I spat. "The trees are horny. I repeat, the trees are horny!"

"How peculiar," said Blayde, unperturbed, actually rather excited. No, not that kind of excited. "A Krimoge cluster! Here, of all places!"

"What the heck is a Crimo thingy?"

"A race of stationary carbon-based life forms with chlorophyll," she said. "Conscious plants, if you will."

"Are they usually this ..." I couldn't find the right word. Well, I could, but I didn't want to utter it in polite company.

"I dated one a while back," she replied, shrugging. "I wouldn't say they were any more obnoxious than anyone else. Well, maybe a whole lot less than the Hemocrymptin of Balgeous. Insatiable, that one. Actually, a huge problem, has been driving the price of strawberry lubes up across three galaxies. Be lucky it lives far away from Earth."

"You dated a forest?"

"I tell you about the insatiable Hemocrymptin of Balgeous, and you want to know about my experience dating a few trees?"

"You dated trees."

"It was a very cute forest," she said. "Was really into me wearing flower crowns. But I digress."

"Touch my bark. Come here and touch my bark," said a voice, to my left. "Rub my leaves up and down your dirty face! Oh god! I'm going to pollinate all over you!"

"This is making me really uncomfortable." I wanted to cover up. Don't they always say that the forest has eyes? Or is it ears?

"You try telling the trees that."

"How are they even talking? Do they have ears?"

"They communicate through careful rustling of their leaves," she said, "which we only understand because, you know, high-tech translators. The people on this planet were probably driven mad by the ghostly, incomprehensible come-ons."

"Is this what my life has become?" I gagged. "Listening to treegasms?"

"Well, look on the bright side, now at least you'll have ample warning when allergy season starts up."

I chose to ignore her, though on any other day I would probably have found that hilarious. Instead, I took her advice spoke up.

"Yo, trees!" I said, trying to project my voice as far as possible. "Krimoge cluster? We're here to find a lost cat! It could be cool if you could avoid hitting on us until we leave. I'm having a really bad day here."

"You think you're having a bad day?" asked a sad voice, wafting on the breeze. "Did you hear about Helgry? She's got squirrels."

There was a loud shifting in the leaves, like an incredulous gasp.

"I'm really sorry to hear that," I said, "but have any of you seen a cat run through here? His name is Magnus. I would say he answers to Magnus, but he's a cat, so answering's not really in his nature."

"Ah, humans," scoffed a voice. "Only caring about themselves. What have you ever done for us? We used to spread across the entire continent. And now there's only two hundred of us left."

"That sucks," I said, and I meant it. Deforestation was not a pleasant thing.

"'*Let me entwine my roots with yours.*' Byan *really* said that. Like really."

"Maybe her roots were cold. It *is* winter, Frey."

"She's also a voyeur. You saw her eyeing that couple the other day ..."

"Take off your clothes!" screamed a voice.

"Shut up, North," came a reply. "She did ask nicely."

"I'm about to burst here. It's pollen season, baby!"

"Fuck you, North," most of the trees said, with varying degrees of vulgarity.

"Sorry about North," said Frey, or at least I think it was Frey. It was quite difficult to place names to voices. "Everyone's a little antsy right now. We're not sure if spring is here yet or not. And most of the time we hold it in until we're sure to annoy the most people as we can. A little retaliation for what they did to our land."

"They took our bogs!" said a voice.

"Does this twig look infected to you?" a branch swung toward my face, and I ducked, narrowly avoiding it.

"What am I supposed to be looking for?" I asked.

"Spots, bruising, swelling, uncharacteristic color," the owner of the branch said nervously. "We've been having a lot of rain lately, and it feels funny."

"It looks rotten," I said, honestly. "I mean, like rotten wood, from non-sentient trees?"

"Aww shit," it said, crestfallen. "Tell me, human, if one of us falls, and we're the only ones to hear it, did he make a sound or not?"

"I would think so?" I replied.

"Stop crumbling to their whims," said Blayde, patting her restless horse. I doubt the confusing whispering was making the beast comfortable. "Ask about the cat!"

"Ah, yes, the cat," said Frey. "I did see a cat come by here. Big fellow? Lots of fluff?"

"That's him!" I grinned. At last, some luck being thrown my way.

"Oh, finally, someone's here to get him," said another tree. "That beast has been creating havoc. Scaring off the birds and such. I think the robin in my branches wants to move. Get the creature out of here before Svenson packs up!"

"Stop talking about your birds," snapped Frey. "You're a creepy bird hoarder, Byan."

"But it's Svenson! You like Svenson."

"Just let him effing move!"

"Yo, we're making a deal, here," said Blayde, leaning forward on her horse. "And what will she get in return if she takes out this cat? Pest control does not come cheap, you know."

"She gets out of here alive," said one tree.

"We don't absorb her into the cluster," said another.

"A big nada on the germination," said North.

"Shut up, North," I snapped. "You guys aren't making this any easier than it should be."

"Is that a weasel?" asked a voice, a younger, high-pitched voice. "Is that what a weasel looks like?"

"No, youngling. That is not a weasel," said Frey. "They're human."

"That's what a human looks like?" the tree seemed to scoff. "They sure look like a weasel."

"That is not what a weasel looks like."

"Have you ever seen a weasel?"

"No. My grandfather saw one."

"But that was a millennia ago. Weasels could have changed. Maybe we are what weasels have become?"

"We are oak trees. Not weasels."

"Okay ... Is that one over there a weasel?"

"No, youngling. That is a deer. And what is this fixation with weasels all of a sudden? This not the right moment."

"How do you know?"

"I just do."

"Will I ever get to just know things?"

"Maybe in five hundred years time," Frey said, proudly. I could almost imagine it smirking, if trees could do such a thing.

"Wait, hold up," I stammered. "You've been on this planet for quite a while, correct?"

"Thousands and thousands of seasons," said Frey. "Winters and summers and all over again. Why do you ask?"

"Then you've survived the Sky People," I said. "You've seen them. You know what we're up against."

"Sky People." There was a shiver that ran through the forest, a wave of leaves rustling in shock. "The fire that rains from above."

"We know them," said Frey. "Our roots tell the story of the last times they tried to decimate the cluster. Not one of us was alive the last time they came, but our ancestors were and they live on below."

"As we will," shouted North, "which is why we should cut loose! Free our pollen! Germinate with the humans! Come here, hairy one, touch my trunk!"

"Calm the fuck down, North," snapped Frey. "We're better than this! Anyway, humans, you would like a deal? We tell you all you want to know about the sky fire, and you weed the large cat from our cluster."

"Quite fair," I agreed, glancing at Blayde for support, and she was nodding along too. "Right. A win-win, really. Now where's this cat?"

A loud creaking filled the air as trees moved and resettled themselves. They turned their branches, delicately pointing the way deeper into the underbrush.

Deeper into the darkness.

"Well, let's go wrangle ourselves a cat," said Blayde, giving her horse a gentle kick to urge it forward. Mine trotted casually behind it without any kind of command. I guess it could tell who was really in charge.

"Okay," I said, clearing my throat. It was starting to itch, and I sure hoped it wasn't from pollen. I would never make it through spring the same way again. "We have some gaps to fill in. The locals say the Sky People show up every five thousand years."

"Sounds about correct," said Frey. "Our roots go deep. We might burn away, but we'll always live below."

"Aren't you scared?" I asked. "It doesn't sound pleasant."

"We don't talk about it. There isn't anything we can do. This has been happening since we were a single seedling."

"And what exactly ... happens? Before the fire?" I urged.

"A large silver tube glides through the sky," Frey replied. "It says, *Show yourself*, over and over again. And we wait for something to answer, but they never do. And then, poof, there's fire."

"Lovely," said Blayde.

"And they don't give any clue to what they're searching for?" asked Blayde. "Or whom?"

"Only those two words," the trees replied. "*Show yourself*. Probably not to us; they can see the cluster very clearly, of that we're sure."

The cluster muttered in agreement, shaking leaves at each other with purpose.

Is there anything else you can tell us?" I asked.

"Anything about ... Selena, maybe? Or this prophecy stuff?"

"Oh, Selena we know quite well," said Frey. "She hangs around this planet with quite an attitude."

"Selena's *real?*" I stammered. I turned to look back at Blayde, dumbfounded, and her eyes were wide as saucers. She caught my gaze. She was as incredulous as I was.

"Quite real," said Frey, "though she never talks to anyone. Most of the time, she's the moon, and she seems out of it. A little ... sad in the head, if you know what I mean."

Yes. I think I know a thing or two about being *sad in the head.*

"And the prophet?"

"Only other ship to ever visit," said Frey. "Little ship landed here, a thousand years or so ago. Didn't see much of that, but he came to say hi. Young little human, though you all look quite young to us. Told us to keep an eye open for a smart-looking human girl who's trying to save the world. Didn't count on the fact we don't have eyes, though."

The trees laughed. Or, at least, I think they laughed. It was a different kind of rustling, and it was cheerful sounding enough.

"Did he have a message for the girl?"

"He did, in fact," said the trees. "He told us to tell her to take a *great leap of faith.*" There was a pause, like the entire forest was thinking and holding its breath. "He told her to *jump and to take it all in.*"

"What now?" I stammered. It went from incredibly vague to oddly specific really fast.

"Up ahead," said Frey. "The cat. It's right there. Nasty beast."

Blayde stopped her horse, and mine followed suit. I hopped off, teetering on weak knees as I adjusted to walking on solid ground once more. What a relief it was. My butt tingled from sitting on the horse for so long.

"Right, which way?" I asked the trees.

"Right ahead," said Frey. "Are you sure you want to do this?"

"It's a cat, how bad can it be?" And yet, I was the only one on foot here. I couldn't help but notice that Blayde hadn't decided to hop down. "Blayde?"

"You've got this," she said. Did I note a hint of nervousness in her tone?

"Dude, come on, it's a cat."

"You Terrans," she scoffed. "Always for the cute and cuddly. Cats are some of the most dangerous creatures in the universe. How you, of all people, can be so calm right now astounds me."

"Thanks for your vote of confidence." I glared back at her. She shrugged me off.

"Frey? Is it still here?" No answer. "Frey?"

Even the trees had deserted me.

"Right," I stepped forward, crouching down with my arms out wide. "Here, kitty kitty kitty ..."

I chanted at the trees, coaxing the cat out. I could hear it, gently moving the foliage. It must have known I was here. It could probably see me and was judging whether or not to trust a total stranger. Did I smell reassuring to a cat? Did I sound pleasant enough? Was I a surefire way of getting cuddles?

"I know you're in there, Mister Magnus," I chided.

"Come here, kitty kitty! Who wants a belly rub?"

There was a tremor in the brush, and the entire forest went silent. There was a second where the air itself held its breath, and a thick hand reached around my heart to stop it. And then, with a sudden, spectacular roar, Magnus the cat burst forth. The horses screamed behind me, and I fell over backward, as a magnificent tiger reared, flying toward me like a line out of a Bowie song.

The beast was massive, easily four times my weight, a single paw the size of my face. The only reason I knew this was because he had me pinned down, a massive foot on my chest, pressing me into the earth and completely at his mercy.

"Sally!" shouted a voice from somewhere behind me, though I couldn't locate it what with the massive beast on my chest.

I said nothing. Any false move on my part could have me mauled by this thing. A massive tiger with a thick leather collar and breath that smelled like week old tuna cakes. The kind with a lot of mayo in it and left out in the sun.

The forest remained silent. Blayde said nothing, did nothing. I laid on the ground, staring up at the tiger, trying not to show any fear.

Did I imagine it, or was the beast smiling? He reminded me of the cute strays that hung around the front of my apartment, sometimes claiming the terrace as their temporary palace. He was making eye contact and holding it, and, for a second, I thought I saw a playful look cross those big brown orbs.

It was a well-known fact that cats liked to play with

their food, after all.

I lifted my hand, slowly. It trembled, and I could do nothing to make it still. I was more of a dog person, but even I knew that this was a sign of power, and perhaps ... if I earned it ... respect.

My fingers reached the tiger's coarse fur, and I bent my fingers, giving it a scratch. Magnus's eyes lit up, and I felt a vibration through his paw with a sound not unlike a lawn mower warming up. The big cat started purring.

"Oh, who's the handsome boy?" I gushed, my voice dropping into the familiar cute pet register. He lifted his paw from my chest, and I slid myself up until I was sitting. My hands moved to his neck and ears, and, boy, did he like that. The purring grew more and more as I gave the massive beast the cuddles worthy of its stature.

I was petting a tiger.

This was awesome.

"Holy hell," said Blayde. "I can't believe I'm seeing this."

The tiger gave me a sharp push with his head, like a big dog digging in for more. I grabbed him tight in a warm cuddle. His purrs ran up through my chest, warm and welcome. For a moment, I forgot this beast was supposed to be a dangerous monster. Right now, he was just a big cat wanting good pets. And I was dying to give it to him.

I stood up, wrapping my arms around the big boy and scratching all over. He loved it, rolling over and showing his belly for more rubs. A giant paw swung lazily in the air, the toe beans as big as my own hand.

I scratched warily here, careful of the sacred kitty

belly, and Magnus playfully put my arm in his massive mouth. He was gentle, content, and now I was slobbery.

"You have our eternal gratitude," said the forest. "It appears you have this ... thing, under your control. Thank you for ridding us of the beast."

"Don't mention it," I replied, giving the tiger more happy-pats. "Thanks for the info."

"You Terrans creep me out sometimes," said Blayde. "You have some serious problems you need to work out. Like, the difference between cute creatures and the ones that'll rip your head off."

"But Magnus is a good kitty," I said, my voice dropping to baby babble. "He loves the belly rubs."

"Well, your horse doesn't like the kitty so much," she said, pointing to the empty space beside her. My ride had deserted me.

"Oh, come on," I said. "You didn't catch it?"

"It'll be fine," she said, twisting on her high horse to peer through the trees. "It will most likely go back to the stables."

"And I'll get back, how?" I asked. "Sharing with you? Not super godlike. Plus, we need to get this big boy back to his momma."

"I think I know a way to get two birds with one stone."

"No." I glanced at Magnus, his massive paws swinging in the air. "Really?"

Really.

# CHAPTER ELEVEN

## *WE COME IN PEACE AND LEAVE IN PIECES*

Riding a tiger was badass.

Magnus didn't give a single crap that I was on his back. He just wanted to get home in time for num-noms. I clambered on his massive hide and gripped the collar, and he took off like the wind itself was after him.

The trees were happy to see him go.

It only occurred to me on the ride back how incredibly familiar this all was. The way this random planet not only had evolved humans but tigers, just like the ones back home. Ones that acted like any cat I had ever met, again, back on my home planet, which was meant to be thousands of light years away.

I had to force myself away from that line of thought. It wasn't healthy getting stuck on the things I couldn't change. I didn't want to think about what it would mean for me if my doubts were true.

So, I avoided letting the thought reach its inevitable conclusion. I couldn't dwell on it if I never thought of it in the first place.

Blayde rode hard, but Magnus didn't seem bothered by the fast pace, always two strides ahead. The horse struggled to keep up with the massive beast, not that it wanted to. I heard it panting behind me while I was having the time of my life. The wind whipped through my hair, my hands digging into the fur. I felt magnificent, like I could ride into battle, and strike down my enemies with just a flick of my wrist.

Then again, I had no control over where we were going. I had to hope Magnus wanted home as much as I wanted an audience with his mommy.

We were getting close to the pyramid now; its worn top tier peaked out from above the thicket of non-sentient trees. But there was a sound rising in the distance: shouting, screaming. Voices drifted through the trees to each us, loud enough to hear even over the panting of the racing tiger.

"Stop! Halt!" I cried, pulling at the scuff of Magnus's neck. How did Bismuth stop this thing?

The tiger didn't like being told to stop. He cried out, hissing, but the race came to an end. I clung to the tiger to stop from being thrown off.

"Sounds like they've been busy in our absence," said Blayde, riding up alongside me. Her horse was foaming at the mouth, exhausted and sweating. Even she seemed to glisten a little in the hot, sticky air.

"Who's fighting who?"

"Whom."

"Shouldn't my translator be taking care of that? We have bigger fish to fry!"

"It's doesn't fix broken grammar," she said, rolling her eyes. Even if we were friends now, that didn't mean she had patience for my humanisms, not while lives were at stake. "And to answer your first question, I don't know."

"Did Zander—"

"Get himself captured as part of a poorly thought out rescue mission to save your ass? Yes. Yes, he did. Of course, he did. Don't you know my brother?" She grinned. "A reasonable deduction. That man would easily start a war to save you. See what I meant, earlier? But I digress. Don't you think this is the perfect opportunity for the goddess to bring peace?"

"Wait, you mean whatever's happening down there..." I gulped, rather audibly. "You want me to come between two warring factions and tell them to stop?"

"Yup."

"You think I'm ready?"

"Nope."

"Then why—"

"Because I believe in you?" She let out a heavy sigh, almost masked by the sounds of her tired horse. "And right now, I might be the only now who does. You need them to believe in you too."

"I just..." I ran my hands through Magnus's thick silky fur. Closest thing to hugging a teddy bear right now. "I don't know how."

"Sally Webber, you are a literal goddess right now. Believe in yourself, or no one else will."

I sat up taller, and Magnus took this as a command to start moving again. I looked back at Blayde for support, but she was as stoic and cold as always. She didn't need to put her emotions on display for me to know they were there: I needed that same confidence right now.

"Riding in on the back of a tiger will probably help," she added, cocking her head sideways. "And, hey, what's the point of being a goddess if you don't have a few worshippers? Knock 'em dead, girl. Though not literally."

"Good advice, I guess?"

"You were meant to be here. Now do your thing."

Magnus didn't need to be told twice. He took off toward the clash, his paws moving so quickly I could hardly feel them hitting the ground. I was riding into battle, armed with nothing but my voice. Blayde either had a lot of trust in me, or this was her plan to get rid of me all along.

Pep-talk Blayde wasn't one I was too familiar with. But I hoped she was reliable.

At the foot of the pyramid, the two villages were at war. An army of bronze-clad men with electric spears was facing off against an army of leather-clad soldiers with swords in each hand. Aquetzallians? I didn't know how they had gotten this far without the superior technology of the Atlan war machine.

Before I had time to think, Magnus dove into the pack, dodging blades and spears as he raced to find his mistress. I clung to his back to avoid being harpooned by friendly fire.

Not that any of it was friendly at this point.

"Sally?" I heard my name as I rode by and sprang up.

"Zander?"

He lowered his sword, staring at me with wide eyes, shrinking into the background as I rode away. That explained a lot of things, like how the city of Aquetzalli could stand this long against an enemy with superior technology.

But I couldn't stop Magnus. He was on his mistress's scent, and I clung on to him for dear life. We found her holding off two men, double-pointed spears in both hands, sending electrical shocks into the enemy. They were only barely phased. Somehow, they were insulated, and I'm pretty sure I knew who was behind that little technological advancement.

"Selena?" she asked, her eyes wide with terror. I guess I had made the entrance I wanted.

"Do I get an audience now?" I asked, sliding from Magnus's back. He rushed to her, swishing his tail back and forth with small flicks at the end of each swing. The chancellor looked more awed than happy for his return. The men who had been fighting her turned to run.

"Magnus, dear," she said to the cat. "Where have you been? Come to mommy."

The cat obliged, letting her climb astride its back. Now that it was here, a circle had formed around us no soldier even attempted to strike.

"I guess I should be thanking you," she spat. Not much for thankfulness. "Though I suppose you are to blame for this little attack."

"I was caught as unawares as you were, *though I suppose* that's what happens when you kidnap a goddess."

"Well, then, it's time to make a decision." Bismuth scowled. Magnus stood to his full height, even with her on his back. It amazed me that I had been the one riding him just minutes before. Riding a tiger shouldn't be possible, no matter where in the universe you are. "Are you with us or them?"

"Neither," I said. "Bismuth, I want this fight to end."

She let out a snort. "We're not retreating."

"I'm not asking you to. I call for a ceasefire. We all want the same thing here: to stop the Sky People, whatever their motivations may be. Or have you forgotten about them? Fighting each other just leaves fewer of us to stand in their way."

She said nothing at first. Around us, the sounds of war were loud and echoed against the backdrop of the pyramid. I did not tear my eyes off the chancellor. If I did, I would see men gutted, impaled. I didn't have the stomach for death, but I needed to re-enforce my gut with a lining of steel.

"We are not retreating," she repeated, slowly. She, too, had her eyes fixed solely on me.

"Do you not believe me now?" I asked, extending my hands in a plea for peace. "I found Magnus. I passed your stupid test. You said that would be enough to earn my trust. We might not be who you expected to come and help you, but we are the best chance you've got to get your people out of this mess. To survive."

Bismuth nodded slowly.

"You do realize that your appearance throws our entire religion, our entire way of life, into jeopardy?" she asked, raising an eyebrow very much like Blayde. "Your presence alone brings into question so many of our practices. I need to think of my people first. If they were to know your true nature, there would be panic."

"Would you rather have them question their practices or survive?" I asked. "Practices that involve throwing young women into volcanoes?"

The chancellor looked offended. "I wasn't refuting your offer for help, just warning you of the barriers we'll face. Not everyone will be as accepting of your help as I am."

Yeah, because she was *so* helpful. Anger boiled through me, fury enough to make my hands shake.

"We don't have time for this," I said. "Any of this. Your people are dying. Your possible allies are dying. The Sky People will be here in days, maybe hours. We have no time for this. We need to get your people to safety. We need the battle to stop."

She said nothing, instead taking her cat and pouncing away, leaving me alone on the field without the protection of a terrifying tiger.

Oh shit.

They rushed at me, and I did the only thing I could think of: I ducked. I threw my hands over my head and tossed myself into the mud, hoping that my end would be swift, if anything. Swords clashed overhead—literally. When I looked up, I realized they were now fighting themselves—over me.

I crawled away, slipping through the sleek mud, trying not to think of how I was going to look after all this was done. Trying not to think about the blaring alarms of panic ringing in my head. Just one arm in front of the other, that's all it took to scramble away. Avoiding the legs of the battling soldiers would prove to be another question entirely.

Until I felt cold metal against the back of my neck.

I froze. I couldn't turn around, couldn't see who it was. I squeezed the mud beneath my hands. This was the end. Killed by one of the strangers I was trying to save.

"Halt!"

Her voice echoed across the battleground, punctuated by the shrill blare of a horn. All around me, the sounds of battle dropped to a distant whisper. The metal on my neck didn't lift, but it didn't dig any deeper either.

"I call for an end!" shouted the chancellor. "We must stop fighting—until the threat of the Sky People has passed."

"Finally!" came a voice from the crowd. Zander? "Are you finally listening to reason? And what of the goddess?"

"She's fine. See for yourself," said Bismuth.

"I will be, once you move that fucking sword," I snapped at my attacker. He pulled it away, and I rose to my feet: my entire tunic covered in mud, blood, and apparently some pollen. Gross. Not a great sight for a goddess.

"Lay down your weapons," I ordered, spitting out mud. "We shall not fight amongst ourselves. We will fight against our common enemy. We will save the children from the Sky People, save our world from their fires. I'm not asking you to get along, only to fight side by side when the time comes. If you cannot pick up this banner of unity, then you are on your own. Take it or leave it."

I didn't even look at the crowd: I couldn't bear to see how they were looking at me. I turned on my heels, marching toward the pyramid, to Bismuth and Magnus, to where I would find Blayde and Zander and hopefully Nim. Aquetzallians bowed as I passed. Atlans placed down their arms. If I hadn't been so terrified, I probably would have been touched.

I reached the pyramid steps, and there he was, in the flesh: Zander. Alive. With a sword on each hip and his shirt slightly torn, he looked almost like a pirate. Seeing him, here, now, after all we had been through, to be reunited made me want to wrap him in my arms and feel his warmth around me.

But I was a goddess, and the world was watching. I wasn't allowed to feel any of this. All I could do was nod and watch him nod back, hoping it was conveying all the words I could not say.

The second we were inside the safety of the pyramid, Zander wrapped his arms around me in a tight hug, getting muddy hair all over his armor. The warmth of his grasp was enough to release my tense muscles.

"How bad was it?" I asked Zander as we slowly made toward the main chamber. "After the raid, I mean."

"The city was decimated. We took every last man and woman able to hold a sword to come to your rescue. If you don't stop the Sky People, Aquetzalli will be wiped off the face of the map. They cannot survive on their own."

I knew it was going to be bad, but hearing those words tied a knot in my chest. I held back the urge to vomit. This was much too much for me to bear. Not that I had anything in my stomach left to retch; I still hadn't eaten. Between hangovers, sugar crashes, and now war, I didn't know which way was up.

But then there was Zander. He was here, within arm's reach. Just that was enough to reassure my soul.

"And Nim?" I asked quickly. "Is he safe? Where is he?"

"He wanted to come along and fight," he replied, and my heart caught. Zander shook his head. "Don't worry. I convinced him to stay off the battlefield. He was given the role of Ancha's ... squire, for lack of a better word."

As if summoned by our words, Ancha herself pushed past us, not seeing Zander or me. She stormed into the chamber, Nim close at her heels. He turned back to glance at me before dashing after his new boss. The relief in his eyes reflected my own.

"And you? You're okay? Did they hurt you?" asked Zander. He placed a hand on my shoulder, glancing me over head to toe. I needed to ignore the flush of my skin under his touch.

"I'm fine," I replied, smiling dully. "Better than fine. I rode a tiger! Did you see that?"

He nodded. His smile was so wide I could have drowned in it.

"You seem to have a handle on this," he said, suddenly letting go of me. I hadn't realized how warm he was until he was gone. "Maybe you were right. Maybe this is what the universe was bringing you to."

I wasn't sure I liked that idea. Fate was one thing; but Destiny with a capital D planning for me to help strangers on the other side of the galaxy didn't sound like the usual realm of possibility.

The throne room was different now that it was being turned into a command center. Bismuth had already ordered her attendants to take out the thrones, placing a large wooden table on the dais instead. She and Blayde were in deep conversation by the time we arrived, with Ancha shoving her way into their midst.

"We have over three thousand well-trained soldiers," said Bismuth proudly, glaring at Ancha across the table. "What you saw at Aquetzalli was nothing but a small show of force—a fraction of our true strength."

"Eyes on me," Blayde snapped as Ancha glared right back at Bismuth, echoing expressions of hatred on their war-torn faces. "This isn't a pissing contest. This is a list of our resources. Emphasis on *our*."

"And how many of those Cyclopes things are left?" I asked the chancellor. "Those are remarkable."

"Only about... forty," she said. "They are difficult to make, and *someone* seems to be destroying them of late."

She knew better than to glare at a goddess, but her face said it all. It took a lot of self-control not to shy away from the heat radiating from her face.

"Here's what you're up against," I said. "You've got a bad case of Sky People, and they're coming here to steal your children and set your planet on fire. I have to be honest here: It's not looking good for you."

"Which is why we implored our goddess," said the chancellor. "There is only so much us mere mortals can do. *The Great Selena* was supposed to be our salvation, which is why we've continued to worship her, even if it defies all logic and reason."

"And yet you massacre your neighbors," Ancha

muttered, "people who want the same thing as you do: survival."

"The Aquetzalli are old-fashioned," she scoffed, "weak. They spent their time praying for salvation instead of working toward a solution. If anyone should survive, it should be us. We worked harder and gave up more than those peace-loving freaks could ever have wanted."

"We are not peace-loving freaks!" snapped Ancha. "We do not have a reason to fight. That doesn't mean we cannot when the time comes."

"We need you united," said Zander, "and anyone else strong and able-bodied. The only way to survive this encounter is to fight."

"Against aliens who have ships and weapons?" I asked, then regretted it instantly. I was breaking character. Showing weakness. But the chancellor seemed too preoccupied to care.

"As of yet, the only thing we know is that they want the children," said Zander, "and I don't suspect you give them up freely."

"We try to protect them," Bismuth's voice weakened, her eyes glazing over, "but the Sky People... they send down a stone. And the stone calls to the children, no matter where they are. They are drawn to it. Then they fly into the air and are never seen again, or so say the accounts left in the histories."

"The whispering forest said the Sky People are searching for something, or someone," I added. "Do you have any idea who?"

"The Evil One, maybe?" the chancellor suggested. "In our religious texts, it is said that there is always evil to balance the good. If Selena *is* in fact flesh, then the Evil One might be flesh as well. Though this is only speculation."

I glanced over at Zander, and he shook his head, slowly. This threat couldn't just be a religious battle, could it? Probably not. If the Sky People were aliens and Selena hung out on the moon, but I was Selena as well, what then could the Evil One be?

"We have quite a few texts in our temple which might help us track its location," added Ancha, "and *we* have no doubt the Evil One is real. If we can find him, we must."

"Tell us more about the myths," urged Zander. "How do they describe it?"

"I don't think this will be of much help," she said. "It is a literal incarnation of pure evil. Supposedly he lives underground and corrupts the mind and soul of the weak of heart."

"So, the devil?"

"That is one name for him, yes." She nodded. "As you can see, not exactly something we can fight. Not with the few men we have left."

"Maybe with our technology, we can," said Bismuth. "I'll have our engineers look into it."

"Our focus has to be on protecting the children," said Zander. "We need to stop the Sky People from getting what they came for. That will give us time to take them down."

"We should find shelter for everyone too," said Blayde. "I would suggest using this pyramid. It's sturdy, made of stone, and if you clear it of anything flammable, it might be enough to ride out the sky fire."

"Bring all of our people here?" the chancellor asked, incredulous.

"Deliver our people into the hands of the Atlans?" scoffed Ancha. "Fat chance!"

"Here, and anywhere impermeable to fire," suggested Blayde, ignoring their qualms. "Perhaps the prison could be adjusted. The temple at Aquetzalli too."

The chancellor inclined her head. "Very well. And what of you?"

"We are going to try and parlay with the Sky People," Zander replied. "See if we can give them what they want so they can leave and never return, and avoid setting your world on fire in the process."

"Very well. The histories show no successful attempt at communicating with the Sky People, but then again, we had never had such ... divine intervention. Do what you must do. I will inform my people of what we are about to attempt."

Her golden circlet slipped a little, and she pushed it back on her forehead. With a turn, she left the room, not another word spoken. Magnus got up and followed her, giving me one last look before he disappeared through the door, which turned back into a wall as soon as he passed through it.

Well, that ended that.

"You cannot possibly expect us to work with this ... murderer," said Ancha, turning to face us finally. She was shaking now, her bony fingers whiter than I remembered.

"You have to," said Zander. "If you want to survive, then you need to work together. There's no way we'll get through this alone."

The Wise Woman finally turned to me. "I am glad to see you well, Goddess. You truly are the war bringer that was foretold."

"Hopefully the prophecies tell of peace, as well."

She said nothing, leaving the room to return to tell her people about the newly formed alliance. My worry for her was growing into an entirely new organ.

"That went well," I said aloud. Zander gave me a half-smirk. I think he might have been impressed. I sure was.

Nim let out a long, heavy breath, his shoulders relaxing. As he met my gaze, I was overwhelmed by a feeling of relief. Once again, I was comforted in knowing that he was alive and, it seems, thriving. He stood tall in his crisp tunic, an unused sword hanging at his hip. So different from the child we had accidentally kidnapped from his homeworld.

"We need to talk to these sky-fucks," Blayde interjected, grabbing me by the arm, "and ask what gives them the right to come here and do as they please."

"The Sky People?" I asked. Somewhere there, I had forgotten what this had all truly been about: an alien invasion. "What do you have in mind?"

"Well, building a radio and yelling at them, for starters." She smiled slyly. "But you're going to have to do something first. If you don't, we'll never get a signal out to them."

I let out a heavy sigh. I had enough of those to spare, lately.

"What is it, Blayde?"

She smiled even wider. "Well, Selena, you're going to have to kill me."

# CHAPTER TWELVE

## MURDER AS A FORM OF STRESS RELIEF

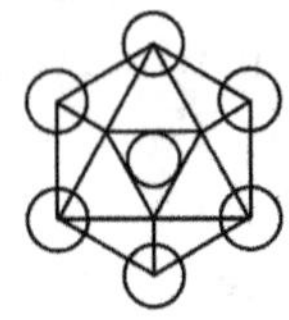

I couldn't help myself: I burst out laughing.

"You that bored?" I asked, grinning sheepishly. "Or, wait, hold on. Let me guess. You need to get some pent-up energy out there."

She glared at me with a very Blayde stare, turning my heart to ice in an instant.

"No, dumbass," she said, "you're going to have to *kill* me."

"Wait, what?" I shuddered. This was no joke. "Wait, you're serious?"

"Deadly." She nodded sternly. She had grown cold in the war room, all warmth between us placed on a back.

"May I ask... why?"

"Simple." She looked up and down the room, checking that we were alone. The other generals stood at the edges of the hall, averting their gaze. "You've got no credibility, not with these people. Giant cats and whispering forests only get you so far. They don't see you as a goddess; they see you as a weird guest. They might listen to you, but they will not obey you. Not without question, at least."

"But I don't want them to, I don't know, blindly follow me around. I'm not a goddess!"

"Keep it down! To them, you are, and you'd better start looking the part. First step? Kill me! We have no privacy here." She pointed to our guard. "And I need some space to investigate while you keep everyone from going around in a panic. I'm never paranoid, and even if I were, that would be a good thing. We need to get those eyes off me. They can stay on you all you like. The only way for that to happen is for everyone to think I'm dead, and the only way for *that* to happen is for me to die. If I'm dead, there's nobody left to watch. Hey, presto!"

"Fine," I replied, stepping away from her, "but can't you fake a heart attack? Why does it have to be me? I'm not a big fan of this killing thing."

"Oh, Sally," she scoffed, "how does someone so nearsighted make it so far in the universe?"

"By not being an idiot," I snapped. "Don't insult my intelligence just because I don't agree with you. I happen to think it's a brilliant idea. I just don't see why I should be the one doing it."

"I'm one of your attendants," she said, sounding slightly ticked off. She probably hadn't expected an argument, let alone me being difficult. Not with our new budding friendship. "I can't just drop dead. It's such a mortal thing to do."

"So, I snap my fingers and curse you to die. Simple."

"That would have been fine if you weren't going so easy on these people. Maybe in Aquetzalli that would have flown. But here? The Atlans probably think you're just some weird pale chick."

"So I have to kill you."

"Yes."

"In some kind of battle to the death?"

"Now you're getting it." She grinned. "I'm glad we're on the same page now. I've always thought that what you're missing is a good flair for the dramatic."

"You can't seriously expect me to kill you!"

"I won't stay dead for long! It'll be good practice for you."

"Practice for what?"

"Defending yourself in combat, *Veesh*. You do realize this isn't a joke, right?"

"Well, the Atlans need a damn good reason for me to have at you. So you better have *that* thought up, too."

"Easy! Just tell them, that, um, you need to release my essence back to the heavens." She grinned from ear to ear. I wasn't mistaken, was I? She was enjoying this? "Or that you need to free me from my earthly body so that I may consult with my immortal brethren. I mean, if only it were that simple, right?"

"Okay, fine, I'll kill you," I said, looking into the eyes of the woman I was about to murder. They were on fire with excitement. "What's the best way to do it? A good stab to the heart?"

"Oh, no." Blayde shook her head. "I don't think you have the arm strength to tear through a ribcage just yet. Burn me with heavenly fire; that should do the trick."

"And by heavenly fire, you mean..."

She brandished her trusty gadget, her laser pointer. How she had been hiding it, through the baths and everything, I would never know. I didn't really want to know.

"You'd trust me with your pointer?" I stammered as she handed me the tiny weapon. She closed my hand around it with her own, smiling a winning smile and topping it off with a wink.

"Lightning from your hands," she said. "Coolest effect ever. More theatrical. More impressible. More... godly. Works like a charm on people who have never seen this technology before."

"This sounds like it's spoken from experience."

"Experience is something I have lots of, though you won't see me share it. Right. Let's get this show on the road."

"What? Here, now?"

"Well, there, ish." She indicated the wide room. "Out in the open and very theatrical. Aim for the heart or where the heart should be. It'll look super credible. I've got the settings all right so don't mess with them, or I will cut you. Okay?"

"Okay," I said.

And with that, she pushed off my shoulders, stumbling backward like a haggard drunk. Or, apparently, like a woman I had just given a harsh right hook to. She raced down the stairs of the pyramid, throwing her hands up high into the air.

"My soul is done with this world!" she wailed. "I must be freed of this mortal envelope so I may convene with my heavenly brothers and sisters!"

I lifted the pointer, but my hand was shaking. I reached the other one up to steady it.

"Don't worry about it," said Zander, who I had forgotten was standing right there. "Just point and shoot."

"I'm killing Blayde," I muttered. "I'm killing your sister."

"She'll only be dead for five minutes. You're doing her a favor."

"You're in on this?"

"I wasn't, but it makes sense," he said, his voice low enough for only me to hear. Meanwhile, Blayde was wailing nonsense at the ceiling, waving her hands around in the air in random circles and giving the stink eye to anyone who stared a little too fervently. A nice crowd was gathering for the show, forming a wide ring around us.

"It feels wrong," I said back to him, taking in the small crowd, which was growing with every passing second. The people looked different than those at Aquetzalli: taller, dressing a little more like Vikings than Greeks. There was less gold and more bronze.

"The murder part? Or the lying? Because either way, I think the end justifies the means."

"If you say so."

"Release me, oh wise Selena!" Blayde implored. "My mortal frame cannot bear this torment."

I took a step forward and faced her. Cue the

theatrics, right? I lifted my arms to the heavens and called upon the only words of wisdom I could think of. *Ma-ia-hii, Ma-ia-huu, Ma-ia-hoo, Ma-ia-haa.*

Who knows if that translated. I didn't wait to find out. I lifted the small laser pointer, aimed it at her chest, and with a deep breath, pressed my finger to the trigger.

And absolutely nothing happened.

"Zander?" I hissed. "It's not doing anything. Is it supposed to not be doing anything?"

"It's supposed to be doing something," he said. "Something must have happened to it."

"At the bathhouse," I realized. "It must have gotten wet when they sent us to the spa! If one of our hosts mistook it for jewelry in need of cleaning..."

"Oh shit." He shook his head. "This isn't good."

"You're telling me."

"Blayde's going to kill you."

"What? Why me?" I stammered. "Aren't I supposed to be killing her? And let's not forget I'm not the one who brought my priceless laser pointer to a spa!"

Speaking of the terrifying woman, she was standing in the middle of the throne room, aghast, staring at the two of us bickering over her prized possession. She must have seen something was wrong. Zander appeared by her side, much to the amazement of the crowd, and then back to mine a minute later, disappearing and reappearing at his leisure.

"She said she can probably fix it," he said, with no prompting from me. "She won't hold it against you."

"Why would she? It's not my fault."

"In any case, she's definitely pissed. Not at you specifically. But she needs to release some pent-up anger, and she regrets telling you that you couldn't break through her ribcage earlier. She says, and I quote here, *I spoke too soon. You'll have to stab as hard as you can.* Sound good?"

"No, it does not sound fucking good. Sorry, I didn't wake up this morning expecting a knife fight to the death with the immortal sister of my best friend."

"I'm your best friend?" asked Zander, perking up.

"As good as, right? And that's what you picked up from that sentence?"

Only enough, he was beaming now. I would have smiled back if the dead laser pointer in my trembling hand wasn't drawing all of my attention.

"So, what now?" I asked.

"You fight to the death." He handed me a bright dagger, slightly curved, the hilt glistening with gold. Where he had stolen it from, I had no idea.

"I don't know how to fight."

"But you know how to dance. Think of it like dancing, with an element of danger."

"I don't know how to dance, either, man." A shiver ran through my spine as I clutched the cold hilt.

"Then just do us all a favor and kill Blayde, okay? Look, I'm sorry, but she's right. It has to be done."

I looked away, my eyes falling on Nim in the crowd of people. The poor kid had eyes the size of dinner plates. I didn't want him to see me massacre Blayde. I didn't want anyone to.

Angee looked as angry as ever, but I couldn't blame her after almost being thrown into a volcano, only to discover me impersonating the goddess she had devoted her life to. I hadn't even seen her in the war room until now, and suddenly I couldn't take my eyes off her.

"Come on, Sal, I'm sure you've wanted to on more than one occasion, right?" he urged. "Trust me, you'll both be fine. You'll probably even learn something in the process."

"I'm on board with the murder part, not so much on the mechanics of it. You don't need to convince me, just tell me *how*."

"Shall we make this quick or interesting?" Blayde shouted over the mutters of the crowd. She had a short sword, practically identical to mine. She bared her teeth at me across the wide distance between us. "Why not show the people your power?"

This was not good.

This was shit. She had years of practice, combined with an inability to never wear out. Not to mention her ability to jump anywhere that was sure to inflict the most horrendous treatment on my normal, human body.

"Here goes nothing," I muttered, more unsure of myself than ever. Not waiting for any more doubts, I lunged at her. She expertly sidestepped out of the way, making me land to her left, her sword on my neck.

"I'm not going to hurt you," Blayde snarled. "But they want a fight, and they'll get one. You'll have to beat me fair and square."

She flew to the other side of the crowd, looking out of place with her stunning beauty and her vicious sword. I spun to face her, trying to remain steady but struggling just to stay on my feet.

"Come at me!" she barked, her feet poised on the

stone like the temple itself was giving her strength. Unfazed by any of my movements, I knew, even if she wasn't going to kill me, that this was going to be the most terrifying fight of my life.

I sprinted at her, and just as she sidestepped away again, I leaped to her side, though she was expecting this. I couldn't tell if she was teleporting or running; she was that fast, moving from point to point to wear me out. I must have looked like a complete idiot, not a deity, as I ran around the ring with my sword held high.

We met in the center of the circle, our swords clashing upon their encounter, their shrill sounds echoing at every strike of metal as we fought, the sweat brimming on my brow, the gnashing of our teeth like a rockslide. She was playing me; that much was obvious. I attacked and she parried the blows, as easily as swatting away a fly. Blayde was always on the defensive, playing for the show, of course. This one was good enough for Vegas.

"Any advice?" I hissed to Zander, out of breath and exhausted from my brilliant five minutes of fighting. But before he had time to answer, Blayde plucked me up off my feet like I was a rag doll and flung me on the war table.

I managed to twist and land with both of my feet on the surface in a crouching position. Probably exactly what she was going for. My knees smarted as my weight bore down, screaming from lack of exercise. If I was in shape, then I was in the wrong one.

I spun around as quickly as I could, my hand a fist as it collided with Blayde's shoulder. She returned the blow by elbowing the small of my back, pain erupting where she hit, my head bursting as I gritted my teeth to keep my composure. Yet I knew she was holding back—this was just for fun, an act. I sprung back, my spine in agony, wishing this would end.

I needed something to stop her. I needed an advantage.

I needed—the force.

Placing my foot firmly on the table, I lifted my hands to the heavens, the golden hilt glinting in the noon sunlight.

"Oh, light of the heavens," I shouted, spitting as I spoke, "grant this mortal body the powers I am owed. Let me use them to bring this sister home!"

They wanted a goddess. Blayde wanted a fight. I had nothing left to give but myself. Me, a terrified Earth girl with no sword training, facing the universe's greatest warriors.

But I had something she did not—a fourth grade Bridgeton Elementary karate medal.

I was unskilled, but I was determined.

And Blayde wasn't allowed to kill me.

This time, when I attacked, I held nothing back. I sprung up, lifting my dagger high as I flew at her. She had ample time to move, so I landed the best I could, turning to avoid her blow. We parried back and forth, with more energy than ever before, though she gave no sign of tiring.

So I did the only thing I could think of and stepped down, hard, on her foot. Steadily, I feigned in her direction then spun, putting all my weight and power behind my arms, and drove the blade straight into her heart.

The crowd cheered as I pulled the blade from her body, dropping her cold, lifeless body to the ground. It toppled off the table, limp as a rag doll, smearing blood on its way down.

I had won. Blayde was dead.

It hard to look at her corpse, knowing that this time, I had been the knife-wielding maniac who caused her death. Nausea rose up my throat like burning bile, even though I knew she would wake up in a few minutes. The blossoming red on her left breast spread over her blue dress, her face a mixture of laughter, victory, and shock.

"Her soul has been freed!" I declared, as loudly as possible. I held my dagger in the air, the blood trickling down the blade and up my arm while I silently prayed that she was regenerating as we spoke.

A cheer erupted from the crowd again. Every person clapped or shouted with glee. There was something fundamentally wrong with the cheering, though. I had killed someone in cold blood in their town square: How could that be admissible?

"You know, you wouldn't expect to hear this from the brother of the woman you just brutally murdered, but nice swordsmanship." Zander was at my side in an instant, grinning from ear to ear as he lifted my hand in the air, high in victory, raising it for all to cheer one last time. It was only then that he crouched to pick Blayde's corpse off the ground, holding it delicately like she was only asleep.

"Nimien," he called, and Nim tore his eyes from Blayde's body. He stared at Zander, his mouth opened to speak but no sound came out. He stood with his back to the crowd, visibly shaking.

"Come on," Zander urged, to me or to Nim I wasn't sure, and he carried Blayde through the crowd. They spread to let us through, hands reaching to touch me as I passed. It was chilling, yet it was good news: They believed the farce now. They would trust us.

"What now?" I asked Zander as we made it through the crowd. Many of them were still following us. Angee pushed them aside until she was right behind us and slipped an arm through Nim's. His face turned bright red.

"That was spectacular!" Ancha rushed to catch up with me. The leader of the Aquetzallians looked more like a fangirl than a ruler, her eyes wide and awestruck by our little demonstration. "Truly, it was amazing."

"Thank you," I tried to sound flattered, but I was disgusted by her reaction. At least they weren't chasing me out of town for murder. "I am glad you and your people are all right."

The urge to hug her was overwhelming now. I put a hand on her shoulder, urging her to stand, but she only seemed to bow deeper. "I came here to seek the help of the Atlans as well. "

I wanted to tell her how sorry I was for assuming they all were dead, for getting myself kidnapped by the enemy, for stepping into their fight, but the words would not come. Which was a good thing, seeing as how I wasn't supposed to admit anything other than complete and utter omniscience.

Instead, I gulped. "Now, please, we need some time alone. To send her to the heavens."

"May I take the body from here?" she asked—no,

pleaded. Like taking Blayde's body would make this the happiest day of her life.

"No, thank you," I replied sternly. I didn't need them to see Blayde returning from the dead, thank you very much.

"I know *all* the proper funeral rites," she boasted.

"I have no doubt about that," I said, still trying to follow Zander up the steps as she sped up. "But I suspect you don't know those that apply to a half-mortal, not having recognized them on sight when we first arrived."

"I do. It is required, but I had never seen a half-mortal before yesterday, which is why I didn't know what she was." She scratched her head awkwardly, and it seemed like she was bullshitting just as much as I was.

We were running out of time. Blayde was healing as we spoke, and my minutes were almost up. "I have no doubt you are well rehearsed in your requirements as ... a Wise Woman."

"Then why am I denied the honor of tending to her?"

"Because we must tend to her body in case she decides to return to it," Zander interrupted, his voice conveying power and inciting confidence.

"Really?" Ancha sounded confused. "I have never heard of that before."

"Well, how many gods have you met?" Zander asked.

"Oh ..." she said, dropping her head. "I know of the theory but none of the technique."

"And we know both. Now please, privacy?"

"Of course," she said, making a sweeping motion with her hand, "but... how is she still breathing?"

# CHAPTER THIRTEEN

## ANCIENT ALIENS WOULD HAVE A FIELD DAY
## WITH ME

You know how sometimes a few words can hit you harder than a knife to the stomach? Well, this was one of those times that made you wish for the knife. Maybe even death by spoon.

"What did you say?" I stammered, my eyes growing wide. And her eyes were growing too, meeting mine, holding my gaze, making my blood run cold. As in, cold enough to chill a beer. I held back a shiver.

"She's ... she's alive?" It wasn't an answer, more of a dawning. But before Ancha could say anything more, Nim grabbed her arm and gave her a sharp tug up the stairs.

"You, come with us," he said and started running.

"No." The Wise Woman, much stronger than Nim, ripped her arm from his grasp. "No, you're coming with me. I have questions."

"You'll get answers." Zander stopped in the middle of the stairs, turning and readjusting the corpse in his arms. Blayde was beginning to stir and he glanced back at Nim, saying nothing. "So long as you don't panic, stay quiet, and find us somewhere quiet where we can chat."

"I know just the place." She shuddered. "The top of the pyramid was left for Selena's return. We've been fighting over it for centuries. You'll have privacy. I'll bring you there, so long as you tell me what's going on."

"Fine," I breathed. "Just hurry."

Blayde was beginning to twitch now, maybe too much. I glanced down the stairs. The crowd from the war room, which had been doing such a great job of ignoring us earlier, now wanted nothing more than to watch us climb away. So much for getting their eyes off our backs. Blayde had seriously miscalculated that one.

I spun around, threw my hands to the heavens, and took the steps one at a time, shouting nonsense about Blayde's mortal death as I rose. It was the weirdest cover up I had ever been involved in, trying to prove that I had murdered a woman who could never die, all while pretending I was a goddess. I blew kisses into the crowd, climbing backward up the stairs, while trying to avoid stepping on the hem of my muddy tunic.

In our attempt to look celestial and unrushed, we adopted a kind of speed hustle up the stairs, making us look like a nice group of mall walkers. Well, all of us except Blayde.

The room at the top of the pyramid was straight out of El Dorado, and I rushed in, hitting the stone door release and effectively slamming the door behind us so I could pant in peace. My legs were on fire. Whoever had designed those stairs so steep should have won the Poky Award for torturer of the century. The five of us were now six. Blayde was draped on the bed, apparently still dead, with Zander and Nim dealing with the too-wise-for-her-own-good Wise Woman. She had her eyes closed now, squeezed painfully shut as she muttered prayers under her breath.

The room had recently been furnished, almost as if expecting our arrival. The bed Blayde had been placed on was a wide four-poster thing with gorgeous gold trimmings, and the only one in the room. The rest of the room was decorated with gilded shields, beautiful silken cushions, and bowls of fruit on small wooden tables. With the front door closed, the only light came from the open skylight, a large stone square like back in the prison.

"What do we do with Ancha?" Nim whispered, shaking. I didn't think he had it in him to even attempt to be intimidating, but he was reacting well under pressure, all things considered. "We're not going to ... hurt her, are we?"

"No, no, of course not," said Zander. "We've just got to ... talk sense into her."

"She' a *Wise Woman*," I said, "By definition, she should be pretty wise, right? I think she's smart enough to see what's going on."

But the problem wasn't just Ancha. It was Angee,

who was watching a woman's skin stitch itself back together. Angee's hands knotted through her hair as she muttered another prayer under her breath. Ancha flew backwards at the sight.

"So you are gods," hissed Ancha, "or are you demons?"

"Oh crap, don't look at that," said Zander, reaching for her hand or any point of contact. She ripped it away. "It's all right, don't freak out. You're safe here."

And the praying grew louder still.

"Oh, great ones," Ancha pleaded, her hands dropping to tight fists by her side. "Protect me from these demons. Protect me from those who wish to blaspheme. Protect me..."

Which was precisely when Blayde came back to life. With a ghastly breath, air rushing into empty lungs, she flew to the floor, arms out and ready to do battle. She looked like someone had plucked her out of the ending scene of a horror movie with blood slashed across her belly and soaking into the fabric.

"Demons!" Ancha stammered. "You're demons!"

"Ugh, come on," said Blayde, falling back onto the bed and rubbing her eyes with her clammy palms. "Could you turn it down? Some of us just came back from the dead, here." She sat up, slower this time, leaning forward and pressing her elbows into her thighs.

"It's all right," I said to Ancha. "It's okay! We're not demons!"

"Yeah, right," she snapped. "That's what a demon would say—deceiver, deceiver!"

"Call us what you want," I said, "but it's your prophecies that wanted us here."

She nodded. Slowly. Very, very slowly.

"And I'm the woman from those prophecies, right?" I asked, this time to Angee. And she nodded again.

"But you're not ..." Ancha didn't have to finish her sentence. I shook my head—no.

"I'm not a goddess. I don't have celestial powers. But I am here, and I'm going to help. Your prophets knew I was coming, somehow, though I have no idea how since I didn't know myself. So maybe I'm not the goddess of the moon, but she as good as sent me."

"The great prophecies," Ancha scoffed, "the ones I've believed my whole life to be false. Yeah, great. You guys really suck."

Ancha took a step toward me, holding eye contact as tightly as she could, dropping any pretense of devotion. When she broke it, it was to take a look at the other people around us: at Zander; at Nim, terrified; and at Blayde, who looked oddly hungover.

And maybe she spared a glance at Angee in the corner, who, with crossed arms and a wicked smile, took this all in like it was the best thing Netflix had to offer. Her eyes never left Blayde. All fear had evaporated, replaced with what could almost be envy.

"I'm Sally."

"So, you are not a goddess?"

"No, and neither are my friends—Zander, Nimien, and Blayde here."

"She died, though," Ancha pointed out.

"She does that sometimes." I looked back toward Zander, knowing some stories were not mine to tell.

"For all intents and purposes, Blayde is dead," Zander explained to Ancha. "If anyone asks, her soul has been released to the heavens."

"Why fake your own death?" Ancha's head snapped to stare at Blayde, who was gathering a wide assortment of random things from the room. Gold shields from the walls, a bunch of bananas, and pillows and wooden ornaments from the bed depicting me reigning fire from above.

I thought I was supposed to be a caring moon goddess. Seems like I had an evil streak.

"Oh, the death part was entirely real," Blayde boasted, ripping a nail from the wall. "I need some privacy. I'm going to build a radio antenna, and I don't want any interference."

"A what now?"

"To speak to the aliens—I mean, the Sky People. To figure out why in the universe they want to, I don't know, decimate the planet and steal a bunch of random children. It makes no sense. Abduction is usually more secretive to avoid creating a panic. And ritualistic, or systematic; culling usually doesn't bother with children."

Ancha looked a little pale. I shot a glare at Blayde, but she was already at my hip, grabbing for her laser pointer.

"You better not have broken this," she snapped, waving it in front of my face before hiding it in her chest. "You were great. That probably looked real to them. Very believable."

"Blayde, it was real," I sputtered. "Technically, you were dead."

"Meh, been there before."

"So, what the hell is an *alien*?" asked Ancha, stabbing a delicate finger at Blayde's shoulder. She turned around sharply, and Ancha retracted the appendage.

"What I'm about to explain," said Zander, making sure Angee was included in this with a glance, "only an infinitesimally small number of people know. It's more than a secret. If I'm telling you now, it's because I trust you, and you yourself told us you have nowhere else to go. If you're going to pretend to be one of Selena's attendants, you should know what's going on. But if you were to tell your people, it would destroy everything you and the holy members of Aquetzalli are trying to do. Trust us—and don't breathe a word."

"I want the truth," she spat. "I've seen things today that cannot be explained. If silence is the price to pay for the truth, then so be it, but if I believe you are putting my people in danger, I reserve the right to tell them what I think they need to know."

"Of course," said Zander. "We want your people safe too. That's why we're here, why we're ..." He sighed heavily, giving me a mournful look. "We came to this world by accident, only to find you were expecting us. We stayed because we thought we could make a difference, that we were needed."

"I swear, in the name of my gods—those of the sun and moon, the real Selena"—Ancha shot me a death glare—"and the gods of the dawn star and of war, that I will not tell another living soul what you have told me here."

"We're from space," said Blayde, standing up and cracking her back loudly.

"Oh, come on!" Zander spat out.

"You're taking too long," she said. "Who cares who knows? They either want us here or not. Look, Angee,

Ancha, the four of us are from space. And we're aliens."

"I don't ..." The words fell on deaf ears. Angee looked even more confused than before, squinting at the undead woman.

"You know that darkness you see when you look up at night?" asked Blayde, "beyond the moon, among the stars? We're from out there. Aliens are from there. We go from star to star, helping people. Doing our bit to make the universe a better place. Visiting. Traveling. Living."

"Up there?" Angee stammered. "So, you're Sky People, too?"

"There are a lot more people in this universe than you could ever possibly imagine," said Zander. "The Sky People are the assholes of the universe. We're quite nice, if you'd give us a chance."

"But, the heavens ..." Ancha squeaked. "Only the gods live up there and the Sky People, the demons of the dark. There is no one else."

"You might want to sit down," I urged. "This is a lot to take in."

"No," she snapped, "if my world is going to turn upside down, then I'd rather be standing for it. You're telling me there are people out there. There are other worlds."

"Yes," I said. "Many. I come from one of them. One very much like this one. And I'm sorry. I'm sorry I am not your goddess. I am sorry I'm using her name. I just wanted to help."

"No." Angee stepped away, leaning against the wall and slowly sliding down. "No. Our prophecies told us you were coming. They were right, and we, we Wise

Women, we've been reading them wrong for millennia. What else have we read wrong? Are my gods up there? Do they care about us? Do our sacrifices matter? Would my death have mattered?"

"Angee?" Nim stepped forward, his voice calm and composed, the first words he had said in ages, "It's going to be all right."

Something in the tone of his voice, in the gentleness of his step—in an instant, he flashed a smile, a quick one, replaced just as quickly with a neutral, thin-lipped expression—and all was well with the world. Angee's full attention was on him now, and so was the attention of everyone else in the room.

"Angee, until yesterday, I had never left my planet before," he said, reaching forward to gently take her hand. She rose to her feet, trancelike. "I was living in a bubble. Pretty much a literal one. Our gods decided everything for us. They told us what to eat and drink. They told us how to dress. They punished us for bad deeds, rewarded us for the good. And I was happy."

She nodded slowly, her entire focus on him.

"Then these people arrived, and my world grew. The bubble popped. I saw my gods for who they really were. I saw they did not care for me, and I left. I followed these people, and now I am here."

"So, my gods are ..."

Nim shook his head. "I don't want you to think the wrong thing. I'm not saying anything about your gods; I do not know them. They could be real, they could be false—that's what faith is for. But if your god tells you to do something you think is wrong or hurtful, then you are not a believer, you are a slave. Do you understand?"

Angee nodded, not saying a word. Ancha stood transfixed near the bed.

"Your gods gave you prophecies," Nim said. "They said we would come. And now we are here. They said the Sky People would come, too. They must be on their way. Now, we promise to help you protect yourself from them—if you want us. I'd say your gods care about you a great deal, if they put all this in motion."

"They wanted to throw me into a volcano," she pointed out, surprisingly nonchalantly. Only Nim winced.

"I've only known these people a short time," he said, indicating Zander, Blayde, and me, "but I trust them with my life. They've already saved it once. Maybe even twice. They might not be gods, but they are good people. They want to help you, if you'll accept that help."

"I will keep your secret." Ancha nodded. "You seem like envoys from the gods. You may not be Selena, but you have been chosen by her. If you can help us, please do."

"We will," I promised. "We'll do everything we can."

"We have one advantage," said Blayde, evidently bored by the conversation and theology. "We know these Sky People are aliens. We don't know from where, but I'm hoping to figure that out quite soon."

"Aliens," Ancha scoffed. "People from other worlds. *Other worlds!* Burn the Sky People. Take their children like they take ours."

"So, what happens now?" I asked Zander. "Blayde's dead, so she's going to talk to the Sky People ... or try to. The chancellor is passing on info to her troops, so

I doubt they need our help. Do we have a plan, like an actual plan?"

"We need to prepare a backup," he said, putting his fingers together, "in case Blayde can't get through to them. We need a way onto that ship, to disrupt things from within. And when I say we, I mean I. You're not going anywhere near that place."

"Oh?" I crossed my arms. "How come? I'm the goddess, after all. It's my sacred duty to protect these people."

"This is a last resort, in case Blayde can't get them to stand down. This is dangerous work, the kind I need to do alone. I can't have you getting in the way or, worse yet, getting harmed."

"I've been in worse. You told me you were impressed!"

"No, you haven't," he replied, perhaps a little sharper than I was used to. "Yes, I'm impressed. Yes, you have a knack for getting out of tight spots. But this is different. These people will burn this planet to a crisp without a care in the world. Humans wouldn't still be living here if they weren't so fucking resistant. I don't want you that close to danger. You and Nim need to find someplace safe to hide. Take Angee with you. If things get tough, I want you to survive."

I swallowed my spit, hard. I was offended, true. But it also hit me just how this could end up if the worst came to the worst. If Nim and I were stuck on this planet as it burned, waiting for Zander and Blayde to find us so we could escape.

Not to mention saving everyone here from aliens from outer space.

I wet my dry lips. "You want me to stay in Atlan territory and ride it out."

"Yes." He nodded ecstatically. "Your presence will rouse their spirits, knowing their goddess is on their side. Stay and keep the people from panicking."

"Erm, isn't she supposed to be in Dorada by then?" Ancha asked, clearing her throat with obvious awkwardness.

"What?" I asked.

"Dorada, the capital city. It's on the schedule. We're to accompany the Lady Selena to the capital to meet with the Emperor."

"There's an emperor in this now, too?" I stammered.

"Bismuth believes you'll be of more help by his side than here," she continued. "As the leader of the free world and all. And although I hate saying this, I agree with her."

"Of course," I groaned, falling down on the bed. I sank at least five inches into the soft mattress. "Of course, I don't get a say in any of this."

"When are we scheduled to go?" asked Zander, on my behalf.

"Tomorrow," Ancha replied. "I thought you knew? There wasn't any kind of discussion about it?"

I shrugged. "Nobody ever consults the goddess."

"Well, I for one can't wait to go on this exciting, new journey," Blayde said. I couldn't tell if this was sarcasm or not.

"Blayde, you can't attend," I said quickly. "You're dead. You realize that, don't you?"

"You're talking to me, aren't you?" She laughed. "So, I can't be all that dead, now can I? Curses, such complete wisdom!"

"Zander?" I asked, worry washing over me. He was smiling at this ridiculous conversation. "Did I cause her any permanent damage?"

"Nah, she's always like this when she wakes up." He said, "Death does that to people. The endorphin rush makes her extremely cheerful."

"You guys are messed up," I said.

Blayde was playing with her laser pointer, fussing over it like it was a Tamagotchi she had forgotten to feed.

"I'll handle this later," she said, smiling again. I always thought her excitement was scarier than when she was mad because at least I knew then what to expect. She pulled a few of her personal items from my duffel bag, stuff I didn't recognize or remember putting inside.

"I'm off," she said suddenly. "Enjoy your trip."

"Off where?" I asked.

"I'm going to do some scans. I may be able to see where we are, maybe even who's coming for a visit. Yes, I have scanning equipment. Don't look so surprised. And don't worry—the city folk won't come looking for me. I'm dead, aren't I?"

"You know, you could have said all this before you had me kill you," I snapped. "I may have been better able to help if I knew what you were fucking doing."

"Don't worry about me," she continued, ignoring my outburst. "Off to run my scans and try to communicate with a shitty alien race that wants everyone here dead. I'll be fine. I'll see you sometime soon, all right?"

And with that, she jumped away and left us in the

stunned silence. But not for very long.

"For ... non-celestial beings"—Angee let out a low whistle—"you can still be damn godlike. Oh! Can I say damn in your presence? Or are you going to smite me?"

"Have at it," said Zander.

"But you're not going to tell anyone, are you?" I asked Angee.

The woman shrugged. "I don't see the point, seeing as how we're all going to die anyway."

# CHAPTER FOURTEEN

## *I FEEL ALL THE FEELS*

Some nights are not meant for sleeping, and that's a damn shame. Sleep should be savored like an elegant glass of wine: dark, strong, and will knock you out if you have too much of it. I quite like that metaphor—or maybe I'm just tired.

Truth is, while everyone else was comfortably asleep in our own luxury room—well, my luxury room, seeing as how I was the goddess—I could only stare up at the ceiling and wonder why sleep wasn't coming for me. I reached for my duffel bag and pulled out my iPod to check the time, before remembering it was a few planets off from the right time zone.

Oops.

I wondered when it was, back on Earth. I had left

at the dawn of the new year, dropping everything for my one and only chance to see the stars. I hadn't taken the time to consider the time delay. Zander had seen two Earth years go by in an instant, and it hit me now, more than ever before, that it was going to happen to me too.

So how long had it been—a week? A month? A year?

A decade?

I shivered. I put that down to the cold, trying not to think about the existential dread that filled me every time I thought about home. How I would have disappointed everyone I loved and cared about. How much I would have missed in their lives, the betrayal they must have felt after trying so hard to accommodate for me.

I could blame part of it on the pills. Sometimes they made me bubbly. Dealing with anxiety made me see the dark side of every choice and decision I ever made, and the pills helped give me the brainpower to realize most were nonsense. But some days, when I was joyful and giddy, they stopped me from seeing any consequences. Now that they were easing out of my system, I remembered why I needed them.

I looked up through the skylight at the moon above and did a double take. It looked exactly like our moon, the one from Earth, which I had seen every day of my life for the past twenty years.

Holy shit.

What if this was Earth? We never moved back in time, so this had to be the future. Somewhere so far ahead that technology was no more and people lay in fear of Sky People. It couldn't be. I couldn't be home.

Not like this.

I felt the attack rising inside me, like a tiger casually sitting on my chest. Something I actually had experience with now. It was coming, The tiger in my chest was rising again. I needed to get away from these people, to put space between us before I exploded. I hadn't had a real panic attack in so long, not since before the incident at the plant. Now one was coming, the second one in a day, and I had to go.

I didn't want to wake anyone to help me. I saw Nim, sleeping fitfully on one pile of pillows, clutching a cushion in his arms like a plush toy. Blayde was sprawled across the bed, wrapped in crisp white sheets. Zander, however, was nowhere in sight. He could have been anywhere.

Let's just hope he wasn't on the roof because that's where I was headed.

I grabbed the rungs of the ladder as fast as I could, hefting myself up. They creaked under my weight, but hopefully not loud enough to wake anybody. With a grunt, I pulled myself onto the ledge at the very top of the pyramid and hoisted up the ladder to keep anyone from joining me. I needed to get away from the skylight, so I forced myself to the edge of the roof, carefully, afraid of missing the ledge in the darkness.

I found the edge and sat down, breathing long, heavy breaths. Once panic wanted to be heard, it would not shut up. I forced myself to focus on details, small things, to try and pull my thoughts away from the darkness that screamed at me to rip off the headpiece, hair and all, the darkness that told me to jump.

And then, it was gone.

It lifted quickly, like I had removed my hand from the fire that had been burning my skin. I did a double take; it had never, ever been that easy. Panic attacks were attacks, not taunts. I held my trembling hands up to my face. What was happening to me?

My bare feet dangled over space, but they were not cold, despite the breeze. I was changing, and I wasn't sure how. In the past few days, I had fallen countless stories, and not just once but a few times, I had survived a spaceship crashing. I had even been thrown out of an airlock. I was doing more than just surviving. There was no internal injury, no brain damage—at least, not that I knew of. And now, panic attacks that abated themselves, like the tiger had come by and thought, *Nah, not going to bother her.*

What was happening to me?

I knew I should have been cold, but I felt sticky. It was more uncomfortable than anything else, like even the cold stopped by to say hi but didn't want to come in. This was really starting to mess with me. While the breeze brought a chill, I was beginning to sweat and felt sticky in places I desperately wanted clean; I was glad for the lightness of the linen. I needed the bathroom, too, but I didn't know about the toilet paper situation here. Oh god, I never thought I would be worried about that in outer space.

Below in the city, a huge bonfire had been erected, and people were dancing in a frantic rhythm. Though the people were small like ants from up here, I could see them swaying their arms in time with the music— music that barely reached my ears. The beating of drums wafted to me on the breeze, fast and energetic.

The people were celebrating.

While the fire was red and orange, the rest of the city was lit with soft blues, like the glowing of their doorways. Was this really the future of the Earth? Was this really what my home had become?

I looked up at the moon once more, daring it to be different. Maybe the craters were off. They had to be, right? Not that I knew them all by heart when I was home; it's not something I thought I would ever have to know.

Little things buzzed around my ears and landed on my skin, and I swatted them away. Mosquitos? It was hard to tell, what with this being an alien world. If it even was an alien planet. I sure hoped it was because I couldn't bear it if this is what the Earth had become.

It was like coming home to find your house had been occupied by a group of squatters. All your stuff was gone. Your family had moved to who knows where. Everything was the same, and yet it was wrong, like the way they decorated the yard or parked their magic carpets.

This couldn't be Earth. Please, no.

A cold hand touched my shoulder, making me jump, but it was only Zander. Of course it was. I turned my head back to watching the people dance.

"How did you get up here?" I asked, but it was a stupid question. The man could jump through the universe. Making it up to the roof was not a big leap for him.

"Blayde was a little hard on you earlier," he said kindly, the hand on my shoulder lingering as he sat beside me, leaving an inch between our dangling thighs.

I wondered why I noticed and why it bothered me so.

"No, we're actually fine, now," I said, blurting out my thoughts without a filter. Dammit. The curse about having a good friend to confide in was never wanting to keep anything to yourself. "We might have actually bonded. That's not what bothers me though."

"Oh?" he asked, sounding surprised. I pointed to the moon, which he stared at intently before turning back to me, confused. "What about it?"

"It's my moon." I bit my lip to hold back the sobs making their way up my throat.

"Nah," he replied, nonchalantly. The hand lifted from my shoulder only to wrap around the other one, drawing me into his warmth. "It's not. It can't be. Have you looked at the stars?"

I did. And they looked ... oddly similar. I was no astronomer, but I felt if I looked hard enough, I could make out the Big Dipper or even Orion's Belt. Maybe I was building constellations out of sand, my mind finding patterns in the infinite nothing, but the stars felt so familiar it hurt. This only made me more worried, like I knew the truth but dared not admit it to myself.

"Zander, what if we missed it?" I looked up at him, but his face was made of stone. "What if we're back, but we're not in 2019? What if this is ... the year three thousand or four thousand or something?"

"Sally, don't think like that," he urged. "This is just some other planet. Some place we need to pass through before we find your home again."

"But they're human, Zander, and the pyramids ... the tiger, the moon, the sky, it's all—"

"Just some other place," he insisted. "Earth is still

out there. Trust me."

I wondered if he meant it. If he was being honest with me or if it was just a comforting lie. Maybe he knew as well as I that this was more than just a few coincidences, that the hope of Earth being out there would be more reassuring than the truth.

"Your home planet is out there too, right?" I asked, glad for his warmth.

"Yes," he said, staring up at the moon. "It's out there. It's just waiting to be found."

"It's just so ... unnerving. I think that's the word," I said, pointing out ahead of me. "You never really know how much you miss your own sky until you have a different one above you. A sky full of alien stars I might know under a different name. Which one is my star, my sun, if we can even see it?"

"That feeling never really goes away," said Zander, staring at the world beyond. "No sky will ever be *your* sky. You never truly belong out here. You'll always be ..."

He didn't finish the sentence. He wasn't really talking about me anymore, anyway. Instead, he removed his arm, lifting away the soft warmth. I fiddled with my hands on my lap, pretending I didn't care when, in fact, there was nothing I wanted more than for him to draw me in again.

Only that would never happen. He couldn't be interested in me—a mortal who would die off so quickly I would be a blip in his infinite lifespan. I was so small compared to him, and the thought of it hurt me inside so deeply it was like I was trying to hold a gaping wound together, one that would never heal. No matter what

Blayde said, he didn't see me as anything more than a friend, and I would hold him to the same."

But I wanted to be around Zander. Even if a romance could never happen—who am I kidding, it would never be possible—I liked him. Other than Marcy, this man was the closest thing to a best friend I had. And, other than Blayde, I was the only person to know his secret, to see his true face.

All I wanted was to go home. But I wasn't sure how I would like living there without Zander by my side. Without him constantly questioning the weirdness of Earth.

I had spent two years in some kind of limbo, not knowing if Zander was alive or dead, if he would ever come back. I had lost the two men in my life I cared for the most, so soon after my brother had died, and I hated living my life without the friendship we had shared. I wasn't ready to lose him again. But if I had to choose between him and Earth, my home—could I ever really decide?

In the moonlight, I really saw him. He was a beautiful man. The hair on his head refused to obey gravity, standing up and reaching for the moon just as I wanted to do. The light fell on his cheeks, illuminating the sharp cheekbones, the harsh features of a chiseled Adonis, the little five o'clock stubble he always seemed to have, though I never saw him shave, nor did I think he ever had the time to.

He pulled his eyes away, and I went back to looking at my hands, trying not to think about the confusing, contradicting feelings in my chest.

"Hey, you want to go somewhere?" he asked,

looking up to meet my gaze. Those eyes contained the entire universe in them. I smiled awkwardly.

"What, and leave Nim alone with Blayde?" I said, desperately trying to keep my cool.

"He's asleep. He won't mind." He shrugged, holding out his hand: an invitation. I hesitated slightly before taking it, and suddenly we were someplace else entirely.

The beach.

An empty stretch of beach, beautiful and calm. No bonfires, no people. Just bare coastline lit by moonlight, the kind of place you almost only saw in travel brochures, places staged to hide the tourists.

I dropped Zander's hand and stepped toward the water. It was icy against my bare feet, but a relief all the same. I didn't realize my skin had become so hot. I let the waves tickle my toes, gently sinking into the wet sand.

"Is this better?" he asked, and I could almost hear him smiling. "No creepy pyramids. No one expecting you to be their goddess. Just a plain, old beach."

"Much, much better." I clutched the hem of my dress to avoid it getting wet. I took a step deeper in the water, letting its icy touch cover my ankles. Fresh.

I stood there, staring at the moon's reflection on the ocean, wondering what lay beyond the horizon of this foreign world. If I was stuck here, I would much rather be exploring than playing god. I'd rather do anything else than play god.

I realized then that Zander hadn't said anything in a little while. I turned my head back, taking in the vision of him sitting on the sand, his face glowing in the moonlight like it was a beacon. I could make out the pyramid beyond us, sitting atop the hill and hiding behind the trees. I preferred not to look up there.

"Is everything all right?" he asked.

"I don't know." I stepped out of the water and walked toward him. I dropped myself into the sand beside him, the tiny grains sticking to my wet skin.

"What's up?"

"Everything." I dropped my head on his shoulder. He didn't try to move me. He didn't say anything, in fact. "I don't want to fight an alien invasion. I'm afraid we're on the losing side."

"We probably are, but we're trying to even the scales."

"Are there even scales to even?" I shuddered. "An alien vessel with incredible technology versus—what was it again? Three thousand soldiers, a few Cyclopes, and two immortals."

"Throw in a prophesied goddess, and I'd say that's pretty balanced."

"Come on, I'm being serious."

"So am I," he said. "You'd be surprised what a little motivation can do to people. Have you ever heard the story of Golar's Last Stand?"

"No. I'm not exactly a citizen of the big, wide universe here."

"Well, as in most stories like this, there was a war," said Zander, "over a small comet with an abundance of suclienor. Both sides started off evenly matched, but over the decades of fighting, the Golarians were reduced to only a dozen soldiers."

"A dozen?"

"Against the Foorna army, three billion strong."

"So you're going to tell me the Golarians rallied together and decimated the enemy."

"Oh no," he scoffed. "They all died horribly in a gruesome explosion. But they took the comet with them. They lost the battle, but they won the war."

"They all died?" I squeaked, jumping to my feet. "That doesn't sound like winning!"

"The suclienor was essential for the survival of the Foornan. Their entire race went extinct soon after their defeat."

"So, basically, everyone in this war of yours ended up dead, and a comet was blown up in the process. Lovely pep talk, Zander."

"I'm not one for pep talks."

"I can't disagree." I crossed my arms in front of my chest. "Don't you have any war advice for a girl who's never been in a battle before? Is there any way we can, I don't know, trick the Sky People into leaving without burning us all in the process? Can you and Blayde ask them politely, like we did with the Killians?"

"Blayde is trying to get in contact with them. We can't make any major plans until we see how that goes."

"So we wait. We go to this Atlan capital of theirs and we wait."

"This prophet called you out for a reason. There's probably something there. Don't panic, please?"

"Don't panic," I said. "Don't panic because a weird monk told everyone here you were the embodiment of the moon, and you were going to save them all."

"He predicted your arrival down to the minute." Zander stood up, brushing the sand from his hands. "Your name was carved in stone on their walls. I'd say that's a valid reason not to panic. The universe wants you here, Sally."

"You talk as if it has a will of its own."

"I didn't used to think so. But after meeting you? I'm beginning to see it more and more. The hot air balloon. Matt Daniels and Captain Kork. Everything leads back to you."

"Stop it, please," I begged. "I have enough to deal with as it is. I don't want to be this major thing in the universe. I just want to be me. What would the universe even want with me? I never finished college, I have a brain that doesn't work right, and I can barely keep myself alive. What good am I?"

"You're my friend," said Zander, awkwardly reaching for my hand. I stared at it as my face went red. "You're reckless and resourceful and you care way too much. You could pluck the stars out of the sky if you put your mind to it. That's why the universe wants you—because you want nothing more than the universe itself."

"Dude, chill." I laughed awkwardly. "As much as I'd like to believe all that, it's not accurate. No one has that kind of power."

"Stay calm," he said, his voice so low I could barely hear it. "Go with the flow. Stay alive. And dance with me."

"What?" It wasn't a question; it was an assertion. And it was so sudden that I didn't even notice when he swept me off my feet and started leading me in a simple dance, stepping back and forth on the sand in rhythm with no music to go by.

"My mind's racing," he announced, about two

minutes in. "I have too much pent-up energy. You don't have to join me—but I'm going to dance."

"You dance to let off steam?"

"Dancing helps me think."

And so, together, we danced, the cold waves crashing against our bare feet while we stared at the stars that would never be ours.

# CHAPTER FIFTEEN

## *ANSWERS TO PRAYERS AREN'T ALWAYS THAT GOOD*

This morning, I woke up with spoons.

Maybe I should clarify: I was the small spoon. There were arms around me, holding me close against a perfect chest, and as I awoke, the most perfect sense of well-being flowed through me. I wanted to curl in away from the bright light that shone directly in my eyes and just lie here, fully content, fully happy.

Then I remember there wasn't anyone I should have been spooning and, poof, good feeling gone.

I rolled away from the arms, out from under the blankets, and into the cold of the morning. Instantly, I pulled back the blanket as the chill brought goosebumps to the surface. There was no memory of where I was, who was with me, or who was supposed to be with me. I tried to open my eyes, but the light burned, making everything look fuzzy. I reached out a hand, thwacking something soft. I had the dreadful feeling that it might have been a face.

"Stop that," came a mutter of muffled annoyance next to me.

"What the?" I stammered as I watched Blayde slowly wake up beside me. She opened her eyes and smiled at me, one of her twisted grins that showed too many teeth.

"Morning sunshine." She grinned, and I had a sickening feeling in the pit of my stomach.

"Oh damn, Blayde," I said, "did we ...?"

"Did we what?" She pushed herself up on her elbows. "I'm pretty sure I didn't sleep with you. Why? If that something you see happening?"

"It's just, well, you were spooning me?"

"Because you asked me to."

"When?"

"Last night."

"When, last night?"

She dropped her elbows and collapsed back on the bed. "When you got back, all sandy and gross, from wherever you and my brother were off to," she said, shuffling her shoulders in what I guess could have been a shrug. "A few harsh words were exchanged *a propos* of this bed. Mainly, me not wanting to move or share. I got here first, why should I move?"

"So ... *what* happened last night?"

"You mean after the two of you stumbled in, you

threatened to kill me again, and told me that if I wasn't going to move, the least I could do was spoon you?"

"Yeah?"

"Nothing." Blayde grinned. "You just slept."

"And why is Zander in the bed?" I asked, glancing one person over and seeing Zander sprawled beside his sister. His gravity-defying hair must have been as exhausted as he was because it fell on his face, shading his eyes from sunlight. His face twitched; our voices must have woken him.

"He was tired?"

"And why is Nim here?" I asked, seeing the teen down the lineup. Somehow, the four of us had managed to squeeze into the only bed. Exhaustion does silly things to people.

"He was here first." Blayde shrugged again.

"I thought you said you were here first?"

"No, I was first compared to you. And you felt bad about kicking the kid out."

"Don't call me that," grumbled Nim, proving once and for all that he was awake.

"You're fifteen, and I've lost track. You're all kids to me."

"Sally's not that much older than me," he mumbled. "I think?"

"Stop it, please." Zander sat up, taking the blankets with him. "We're supposed to be putting a plan in place today to save thousands of people ... I think. I'm not quite awake yet. I need coffee."

"There's never an instance when coffee's a good idea for you," I pointed out.

"This is too weird," said Blayde, pushing past me

and hopping out of bed. She started to climb the ladder to the roof, then let herself fall back against the rungs and started a series of intensive sit-ups.

"Yeah, agreed." I followed her lead and stood up, then realized there was no way in the universe I was doing a morning workout. So now I was just standing in the middle of the wide stone room looking like a dumbass.

"Anyone know where this capital is?" I asked, trying to shift the conversation.

"I have no idea," said Blayde, between huffs.

Another groan rose from the room. This time, Nim's.

"Do we have to?" he whined. He extracted himself from the blankets, lost his grip, and fell out of the bed, his body hitting the hard, stone floor. "I'm okay," he said as he pushed himself up to his feet.

Blayde threw herself up to grab the higher rung on the ladder, grasping it with both hands. She swung herself up, letting go at the peak of her swing, landing gently on her feet, a good five yards below.

"Ugh." Nim grunted. "Can't you just..." He tried snapping his fingers to no avail. "Like, you know, jump us there or something?"

"Doesn't work like that, sorry." Zander replied.

Nimien grunted again. I made better use of my time trying to find something to wear, tired of dresses. I dreadfully wished for my jeans and Chucks again. But one thing these people had in abundance was tunics. As much as I was happy to be wearing something comfortable and clean, I longed for a bra that actually gave me the support I needed.

I came out of the bathroom wearing the same thing as the day before, only a clean version. I still needed to look my part after all.

"Blayde, progress report?"

She did an overdramatic double take, slapping her hand against her chest. "Words I never expected to hear out of your mouth."

I let out a heavy breath. "Have you reached the Sky People or not?"

"Well, they reached me," she replied, "but I won't be reaching them. Not easily, at least. It seems as though they've saturated every frequency with their call. *Show yourself, show yourself, show yourself.* If these people had radio, they'd never get a decent channel."

"Just like your creepy forest said." Zander snapped his fingers.

"You guys get all the fun," said Nim. "I had to sit around listening to Ancha list off all the times birds told her the universe was ending."

"Trust me, kiddo, the forest didn't have anything interesting to say," said Blayde. "Not to mention, we *were* kidnapped."

"Could you not call me kiddo?"

"No."

The door shuddered open, revealing Angee with a large serving plate in her hand, topped with fresh fruits the likes of which would grace a Caribbean Best Western's continental breakfast. She did not look impressed by the likes of us.

"By the moon, if you're going to be impersonating my goddess and her court, you'd better be more careful," she said, practically sneering. "I could have been anyone just there."

"You really think a stranger is going to interrupt Selena's beauty sleep?" asked Blayde, at her side so quickly I could have sworn she jumped there. She grabbed what appeared to be a pineapple and bit into the rough hide, juice seeping out her lips.

"It depends if Ancha can be trusted," she replied, placing the plate on the table at the end of the bed. "If she has told anyone the truth, the news will spread faster than the destruction of an erupting volcano. It would be disastrous. Divide us at our time of greatest need."

"And we'd be killed on the spot."

"To put it lightly." Angee's eyes fell on Nimien, and I could not imagine the shade of scarlet that crossed her face for an instant. Nim smiled back at her, equally rosy in the cheeks.

"Well, warning accepted. That's my cue to leave. Catch!" said Blayde, ripping my attention from the duo just in time to see a jar sailing past my shoulder. Zander caught it just before it hit the floor, making her roll her eyes.

"What is it?" I asked, ignoring the look as Zander handed the jar to me. It was about the size of a newborn, made of clay, and painted a solid blue, no heavier than a sack of flour.

"It's me," she said, grinning. When none of us reacted, she rolled her eyes and continued. "It's my earthly presence. There's a two-way radio in there, so I can relay what I find back to you. I managed to find a frequency the Sky People aren't using so we don't have to worry about that."

"Great idea!" I said, tucking the jar under my arm.

"And you can hear me?"

"You'd have to stick your hand into the jar and find the button, but it shouldn't be an issue. Now I'm off to try and get these assholes to turn around before they make the worst mistake of their lives."

"Which mistake would that be?" I asked. "Kidnapping children they have no right to?"

"Setting a planet on fire for no reason?" added Zander.

"Flying around like they own the place?" said Nim.

"No." Blayde's grimace became a grin. "Attacking a planet defended by us." And she disappeared without a flash or a sound.

"Did I imagine that?" I asked, turning to Zander. "Or did she just say 'us' like we're some kind of intergalactic superhero team? Are we the Avengers now?"

He shrugged. "I'm as surprised as you are. Breakfast?"

We sat and ate our fruit as Angee filled us in with the news of the day. She still hated us but seemed to have realized we were on her side because there were a lot less pointed glares today. Maybe the breakfast was poisoned or something. I didn't exactly care, though it was nice to see her trying to help.

I tried keeping at least an inch between Zander and me, though it was becoming difficult. It was as if we were subconsciously drawn to each other. Every few minutes, I'd realize his leg was against mine or mine against his, and I'd sit a little farther away. Blayde's words still resonated through my mind, but so did the comfort I found from our conversation the night before.

It was all very confusing. Add being part of a prophecy to the mix, and you'll understand why my mind was having trouble with the events of the day.

"So," said Angee, finally wrapping up the morning's debriefing, "what's next in your plan?"

I didn't hesitate. "I'm going to meet with Selena."

All eyes were on me, and I felt them. I brushed a hand through my hair.

"Are you going to make me ask?" said Zander.

"Look." I stood up, leaning on the doorframe and staring out at the land below. Two cities—Atlan and Aquetzalli—both dependent on my every move, both believing in the same prophecy, but in different ways. "If there's a prophecy, there's probably a source, but there's no way to track down that mysterious monk-man the forest told us about. But it sounded like the cult of Selena was established long before he put those scrolls in their hands, so maybe, just maybe, there's a way to talk to her."

"You're saying that as if she's a real person," Zander pointed out.

"The forest sure thought so, and Blayde mentioned that gods come in many forms, so what if she is? It's worth a try talking to her; it can't hurt. Worst comes to worse, I'm just praying into empty air."

"I'll take you to the temple," Angee said. "Show you her shrine. She hasn't talked to anyone in over a century, but she might take one look at you and decide to smite you where you stand."

"Wow, Angee, who's side are you on?"

"Selena's," she replied. "No question. Are we going

now?"

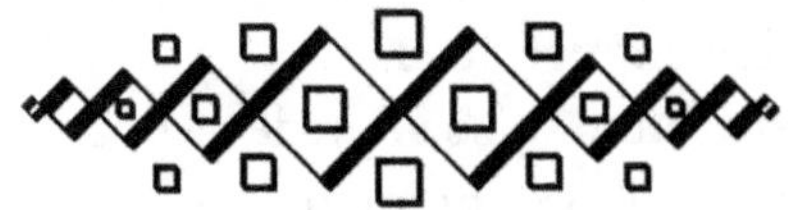

I tucked Blayde's jar under my arm as Angee led our little entourage through the city. The city looked a lot like Aquetzalli, minus the doors. It was built into the side of a cliff, overlooking the ocean, steep steps led us down and around the winding streets. Nobody in town paid us any mind, though some gave me second glances, as if trying to place my face, saying nothing. Not everyone had made it to our battle to the death the night before.

Selena's temple was underwhelming compared to the one in Aquetzalli. Sandwiched between buildings in the city itself, it has seen better days. Even so, people were in and out of the front doors like a grocery store before a hurricane. Unlike my first temple, this one welcomed its community inside the doors.

"This way," said Angee, waving us along the side. She led us to a back entrance, reserved for staff. The narrow way was wide enough only for one person, and we followed her single file through the labyrinthine corridors. Finally, she stopped in front of yet another smooth wall.

"If Sally wants to commune with Selena, she enters this chamber alone." Angee stroked the stone. The door revealed itself in a soft blue shimmer.

"Great." I shoved Blayde's jar into Zander's hands and shot her a solemn smile before walking into the room beyond. It was circular, spacious, and entirely empty. Light filtered in from a small hole on the wall, not even wide enough to fit a fist.

I turned around to see Blayde gazing intently in my wake. She looked disappointed.

"Expecting me to get smited?" I asked.

"A little."

And with that, she closed the door, sealing me in.

I probably should have gone to the bathroom first. Now that I was in here alone, I felt the incredible urge to relieve myself. It was getting uncomfortable.

Maybe that was Selena's punishment for me.

I cleared my throat. Time to give this mad idea a try.

"Hello, Selena," I said. "The real one. It's me, the fake Selena. I'm really sorry about that. I'm not that comfortable about impersonating you, but it's to help these people. You understand that, right? They've been living in fear of these Sky People for so long, and I want them to be safe. Yeah, I know, I just met them. But it's not every day you share your face with a goddess, you know? They needed help so I'm helping them, but ... I'm not sure I'm doing much good. The Sky People should be here, what, tomorrow? And I'm no closer to having a plan in place to stop them. I don't even know what they want. So please, Selena, if you're listening, talk to me. Give me wisdom, a firm kick in the ass, I don't know, anything!"

Nothing.

Was that enough? Did my attempt count for anything? I didn't know how to summon gods or goddesses. That wasn't something that came up in high school. I'd watched enough *Supernatural* to know that divine beings do whatever the fuck they want.

I sat down on the floor and crossed my legs. What did I know about this Selena lady? Well, she was the goddess of the moon, and she looked like me.

And that was it.

"Do you really want your people to die?" I asked, crossing my arms now. "Because that's what's going to happen if you don't help us. I'm not a goddess. I'm meant to be here, sure, by whatever cosmic fuckery my life has become, but I'm not powerful. I need your help."

"Oh, you *need* it, do you?"

I turned, startled. Then my eyes fell on her, and I drew a reverent breath.

She was glorious: beautiful beyond any kind of belief. She literally glowed, her skin made not of flesh but of energy and light, beaming into the universe so bright I thought I would go blind.

The hair, blue beams of light, reached the floor, a floor her feet did not touch. They were hovering a foot above the floor.

I had never seen a person so beautiful, so elemental. Was this what I should have looked like? I stared at my own hands, dismayed to see them confined to flesh and blood and bone. This creature before me, this angel, was too perfect to be human. I was too human to be that perfect.

And, yet, her face. It was so familiar, like I knew it as well as my own. Only, it was my own—thought perfect in a way that words cannot describe. Symmetrical. Blemishless. Made of actual light.

"Selena?" I stammered, recognition dawning in a

part of my mind I didn't think had been working.

"Ha!" She laughed, looking down at her nails. "Oh, I guess it's how you know me. It's just a little unsettling. I thought you might be above all that, seeing how you're pretending to be me and all."

I felt my face flush and ducked it away in shame. "I'm sorry about that." Maybe I wasn't dead yet, but this would be how it ends: at the hand of the goddess I had been impersonating.

If I ever saw Blayde in the afterlife, I would have to have a serious talk with her about the bad advice she doles out.

"No, no, do not worry about that," said Selena, waving me off. "That was always meant to be. The only reason I carry your face is because it has always been this way and will continue to be."

"Wait, what?" I stammered. "You're not saying ... I'm not ..."

She laughed again, a little more melodiously this time. "I'm afraid not. You are still human. Not that that's a bad thing!" She chuckled again. "This is a fixed point in time. You were always going to play the role of Selena, and because of that, Selena would always wear your face. I could show you my true form, but you lack the sensory organs to perceive all of me. See?"

She turned into a mess of triangular fractals, snowflakes of lights inching out of space and time, dizzying my mind. I fell back in shock, and she stopped, turning back into a ghostly recreation of me. Very *Doctor Strange*.

"You wanted to talk," she said, crossing her arms, "so talk. I don't have much time."

"You're a ..." I wasn't quite sure what to say. "Goddess? I thought you weren't supposed to be constrained by time?"

"Doesn't mean I don't want to waste it on some human," she said, glaring at me. And when a goddess glares, you feel it. My body rippled with cold. "I am no goddess. I live my life on a different plane of existence. The kind that boils people's minds to try and comprehend. But do not worry; it's actually quite a 'chill' place, to use your words."

"But ... the people here, they—"

"Worship me, yeah." She flicked her hair to one side, haughty. I was losing awe for her with every passing second. "Side effect from living outside of time. Apparently in the future—my future—I become more generous and loving or something."

"Why can't I talk to that version of you?"

"Watch your mouth," she snapped. "You get what you get. You asked for help, and I'm here. Feel blessed. I don't usually answer to prayers. I'm in the middle of a fantastic healing seminar and following my flow toward the new me. You're blocking my flow."

"I'm sorry about that." I paused, but I had so many questions. "So ... you're immortal?"

She laughed. "My dear, nothing in this universe lasts forever, not even the universe itself."

"But my friends—"

"Flukes of nature," she said. "Not meant to be. But I, like anyone else, have an expiration date. Though when you see time the way I do, you would understand that I've already been there and back again. It simply is. And I simply am. But I will not be forever. Aren't you going to ask any relevant questions? Isn't that why I'm here?" she said, getting more frustrated by the minute. I was too. "I could be leaping off mountaintops right now."

"You just said you live outside time—"

"Even so, stop wasting it. You bore me. Ask me your questions and let me be done with you. I'm only doing this as a favor to that monk."

"A monk!" The monk from the forest. Nothing made any sense, but it was stringing itself together. Even so, I had more important questions. "Right. Tell me about the Sky People. I need to know everything about them so that we can defeat them."

She let out a heavy sigh. "I guess I should start at the beginning, though when you experience time as a sphere rather than a line, concepts like beginning and end are difficult to grasp. For you, I think the story starts when my husband devoured me."

I blinked, incredulous. "He ... devoured you?"

"He devoured entire worlds. I should have expected him to try and devour me, too." She sighed. "I was bonded to him for thousands of years before he snapped. I don't know what set him off. Sometimes, people aren't triggers but fuses. Always bound to burst, to go supernova. We didn't have much of a relationship to speak of, so it meant next to nothing when it was over. He ate our home planet and took me along with it."

I nodded, slowly, pretending I understood what she was saying—I didn't. Apparently, you could marry a psycho who eats planets for no reason. After all, everything is possible in an infinite universe.

"But you're still here," I said, stating the obvious.

"Death isn't really anything for people ... like me," she stated, shrugging. "I don't exist in the same sense as you do. I no longer have a corporeal tether to the lower dimensions, but I *am* in the higher ones. In any case, my husband was arrested for his crimes against the galaxy. I thought it was all done and dusted, that justice was served, and I spent my retirement—and apparent divorce—chasing planets and stars. And then that asshole had to break out of jail and hide out in this dusty arm of the galaxy."

"So you came here to, what? Stop him, talk with him, reason with him?"

"Ugh, worse!" Her silky hair fell in front of her face, and she brushed the strands away quickly. "They thought I broke him out! Sent me out here on exile by the Council of Higher Dimensional Existence! Then my stupid ex was giving me the cold shoulder. That, or he just couldn't see me. Our relationship *was* purely physical, and I mean that in a dimensional sense. Maybe he resented the fact I couldn't give him all of me. Or maybe there was so little to him for me to see. In any case, he was oblivious to me since my death. But I couldn't sit idly by while he was a danger to this world and its people."

"You're the real Selena, then," I said. "You help them."

"I don't do much. Mostly my future self does. I'm still trying to find myself so I can become her, you know? I keep them safe, watch them grow, watch them move on. I try to keep my ex from messing with their lives too much. But my main goal has always been to try to show this stupid retrieval squad where he's been hiding. To send him back to jail. To save these people from his grasp once and for all."

"Retrieval squad?"

And then it clicked. *Show yourself.* The Sky People were looking for *it*, this planet-devouring thing, and they didn't care about anyone who got in their way.

"You brought me here, then ..." I stammered. "That was you, right? I felt ... I think I felt ... a push."

"Not me. In any case, this should answer all your questions. You're going to catch my ex. You're going to trap him, give him to the squad, and they're going to lock him away until the end of days."

"Sounds easy," I muttered.

"I sense some sarcasm."

"Well, if it was so easy, why aren't you doing it? Why can't you turn him in?"

"Haven't you been listening? He doesn't see me! Not to mention I'm busy. I'm supposed to find be finding myself."

And with that, she disappeared, leaving me with more questions than when I began.

# CHAPTER SIXTEEN

## *JUMPING INTO HOT WATER IN A VERY UNSEXY WAY*

I didn't feel quite so bad using Selena's prayer chamber as a debriefing room after that debacle. She didn't seem to care much anyway.

"Let me get this straight," Blayde's voice wafted from the jar, "Selena's real, but going through a mid-life crisis after her husband ate her? I take it the husband is the Evil One everyone's afraid of?"

"Yup."

"And the Sky People are his wardens trying to get him back?"

"Exactly."

"Only they don't know where he is, so they burn the entire planet?"

"Seems that way."

"Then why kidnap the children?"

None of us had an answer to that. Angee stared at the place Selena had appeared, as if wishing her back into existence for a chance to see her herself. The rest of us circled intently around Blayde's jar.

"Then that settles it," said Zander, smacking his leg for effect. "We need to find the Evil One and present him as an offering to the Sky People before they get here."

"And then bring the Sky People to justice for what they've been doing to this planet. Yeah, like that's going to be easy. We didn't even get to the part where this thing has evaded capture for thousands of years. We don't know what it looks like; heck, we don't know anything about it! And Selena's assured me that's all the help I'm going to get, so she's out."

"Hey, you have us." Zander threw an arm over my shoulder. "We've been through worse!"

"Two immortals, two teens, and a girl impersonating a goddess," I muttered. "Fat lot of help we are."

"Will somebody please keep a hand in the jar? I've like to know what you're saying!"

Blayde's voice crackled to life on the floor, and I took the jar under my arm again, jamming my finger angrily into the radio."

"Any way you can tell the Sky People we'll deliver the Evil One to them before they attack?"

"I can try, but as I said, they're clogging all the wavelengths. This one's shortwave so it's fine for now, but it's not going to help us talk to them any time soon."

"We need to go to the capital," said Angee.

We turned to face her, shocked to hear her speak. Up until now, she hadn't offered information voluntarily. She smiled awkwardly before continuing.

"The emperor is the catalyst between good and evil," she explained. She walked around the room until she found the specific icon carved into the wall. "See, Goddess Selena above, Evil One below, and the Emperor in the middle. He'll know how to summon the Evil One."

"That's the Evil One?" asked Zander, running his hand over the indentation. "Sally, come look at this. It looks like that lizard from the scrolls of prophecy."

"The dinosaur?" I asked, but I needn't have. The resemblance was uncanny. "Oh great. So the dinosaur is real too?"

"You know what this means, right?" He grinned. "It means we're going on a trip."

There was a moment there, when the four of us—five, if you counted the jar—shared pure excitement. The feeling that we were moving toward something greater. It's that moment in television when the heroes get a clue so powerful they travel halfway around the world to follow it. Now I knew how it felt, the shared smile, my heart pounding through my chest.

"You guys are joking, right?" Angee rolled her eyes, shattering the moment. "The trip's already on the itinerary. Weren't you listening to anything I said last night?"

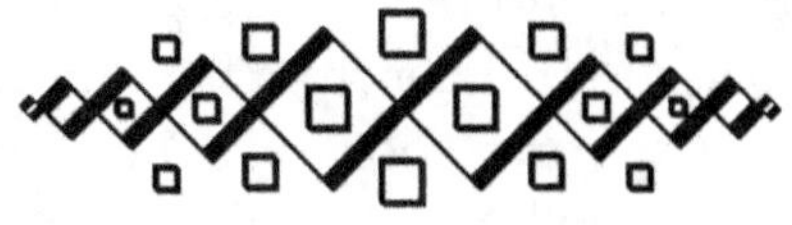

We waited for our departure in the war room, wearing our earthly best. No sense in being impolite when you're the goddess of their world. Dressing well was the least I could do to make up for impersonating Selena.

"Here they come," Angee announced, grinning. She was all smiles today. Maybe it had something to do with the fact that she had irrefutable proof that her goddess was real, even if she had only heard her voice through a wall.

I turned to see Ancha and a few of the wise men and women dressed as fancifully as ever. They resembled giant birds, their heads covered with what seemed to be a mix between a helmet, a cap, and mask of a giant beak. The Wise Woman looked as normal as you could get in these parts, with her lose silk tunic and leather belt. The massive golden crown on her head might have been overkill, though.

Chancellor Bismuth marched in beside her, keeping Ancha on her right. Watching them all stand together was unnerving, seeing as how just a day ago they would have slit each other's throats. It looked like they would rather be doing that than giving each other the cold shoulder.

"As you can see, she is perfectly well," said the chancellor, coolly, folding her arms across her chest. The chest piece gleamed in the light of the noon-day sun. "As are her companions. Except for the woman, but Selena herself freed her from her human form."

"Yeah don't worry about me. I'm just ... eating nachos with the sun!" Blayde replied, her voice reverberating through the clay. She grunted, ripping something with her teeth. "Everything is a-okay in the heavens! We're behind you all!"

The two leaders stared at Blayde's jar, dumbfounded. I groaned internally: Blayde was distracted and overdoing it. It was embarrassing on a deep celestial level.

"I'm surprised the three of you are even talking," said Zander, saving me from more embarrassment, "seeing as your people have spoken so ill of each other."

"It was Selena's will," Ancha said, rising, her palms to the heavens. "The prophecy urged for unification during these dark times. We were surprised the Atlans wanted any part of peace. They do not believe."

"If it's Selena's will… well, she's right here," said Bismuth. "Whatever the path, we must follow it to find a solution. We're running on a tight schedule. We must take her to the capital as quickly as possible."

"The emperor will be excited to see her," agreed Ancha.

"I'm not so sure." Bismuth pursed her lips. "His grasp of religion has been less than supportive. He gives the impression he will put up with it but nothing else. It will be up to Selena to prove her worth."

Of course, it was.

"Shall we get going, then?" I asked, before I could change my mind.

"Let's," agreed Bismuth, and she turned on her heels to lead us out.

The day was beautiful and certainly not one where you'd expect an alien invasion. The sky was a clear blue and cloudless, and the grass seemed to sing below our feet. The air smelled of mint and jasmine, sweet and intoxicating. My flimsy leather sandals slapped hard against the cold stone of the pyramid steps, but the sound was drowned away by the dozen other sandals following my lead.

We walked away from Atlanta, with no one from the city coming to wave us off. Did they know we were leaving? Did they care? I wondered if they were ready to come. I sure wasn't.

Horses were waiting for us, and we rode in silence. We passed the Whispering Forest, which remained silent as we crossed by, preparing for the fire that would burn it down to its roots. I shuddered at the thought. The rest of the expedition seemed wary of the place, though probably because the forest was a creep.

We stopped when the stone road turned to dirt, leaving the horses to turn back on their own. Chancellor Bismuth didn't wait for anyone, continuing down the dirt path alone. Ancha hurried to follow, her birdmen by her side.

And so, we continued on foot.

For ages.

The sun was already hot on our necks. I wasn't a big fan of hiking since the last time I attempted it was on a planet where I was chased by monsters; I wasn't really looking forward to leaving the safety of Aquetzalli and Atlanta. Like a small child, I raised my voice.

"How far?" I asked, trying to keep the voice serene.

"Just over the ridge."

That caught me by surprise. If we were near the big city, their capital, this whole time, why didn't any of us hear it? And why didn't we leave earlier? I kept this to myself, trudging the long path, feeling boredom sinking into my soul. A sugar crash, again, dragging me down and fogging my mind. Heavy beads of sweat trickled down my neck.

"Are you all right?"

Nim marched beside me, seemingly feeling none of the suffering I endured.

"I should be asking you," I said. "You're the one recovering from, well, death."

He smiled weakly. "It's been an odd few days. But considering? I'm all right."

"Did you mean everything you said yesterday? About trusting us? Even after everything we put you through? I can never apologize enough for—"

"I wouldn't be here if it weren't for you, but that's a good thing. If you hadn't come along, I would still be a part of that stagnant world. Out here, there are infinite possibilities. I can't wait to discover them all."

He grinned so wide that I could see every one of his teeth. The kid had the uncanny knack to take a bad situation and turn it to his advantage. A knack I wish I had at his age.

"Thank you," I said. "Thank you for standing up for us."

"I'll always stand up for you, Sally."

The grin disappeared, and he was all seriousness again. The relief of knowing he was all right frayed at the edges. There was something dark about this boy, frightening even.

After walking the long path, the grass on either side of the road grew more unkempt. We climbed the ridge and made our way back down the other side, down steps carved directly into the stone face. I could see almost the whole coast behind me, beautifully green, pristine, and ...

"An island," I hissed. Zander nodded beside me. "We're on an island. And we're heading where, exactly?"

He could only shrug. The rest of our little group was already walking down the steps into a sloping depression, which sounded like my life in a nutshell. We followed, saying nothing.

The inside of the crater was unlike the rest of the island I had seen so far. The plants were lush and thick, the Mediterranean climate suddenly transforming into a rainforest. I shivered at the memory of the last time I was in dense vegetation, chased by towering troll monsters. Zander shifted closer to my side, either sensing my unease or feeling uneasy himself.

The leaders didn't seem nervous in the slightest, though the coolness that radiated from them kept the island silent as we walked. Nim, however, seemed once again overwhelmed by green. His gaze darted every which way in complete and utter awe. Every once and a while, the awe was replaced by worry, and he'd look back along the path in the direction of Atlanta. Angee walked close to him, saying nothing.

In a matter of minutes, we reached a clearing in the underbrush. In the distance, I saw the forest sprout up again, a good tennis court away. But the clearing wasn't grass and plants. A gaping hole stood before us, so wide it could have housed an Olympic pool. And surprisingly, that was what the bottom held: a stunningly blue lagoon, a ledge on its side and stairs spiraling up to the top. Greenery clung into it, a beautiful canopy of vines and leaves dangling above the inviting waters.

"What is this?" I asked, turning to Ancha, who had stopped along with the rest.

"The way."

"The way to what?"

"No. *The* Way."

Already, I could see our hosts taking out rope, tying their belongings firmly to their backs, then tying it around their middle, and passing it along, like on an alpine hike. I was handed a bit of loose rope as I stood pondering the implications these actions entailed, feeling the fear rise within me once again. It was never far for long. Nim shook my arm, pulling me out of my reverie as he and Zander stuffed random items into my duffel bag and politely took the rope from my hand to tie the bag to himself.

"What are they doing?"

"I don't know," said Nim. "Maybe the city's in an underwater cave or something ..."

"In any case, the pool looks okay. Nice and cool water," said Zander, giving my hand a gentle squeeze as I passed him the rope. "Deep, too. We'll be fine."

"Nimien, can you swim?" I turned to him, and he paused for a second, thinking hard.

"In theory?" he replied. "I have time to learn."

We finished tying each other together, making sure the knots were tight. I was last on the line, afraid of the swim, though I was okay endurance-wise. I wasn't keen on the idea that I would have to hold my breath for a long period of time.

The commander made her way to the stairs, and we followed. Well, we had to, being all tied together. My heart pounded like before you try out a new water slide. You know it's safe, your friends are with you, but damn it's frightening. And it got even more so as the chief didn't even take the stairs. He stopped at the rim of the hole, the Wise Men lining up next to him, slightly spaced out. Bismuth rolled her eyes, like this was just some kind of political engagement to get over.

I looked down at the pool below, and all at once the distance fell away from me. Selena, I hated heights. Even falling miles through an alien city and crash landing on a planet from the edge of space hadn't miraculously cured me of the terror I felt any time I was up off the ground. It was like standing on the balcony of a third-floor apartment, planning to jump. Or maybe the fourth floor. You know what? Don't ask me; I was freaked out enough as it was.

And then it got even worse.

Bismuth touched a standing stone near the stairs, blue light radiating forward, and the pool started to shift. The edges waved back and forth, moving, swirling. With a groan like the earth itself was shifting, the water began to spin, a drain emptying into a void. In seconds, the cute little lagoon was a full-blown whirlpool.

"Clear!" Bismuth yelled at the same time as Ancha. They shot each other glares along the rim of the basin.

"It'll be over soon," Nim whispered as soothingly as he could, but it was obvious that he needed reassurance himself. He probably wasn't even talking to me in the first place. Angee grabbed his hand almost violently, squeezing it so tightly I swear I could hear his bones break.

"That's nice to hear," I shuddered.

Without warning, the men fell like dominoes. Ancha took off in a stunning dive, and the Wise Men followed suit, their cheerful cries of glee echoing across the hole as they pulled us with them. As Zander jumped, I heard a rustle in the bush behind me. As Nim dove, a soft hand gripped mine, and as I registered Blayde's grinning face by my side, I was pulled off the cliff.

A few seconds passed with bliss and confusion as the free fall disoriented my mind, air burned my face. Yet I felt free, even as I tried to understand why Blayde was by my side. Then we struck water and were pulled down the drain of the world into the unknown.

# CHAPTER SEVENTEEN

## MS. WEBBER GOES TO GOLD PYRAMID CITY

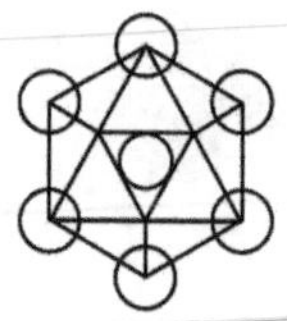

Take it from someone who knows: Leaping into a whirlpool from three stories high was a lot more painful than having your atoms shredded and reassembled halfway across the galaxy. Not that I would recommend either as a fun way to spend a weekend.

The second I hit the water, my body was ripped apart. Then, darkness. My mouth flew open and in went the water, right up the pipe. It was icy and cold, yet it somehow managed to burn my skin and stab my eyes. I forced those shut, the only thing I had the slightest bit of control over.

I wanted to cough out the water from my lungs, but there was already too much of it around me. My body twisted as it was pulled this way and that, a leaf in a water park that wasn't so much flying as being ripped to shreds. A bubble forced itself through my lips, and I realized it was my own scream.

I was drowning. I was dying.

The hands squeezed mine, and I squeezed back. I grabbed them like my life depended on it.

And then, as suddenly as it began, the water stilled.

I forced my eyes open, still feeling the sting of water in my eyes, but I was greeted with something far more rewarding than the dark: light, trickling in from above. I let go of the hands and doggy-paddled to the surface, breaking out of the water and bursting for air.

Hello, oxygen! So glad you could make it to the party!

I coughed before I could breathe. Water spewed from my lips as I gasped for air. It tasted like liquid diamonds when it reached my lips: perfect, pure, and filling me with life. The instant I heard Blayde inhale, she let go and was gone, leaving me alone as I struggled to reach any land. The water was too deep to stand, and the light too strong to see. The rope around my waist was gone.

The journey through the whirlpool had lasted only seconds, but it felt like an eternity. I was physically exhausted and mentally drained. I needed to lie down, to breathe. I needed to make sure my friends were okay. I needed to know where I was.

I breathed easy. Finally.

As my eyesight came back, my feet pedaling to keep me from sinking again, I realized an arm was extended to me. Out of reflex, I threw mine to grab it and was hoisted out of the water on what felt like a flat stone platform. It was shaded here, and I blinked the burning out. Cold, so cold; did no one have towels here? I only now understood the meaning of Ford Prefect's advice. Damn.

I turned to look at my rescuers and almost fell back into the water, with only Zander's arm stopping me from such an embarrassing end.

*Giant birds.*

I stood, staring with my mouth agape, at the tall gold and colorful birds, taller than any of us assembled there. Their long necks craned to stare me in the face as my mouth opened to form a scream, but the people around me laughed.

They weren't birds at all. Men, feet in stilts, covered head to toe with feathers and using sticks to control puppet heads, laughed gleefully at my astonished expression. Was it a ritual? A greeting? Were they hazing me? I had no idea. But I joined in the laughing, the birdmen cheering at the success of their costume.

We were inside a sinkhole, a large one with bright blue water at its base, the same blue water I had just appeared in. Stone steps curved around the outer edge of the hole, our way out of here, though they were draped in vines that sprouted bright white flowers, filling the chasm with sweetness.

So much color, so much beauty. An opulence of gold enough to spare. My friends and I were soaked but so were the leaders of Atlanta and Aquetzalli, and neither seemed bothered by this fact. They exchanged disdainful glances, much tamer than you'd expect after one had almost annihilated the other's city.

I guess the prospect of an alien invasion could cause the formation of even the oddest of alliances.

The bird people began to circle me. They eyed me down, taking in the tunic and painful gold headpiece. There were other men by our side next to the pool. The leaders and wise men were still there, looking slightly nervous as they twitched in place. Their feathers were disheveled or, in some cases, altogether missing, making them appear almost shabby next to the giant birds.

And I forgot to mention the elegantly dressed, head-held-high warriors standing as an escort to the group. Their serrated swords were in hand, ready for a fight, even though there was no threat nearby. They did not smile or frown as I let out my awkward laugh, nor did they have any expression at all.

Unsettling was the kindest way to describe it.

Then, as if choreographed, the soldiers turned and started to march up the stairs, followed by the birdmen, and soon we were a procession, parading up to the top of the sinkhole. At the top, there was the city. And, oh, what a city it was.

It stood a few miles away. Even from here, we could see that it was just as a capital should be: gigantic in size with houses lined up on either side of the main road, all spreading out from a pyramid like the spokes of a wheel. It put the one in Atlanta to absolute shame. This one was a dozen times taller with windows and doors in every direction.

And to top it off, this one was made of gold.

Between us and it, however, lay an ocean of tents. Thousands of them dotted the surrounding landscape, all in different colors, shapes, and sizes. They covered the dusty earth like pimples.

"Ancha, who are they?" I whispered, leaning to Ancha, trying not to draw attention to myself. She seemed surprised I was even talking to her.

"Other tribes, Sally-Selena," she replied as casually as she could.

"Don't they have their own cities?"

"They're here for you. Each tribe has a different part of the prophecy. Theirs must have come true for them to be here."

"They all ... came here?" I stammered. "For me?"

"They don't want to die either. I would do anything for my people, even associate with an Atlan. I expect that they are the same. We all are, anyway. We tell ourselves we're unique, but in the end, we're all humans. And we just want to survive."

I gave her a knowing look as we followed the soldiers down the dusty road, keeping up the fast march of the soldiers as we were  paraded through town. Though it had been early in the morning when our hike had started, it was nearing noon now, and people were out and about, chatting furiously outside their tents and staring  as we walked down their road.

We reached the edge of the city, a massive stone wall surrounding the place. It was vast and sprawling, but it was also protected. The wall itself was crafted with dark black stone, fitted together like a gigantic puzzle to create a barrier no one could possibly hope to break. It was easily taller than a two-story house, so high I couldn't see who stood guard.

I mean, with a wall that size, you'd definitely have guards.

This was proved to be true when we arrived in front of the gate itself. Iron topped with gold had been twisted into the most incredible shapes, telling stories in their craftsmanship. Stories of heroes and heroines doing battle. Giant creatures and small cats.

Four guards protected the gate, two on the outside and two on the inside. Our escort was quick to make their way forward and speak a few words to their colleagues, who only stared at us. Finally, one let out a grunt, turned back to the gate, and pulled on the chain. The guards on the other side helped, and the golden gate slowly slid back into the wall on either side.

Our guards began to walk again, and so we followed. I glanced over at Zander, only to see his gaze darting back and forth nervously. I hadn't seen him so unsettled in a long time, not since this trip had started. Although he looked somewhat composed from the outside, I could tell he was anxious.

"Blayde followed us," I whispered. Instantly, his radiation returned, warmth beaming off his skin.

"How?" he asked under his breath.

"Grabbed my hand as we were going through the whirlpool. She's fine; don't worry."

He let out a huge sigh, a breath he'd seemingly been holding in since we'd surfaced. "That's good. To be honest, I have no idea where we are now. Their capital could be on another moon for all we know. But traveling by water—"

"Water ..." I grabbed my bag from Nim's hands, though he was too mesmerized by the city to notice. I zipped it open, frantically looking for my iPod, and with hesitant fingers flicked it on. "It still works."

"It's survived a lot more," Zander pointed out.

"You sure you didn't somehow make my iPod regenerative?" I asked and got a dopey grin in response. I slipped the gadget into my pocket, feeling the weight of it against my thigh, familiar as it rested there even through the tunic.

We walked down a narrow avenue, small stone houses on either side all connected by bridges and walkways so that the roofs created a network of terraces, maybe even a street above the street. I wanted to explore and to climb, but the guards had one place and only one place to take us: the golden pyramid that lay ahead.

The avenue opened, and we were in a small plaza. In the middle of it sat an odd-looking statue, a cube carved out of dark black stone. If I hadn't known better, I would have shouted that it was a poor replica of the Monolith from 2001. But it was much too large, though nonetheless imposing.

I shuddered. I was pretty sure this was what Bismuth had spoken about, the place the children were sent to be offered in sacrifice to the Sky People.

We walked around it and beyond, to the foot of the pyramid itself. We started to climb the temple steps, the slippery gold and the steepness making it an almost impossible task. But we managed, somehow, reaching the top after a long and arduous ascent. From up here, we could see the city and far beyond.

The approaching danger made me even more nervous, but I tried to keep my cool. We were ushered into the temple, now completely surrounded by the guards, more like prisoners than visitors.

Down the hallway we walked, completely silent, the gold burning red in the firelight. The walls were decorated with tapestries of the same man doing random actions of daily life: signing documents, hunting, sitting on his throne. A whole life story for all to see.

"The emperor's a bit full of himself, isn't he?" I asked Ancha, who had ended up closest to me after the climb.

"Those are the emperors of old," she said sternly, glaring at me like I had said something offensive. As a goddess, I probably had.

"Are they?" I took a closer look at the pictures. "They all look the same."

"They all do after they pass the test of courage."

"What?"

"They come back exactly like that. But they're different men."

The corridor opened into a large chamber, at the center of which sat a throne on a pedestal, both made of, you guessed it, more gold. This place certainly had more than enough of the stuff. The entire palace was overflowing with riches: gold shields on the walls, gold tables, gold platters. The open skylight  illuminated inlaid gemstones all around the room. The only reason our feet weren't slipping was because we walked on plush, finely woven carpets.

More tapestries hung from the walls, large and swooping, that same man's face in every detail. The man in question, looking slightly bored, now lounged on the throne before us on comfortably arranged pillows. I was surprised to think he looked quite handsome, in the flesh. His skin had an ochre tone, his hair black as night and pulled into a high ponytail at the back of his head. He cut a sharp figure, even in the weird position he was in. If he noticed us, he didn't perk up.

The three leaders exchanged glances, glaring at each other with that look I had gotten used to seeing there. The one where their eyes would squint and shift all at once.

"You," said Ancha to Bismuth.

"No, you," insisted Bismuth, glaring.

"No, it was me last time."

"Just shut up!"

The emperor let out a groan so loud I could imagine the pyramid rumbling beneath my feet. He blinked his eyes open slowly, yawning wide enough to show us all his teeth. As he sat up in his throne, his servants scurried to fill his golden chalice with thick wine and bring him a platter of fruit.

"Um, Your Eminence, the Goddess of the Moon walks among us," said Ancha, stepping forward and raising her hands high. "Just as the prophecies foretold. Behold!"

Behold—me. I straightened, hearing my cue. Ancha beamed at me, somehow simultaneously bowing and showing me off with jazz hands. I took a step closer to him.

And he didn't give a single flying fuck.

The emperor looked even younger now, like the stoner younger brother who lived in his parents' basement and listened to jungle music all day, not the leader of a world. He balked, pushing himself up on the opulent cushions, yawning once more.

"Again with your fucking prophecy," he said. "Didn't I tell you to stop bothering me with this?"

"My Emperor," Bismuth stepped forward, slapping her chest with a fist. "You know I would be the last person to support their claim. But this woman, Selena, she can help. I'm sure of it."

I was surprised to hear those words out of the chancellor's mouth. To see her supporting not just me, but the Aquetzallians as well. But desperate times called for desperate measures. Even so, the emperor grabbed an apple off his tray and threw it at the woman's chest. Bismuth stood solemnly still as the fruit ricocheted off her breastplate, chunks of apple and juice trickling down the bronze.

"And just how do you know she's a goddess? Doesn't really look that divine to me." The emperor pouted like a teenage boy, putting his elbows on his thighs and balancing his head in his hands. He scanned me from head to toe, but he was clearly not impressed. I wanted to shrink back from his gaze but forced myself to stand tall, angry at the man for being so nonchalant when his people—and world—were about to burn.

"She exited from the locked room in the temple. It was guarded. No one went in," said Bismuth.

"She can appear from room to room," said Ancha.

"She sings in languages we've never heard."

"The headpiece fits her perfectly."

"She braved the Whispering Forest and rode a tiger across our land."

"She fought a demon with her bare hands," Ancha finished, embellishing a bit. Zander nodded, clearly impressed by their accounts. Heck, even I was starting to feel pumped up by their rendition.

"Could be an illusion," the emperor spat. "How would any of you know what a goddess truly is like?" He stood, readjusting his massive golden headpiece, supposedly a rising sun but looked more like a lemon wedge stuck through his scalp. I stood still as he eyed me down, circling. "She seems rather ordinary to me."

"What about the strange manner of speech?" Ancha pointed out. I was glad to have her on my side, even knowing what she did.

"I've seen stranger. Look, you know as well as I that the prophecies are fables. You hear me?" His voice rose, making all of us cringe at once. We were no longer staring at him but glaring. "There are no Sky People, only the gods. And why would a god send one of their own to stop us from giving them their needs?" He turned to a servant by his side. "That reminds me. Have the children been prepared?"

"They have." The attendant looked uncomfortable. He stared at us apologetically. This must have been commonplace for him.

"Perfect," the emperor replied, rubbing his hands together. He almost looked gleeful. "I will tell you when."

"But the prophecy has come true so far!" Ancha pushed her way forward, pleading. "Selena appeared in the temple room. She wears the clothing laid out for her by the ancestors, and they fit her perfectly. And though she looks nothing like us, she can converse with us fluently. She fights and moves like no person we have ever met before. What other signs do you need?"

"Look, if that's what you believe, fine. But I will not subject the rest of my people to this ... religious nonsense!" The emperor settled himself back into his throne, all the while openly glaring. "But if you really want to prove it to me, fine. If she survives the *Huti*, then I'll agree that she's been sent by the divine. That's the only way to be sure."

"Sounds fair." Ancha turned to me, suddenly calm. It was almost as if she was expecting this answer. "Will you be our champion in the *Huti*?"

The name didn't sound appealing, but what's the worst they could throw at me?

"Sure," I replied, giving them a curt nod, keeping my chin parallel to the floor and my spine nice and straight. Very godlike, I told myself.

Obviously, this had been the answer they had been waiting for. The room burst into applause, even the chancellor, but her face was devoid of all color as she stared at me.

The emperor snapped his fingers, ushering attendants to his side.

"Fine," he said with a roll of his eyes. "Good luck, whoever you are."

At his command, the soldiers moved to a corner of the room, and started to unlatch pieces of the floor, lifting them up and propping them against the wall. Only darkness was below.

"Ancha, what did I just agree to?" I gulped.

"Huti." She didn't even meet my gaze, instead staring at the dark pit that was slowly being uncovered. "The place the emperors must face to prove their divinity. The cave of ordeals, the end of all things good, the ultimate test of courage and strength."

# CHAPTER EIGHTEEN

## *WE ALL FELL INTO THE PIT*

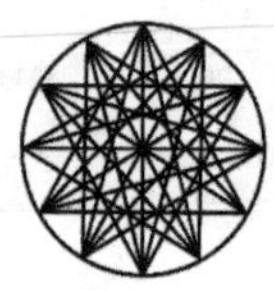

Always read before signing the terms of agreement. Only the price I had to pay for this verbal contract was something called a Cave of Ordeals. I don't like caves, and I don't like ordeals, so put together, I had the worst feeling of what was to come.

I mean, this is coming from the girl who only made it through the first ten minutes of her thirty-day yoga revival. Ordeals were not my cup of tea.

Tea wasn't even my cup of tea. And now my mind wandered from the problem at hand—the problem of what the hell I just agreed to do.

If they had given me something to read, I would never have agreed to this. As the hatch opened in the floor revealing a ladder and a whole mess of darkness, the smell of stale air, or rotting meat and mildew mixed together, assaulted my nostrils. I stepped closer, forcing down my gag reflex, looking at the pit and realizing that there was no end in sight.

Only a whole lot more darkness.

I looked up to my friends. Zander and Nim stood solemnly next to the emperor, staring at me with completely different expressions. Zander, stoic and confident; Nim, holding back his obvious worry with teeth on his bottom lip. I gave them one nod—a nod I gave as a promise, telling them I was going to do this, and I was going to be right back.

I sure hope they didn't take it as goodbye.

Angee just gave me a halfhearted wave goodbye. I shoved Blayde's jar at her; someone else could deal with her.

"Climb," said one of the guards.

"Hey, I'm going, I'm going! Cave of Ordeals here I come. If you want to go first, be my guest."

The man said nothing. Good. I wasn't in the mood for arguing. I wasn't really in the mood for anything, except maybe a day off to fight my still-raging hangover.

And now the doom was closer. I staggered forward, taking small steps to try and hide my lack of grace. All the while the faces of those I trusted, who I had counted on, who I knew, who I had just met, and who I despised wore masks of emotions to hide their truth of what they felt.

Or maybe I was just nervous.

I bent over and lowered myself into the hole. It was awful feeling watched; getting on a ladder is not a very graceful thing, not when the ladder is in a hole of darkness. I grabbed the top rung and took a step down.

And another.

Rung after rung, person after person turned away, not wanting to see the unhidden feelings of a girl sentenced to death, her face pallid and as easy to read as a book. Yay, me.

What an embarrassing way to go: climbing down a death hole.

Rung after rung, they silently judged and placed bets on me.

And rung after rung after rung after rung, I pushed them away, trying harder to crush the panic their faces rose inside of me.

The second my head cleared the top, the cover was placed over the hole, condemning me to darkness and to a pretty awful silence.

I was completely and utterly alone.

I don't know if any of you have ever experienced cave darkness before. Real darkness, the kind of dark that feels like more than just the absence of light. I had once—in the undercity of Da-Duhui. And, somehow, this felt worse.

The darkness was cold, and it coated my eyes like spilled ink. It wanted me to stop. It wanted me to freeze.

I wished I were wearing something other than the tunic, which was light and flowy but kept getting in the way of my feet, and it wasn't keeping my warmth in all that well.

I was five steps into the Cave of Ordeals, and already the darkness was doing me in. I doubted *that* was the ordeal everyone was talking about, so what was on the bottom of this ladder was going to be much, much worse.

I shivered. Whether it was the cold or the terror that ran through me like a stream in spring, I didn't know. It was probably both.

*I'm not alone,* I told myself, climbing another rung down and trying not to think about the depth below me. It was easy to ignore how high up I was when I couldn't see the bottom.

*I'm not alone,* I repeated over and over again. Zander's here for me. He always is. And Nim and Blayde too. They'll be waiting for me when this is all over, cheering me on. And together, we're going to get through this. We'll save these people and be heroes, as a team. And as a team, we would never be alone. I can never be alone.

The thought warmed me up, so I kept climbing, step by step down the wooden ladder. I fueled the thought, pushing the fear of what was to come out of my head. There would be no panic or anxiety from me. I would do this.

But why?

A new thought came into my mind—one that turned the warmth away. A single question: why? Why was I doing any of this?

What was I trying to prove here? I wasn't a celestial goddess. This pit was going to find me , chew me up, and spit me back out like I'm nothing.

This is where lying gets you, folks—in too deep. Literally.

I laughed now, realizing just how much shit I'm in. All I wanted was to help people. To be like Zander and

Blayde and make a difference in the universe. But I'm not like them. I'm not immortal. I have no abilities. I'm a college dropout living in a small town who thinks I can change the world. Change the universe.

Pretending to be a goddess when I can't even make appointments without getting an anxiety attack.

I laughed. I was lying to save an unknown population on an unknown planet from an unknown threat so I could jump over to another place and do the same thing again. Lather, rinse, repeat.

Speaking of which, I desperately needed to wash my clothes. Ugh, why wasn't there any detergent in space? If only we were flying around in some spaceship instead of jumping around blindly in space. Like in *Doctor Who*. Speaking of which, if there was something looking like *Star Trek* out here, wouldn't there be some form of *Doctor Who*?

Or *Star Wars*. Man, I haven't seen a movie in so long! And all this because I wanted to see space with a guy who kinda caused the death of my then-boyfriend and didn't show up for two fucking years.

I wouldn't be the first one to call me crazy.

"Selena?" I called into the darkness, as my laughter died away to nothing. "Selena, the real Selena, if you're still out there, could you pop me back to Earth, lickety-split? I won't say a word of this to anyone, I promise. I'll be good. I'll do anything; just get me out of here. Get me out of the darkness. Get me home. I don't want to be here. Please."

Nothing. No answer. Nada, zilch.

The pit was silent and still.

The world was darkness and made of nothing.

Empty.
Cold.
Nothing, all around, forever.

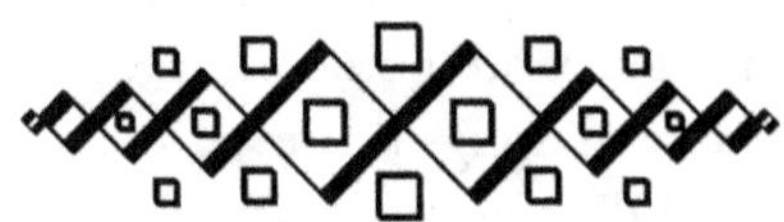

Still nothing.

I stopped counting the rungs of the ladder. I couldn't really feel my hands and feet anymore, anyway, so there wasn't much of a point to it.

What was the point of this, any of this? Would there ever be a bottom to this stupid pit? Was this supposed to be some stupid metaphor, or was I climbing to the center of their planet?

For the first time in years, I wished I were dead.

Maybe not dead—just that I didn't exist anymore. Not existing would be much easier than existing right now.

*I wish I was* dead.

Or was it were?

If were was was, was I dead or do I wish I were dead?

I sobbed a quick, quiet sob. Even my grammar was leaving me.

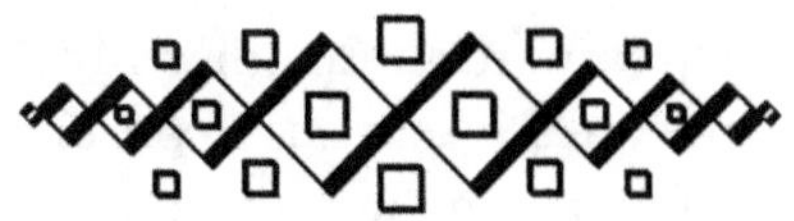

Well, maybe it wasn't all that bad.

I mean, I lived more in the past—how long had it been already?—than in my twenty-some years on planet Earth. I met amazing people who risked their lives for others without a second thought. I traveled to amazing places and had seen things I'd never dreamed of seeing. I made true friends, who I felt safe with, no matter that they always got themselves into dangerous situations.

Who cares if I couldn't get home. I needed to get away anyway. For some, growing up is when you leave your parents' house; for others, you've got to get out of the solar system to find out who you really are.

And I am privileged to have done so.

So who cares if I'm not important? Who cares I'm a human on this foreign planet?

I know who I am now. I know who Sally Webber really is. And the real Sally Webber would try to save these people with her last breath.

And my foot touched sold ground.

Thank your deity of choice! I screamed a cheer of victory as I put my second foot on the floor, thrilled my terrible experience had come to an end. As I dropped my arms to my side, my shouldered screamed, and I laughed, a laugh of pain and joy all at once.

Was this the ordeal? Or was my ordeal still to come? I didn't know, but right now, I didn't care. I was here. I was on the ground. I was alive, and I had made it this far.

I took a step forward and another. My arms reached out to touch the walls. There was a corridor, a very thin one, and it led forward in the dark. So I started to walk.

"Hello?" I called into the void. My voice echoed off distant walls I could not see. There was a vast cavern far ahead, at the end of the hallway. I had to keep walking; the only way out was forward.

I hoped.

Okay, okay, calm down, Sally. I could hear my heart racing and felt it with every muscle in my body. All I had to figure out was what to do next. There wasn't exactly an instruction manual here.

"Hey."

The voice came out of nowhere—quite literally—and I flew into the air. But it was only Blayde.

"Hey?" I said, trying to sound as calm as possible. "Blayde? What are you doing here?"

"I'm bored with pretending to be dead and waiting for an alien signal that won't come. So, I thought, *Sally must be in some form of trouble; she always is.*" She laughed, a shrill tinkling laugh that chilled me to the core. "Just saying. Anyway, when I heard about the Cave of Ordeals, I just had to come. Two of my favorite words in one place? Don't want to miss out on the fun, do I? Now, to business. Got any light?"

"Nope," I replied. "Why do you think I'm standing in the dark?"

"Well, then," she said, but stopped there. Not because anything interrupted her; she seemed too bored to continue the phrase. I felt her presence beside me, even if she was avoiding my touch.

"How did you get here?" I stammered, stepping forward. "Did you follow me?"

"Duh," she said.

"Funny, I didn't hear you."

"You probably were too busy ranting about not wanting to be here to hear anything."

"I said all that out loud?" I felt hot in my face, embarrassed.

"Well, I'm glad to hear you put so much faith in us. But don't expect us to pop up every time you need us. We're not magical fairies, and I'm certainly not a genie."

"That's odd."

"What?"

"You said magical fairy first, then genie."

"So?"

"So, magical fairy's more absurd. Isn't it the other way around?"

I heard the sound of a scalp being scratched. "Not really. Genii are mean. I'd rather be a magical fairy than a genie."

I snorted. "You've met genii?"

"Sure, I think. Once. Lying tricksters, they are. They like coming to Earth because ... well, I think because humans are just so ridiculous in their responses. Did you know they ask those questions for kicks? Before killing their prey, of course."

"So, if they kill everyone who asks for three wishes, who tells the story?" I asked.

"Dead men tell no tales." She sniggered. "Yet the story always gets out, somehow. Only good stories are truly immortal."

"Good stories—and you."

"I'm only immortal 'till I die."

"But you've died before," I pointed out.

"Good point. You got me there."

Silence. Not a silence I wanted any more of. I

cleared my throat.

"So, um, what do we do now?" I glanced around the cavern, but the darkness was so complete that I learned nothing from it. "I mean, Cave of Ordeals. Shouldn't there be more... ordeals?"

"Maybe the ladder is the ordeal. You went through a lot on your way down. I think I recognized the seven stages of grief."

"Five."

"Pardon?"

"There are five stages of grief: Denial, anger, bargaining, depression and acceptance. Count 'em: five."

"What about hillbilly and free association?"

"What?"

"Between anger and bargaining, you start coming up with random stuff in free association: lather, rinse, and repeat, in your case. Then hillbilly is when you lose your grammar. They can be put into one category—nonsense—making it six or seven stages."

"I'm not discussing this with you."

"And why then?"

"Because ..."

Fuck it.

The corridor ended quite suddenly. It dropped away beneath me, and I was on a platform in the middle of nowhere, in the middle of the darkness, surrounded by absolutely nothing.

When I turned around, the corridor was closed. There was now a wall at my back, keeping me trapped on this platform. I was in a dark cave with one of the most terrifying women in the universe, and she wanted to talk psychology. I had had enough. It was dark, it was cold, and she was the last person I wanted by my side.

"Can I ask you something? Since we're alone?" I prided myself on how I was keeping my cool, when all I wanted to do was explode.

"No."

"No, I can't ask you something? Why?"

"No is the answer to your question."

"I haven't asked it yet!"

"Well, the whole us being alone bit means you have two questions in mind. Either you want to ask if it's okay to go out with my brother and my answer is no, or you want to share your feelings about me and, again, I'm sorry to say no. I'm flattered you see me that way, and you're attractive and all, but I make a point to only go out with my own species."

"I don't have feelings for you!" I sputtered. "You're absolutely my type, but why have you gone back to hating me? I don't want to date your brother. He's my best friend, but he's also an immortal, teleporting alien, and I don't think it would work it if we were anything more than that. Is that why you're back to being so cold toward me? You think I want to take your brother away from you?"

"Like you ever could," she snapped, "and look at you, sabotaging the Bechtel test. No. This isn't about you, or my brother, or you and my brother. It's about *me* and my brother. The only other person like me in this entire universe. It's always been *us* against the universe. But then he invites you along, and ever since it hasn't been *us*. It's been him, me, and you. Not us and *you*; him, me and you. And now Nim is tagging along too. Soon, we'll have a posse, and that's insane."

"You can't possibly think I'm trying to drive a wedge between you. You're the most important person in his life. Like I would ever change that or even want to change that. We've talked about this before. I thought we were over these differences."

"What part of *it's not you* do you not understand?" she snapped. "It's not you. It was Earth. Earth fucking did this to him. He turned into a *normal*. And so quickly! You're lucky to be normal, Sally. Zander hates that he took that away from you, and now he's all weird and careful, and it isn't like him."

"I like it better this way."

"That's not what I heard on the ladder."

"I was angry!"

"In any case, I can't handle it. Every time I look at you, it makes me wonder what life would be like if I didn't do what I do. If I had a home and a life and a husband and kids and was dead."

"You *want* to be dead?"

"You have no idea what it's like not being able to die."

"I can imagine it's liberating."

She laughed, sharp and shrill, the sound filling the cavern. "Liberating? I'm stuck in the prison of life. Hardly liberating. I can't feel physical pain. Every time I jump, everything is reset to a display model."

"Sounds liberating to me."

"After a few thousands of years it isn't. I don't even have to care for myself. I haven't brushed my teeth in centuries, and I can't even remember who taught me how to! Did I once have a caring mom, maybe a loving dad? It's like being a video game, always with a simple reboot. But after a point, what's the use? It's boring, that's what. I just want to rage quit."

"Oh, Blayde, come on," I said, reaching a hand out into the darkness but not finding her. "This doesn't sound like you."

"Maybe you should die," she said. "It would be so easy, right? Just jump off this platform, and it'll all be over."

"I don't want to die," I said.

"Again, not what I heard on the ladder."

"What the fuck is wrong with you?" I snapped, again trying to find her in the darkness, but she must have been as agile as a fox, and I kept missing her. "I thought we had finally bonded! You hate me that much that you want me to kill myself?"

"Do it for Zander. Do it so he can move on!"

"That's up to him!" I snapped. "I don't have anything to do with his mind. Are you nuts? I want to go back home as much as you want me out of your hair, but killing myself isn't going to make any of this better. For anyone."

"Just jump, Sally."

"No!"

"Then we'll have to try something a little different."

Her voice wasn't her voice anymore. It was low, deep, and sounded like it was coming from the ground beneath my feet. Blayde was gone, as if she never existed.

The cavern erupted with light, and I fell to my feet, blinded, and screaming in terror.

# CHAPTER NINETEEN

## *MY NEW PSYCHOTHERAPIST IS A THOUSAND TON MONSTER*

You know how you find what you're looking for exactly when you're not looking for it? Well, don't try looking for the Evil One because you might just stumble upon his secret lair in a giant bunker under a gold pyramid.

Or maybe that's just me.

The beast roared, flinging spittle like water bombs against my flesh. I forced open my eyes, breaking the blindness away from them, and was confronted with a hideous face. An open mouth, wide and full of teeth, larger than I was by at least a factor of three.

The mouth closed, and I realized I was looking at a true Leviathan: a dinosaur, larger than any fossil ever found, larger than any creature that ever roamed the Earth.

But this was not the Earth, not in the slightest.

Its proportions were monstrous and completely wrong. It had a long, spindly neck, thick and broad like a redwood tree, carrying that humongous face so it could level with me. It turned, bringing its eye to the platform, eyeballing and sizing me up. The lids could have closed around me.

It was a dinosaur, an actual fucking dinosaur.

Underground.

Speaking to me.

Did somebody say Evil One? I'm pretty sure this thing checked every box.

"I take it the ordeal is to fight you?" I spat, gathering my courage and trying to puff up my size. Not that I'd ever come close to the creature. Its body took up most of the space the cavern had to offer, the glowing blue walls uncomfortably close to its large shape.

"No," it said, pulling its head back and, apparently, grinning. Which was a tall order, considering it didn't have lips. "You sit tight, and I will let you go in no time at all."

"What?" I stammered. "Are you part of this test or not?"

"Oh, yes," it hissed. "You might say I was the one who... created it. It's my test, and don't worry about it. You passed."

I turned to the left then the right. Maybe Blayde hadn't been there at all.

"The offering is acceptable," the creature said, its voice suddenly the same Blayde's. Only it wasn't moving its lips; the voice was coming from inside my head.

I screamed, clutching my skull with both hands. The thing was inside my head. It was reading my thoughts, making me hear things. I had never felt so violated in my life.

"Get out!" I shouted. "You are not welcome in here!"

"Oh, but you can't keep me out," the Evil One chided. "You'll make the most perfect host. Those friends of yours offered the escape I need from this ... torture."

"Host?" I spat. "What the fuck?"

"She is convenient, Master?" asked another voice, mouse-like and frail. My head snapped in its direction, falling on a hooded figure walking up the creature's back, strutting on its spine like a catwalk. The creature remained steady so the stranger could advance, delicate even for its large frame.

"Does she please you?" the cloaked man asked, standing comfortably on the crook of the creature's neck. I felt the thing smiling in my head.

"She's perfect," it purred. "Strong-willed. I like it. But still ... malleable."

"What are you doing to me?" I stammered. "Was Blayde part of this ... test?"

"More of a diversion," it said. "Entertainment as I bonded myself to you. I'm surprised you got so involved with the charade. I guess you have a lot of ... feelings to deal with. No matter. You will never have to bother with them again."

I floated upward, as if some giant hand had gently lifted me into the air, bringing me closer to the beast's head. The cloaked man was floating, too, though he wasn't struggling like I was. Without an actual hand to fight against, it was useless to fight, but I wasn't going down without doing anything.

Or going up. Whatever. Fight me, alien thing.

"What do you want with me?" I shouted. "Put me down!"

"Do not fight, child," said the hooded man. "The Zoesh only wants what's best for you. He will not harm you."

"The Zoesh? What kind of stupid name is that?"

"It's *my* name," said the Evil One, apparently also named the Zoesh, its voice echoing through every wrinkle of my brain, reverberating in my head and in the cavern around me. "I am the Zoesh the Majestic, the last of my kind. And I am weak, my child. So very weak."

"You don't seem so weak to me!" I sputtered, still trying to twist free from whatever invisible grip it had on me. "Now put me down!"

"Not until I have finished with you." I felt its anger inside my head. A migraine was growing, a pressure building that I wanted out—now.

I had never had anyone or anything invade my consciousness before. And it hurt; it hurt so badly. I felt more naked than I had ever been in my life, like the creature was slicing me open with a scalpel and putting every cell on display.

There had to be some way to push it out. But it's hard to shove someone out the door when you're not quite sure how you got in, when you thought that you weren't in a house but a perfectly isolated hypercube.

And that hypercube was on fire.

The Zoesh was an unwanted houseguest, and I had to get it to leave. One way or another.

"You are quite an interesting specimen, Sally Webber," the creature said. "Not from this planet, are you? And stop trying to push me out. You know you cannot."

"No," I snapped, "I *don't* know that. I don't believe that. I believe you want me to think I'm not in control here, but it's my head, and I don't want anyone in here but me."

"Ah," the Zoesh laughed, "but that's not true, now is it? Or you would not be ... medicating."

"That's my business," I said. "My brain chemistry is screwed up, I know. Sometimes my mind lies to me, just like you're trying to do. So guess what? I have experience with foreign thoughts. I have fought this battle against stronger foes than you, and I have gotten away with my life. So what if I need pills to help me with that battle. It's not like you're right in the head, either. Five minutes ago, you tried to get me to kill myself and now you're calling me your perfect host. Which is it?"

"You're the perfect host because you denied me," it said. "I would not want your mind too weakened. You have a strong mind, one I can really sink my hooks into. Soon, that strength will be mine."

"As if," I said, scowling inwardly as well as outwardly. "That's your plan, then? Use me to escape your prison?"

"Prison?" The creature laughed. "This is my hiding place. My safe room. Here, I cannot be found. No. I need you to defend me. I need you to keep me from being discovered."

"It is an honor and a privilege to be chosen," said the nodding figure. Slowly, it removed its cape, revealing a face I recognized from just having met: the emperor.

Only it wasn't the emperor, not unless the man had aged fifty years in the past hour. No, this was an old and weakened form of the emperor, aged and dying.

"My time is up," said the not-emperor. "And your time begins."

"Hold up," I said. "You want me to be some sort of hooded evil dinosaur defender? No, thank you."

"You will not be bothered by it," said the Zoesh. "I can fix you. Fix your mind. You will be free again ..."

"But not from you," I snapped. "Maybe if you had asked politely, we could have given this a trial run. But you had to bust your way in here against my will and refuse to leave. No, thank you!"

"You will be the most powerful woman on this filthy planet," it said. "Second only to the emperor, who is also under my control."

"Oh, that's why you both look the same," I laughed, despite myself, eyeing down the so-called protector. "Your mental influence bends them to your image, right? Which is why all the past emperors look identical, right? Also not part of the contract I want. I like my face, thank you very much."

"He is my voice," the Zoesh growled, "and you will be my protector. I need both of you. My influence is limited. But it is so damn *dull* waiting for things to happen."

"Right," I said, "so you create drama. Are the Sky

People coming or not? The emperor, your puppet, seemed quite adamant that they weren't."

"No, they're coming, all right," the creature snorted. "Every three thousand years they show up, a total pain in my ass. Worst day of the cycle, ever."

"I'm sensing some apprehension here. Oh right, they're looking for you, aren't they? That's why you're underground! You're dying to be worshiped, with an ego your size, yet you're hiding—which tells me that where they want you to go is much worse than this place."

"You catch on fast," the Zoesh said. "I like a fast mind. Those Sky People that have everyone in a fuss? They're my wardens. I escaped their prison long ago, for a crime they have probably forgotten by now, but it doesn't matter. They will not find me. They never do. They haven't in the past twelve million years."

Which, of course, I already knew. The fact he didn't realize that was a good sign. I had to keep him talking.

"But they always come back to this one planet," I said, pushing further at the creature's mind, "which means, they must know you're in this solar system. After that length of time, you'd think they'd weigh their losses and leave."

"They know nothing else," the Zoesh said, nonchalantly. "They have a generation ship and are the most stubborn creatures. Combine those traits together, and you've got a mess of determination."

"A generation ship?" I asked, engrossed, everything becoming oh-so-clear now. "Which means they just keep going generation after generation ... eventually forgetting they ever searched here and came up null, so they check again, right? Or they just keep checking because, as you said, they know nothing else." No negation, so I continued. "They take the children to refresh their gene pool, correct?"

"I would assume as much," said the Zoesh. "I don't care what they do, so long as they leave me alone."

"And they incinerate the surface to draw you out, which explains your digs. You've been hiding here twelve million years?"

"I was not always this big. I can easily change my form to suit my needs. But this is more ... comfortable. Ample space for growth."

"You could live on the surface and be worshiped, but instead, you use pawns—a small number of pawns, only two in fact. You live in hiding, yet you control everything. Well, Zoesh, I'm impressed."

"I am all powerful and all knowing," the Zoesh said smugly.

"So, the prophecy? You planned that, knowing it would draw me here? How does that work? You see the future or—"

"The prophecy is not of my doing."

Surprisingly, this was the first thing in his entire spiel that stopped me struggling and freeze.

"What now?"

"I did not foretell your arrival. I did not write the prophecy of which you speak."

"But ..." I stammered, at a real loss for words. "How did they know I was coming? That any of us were?"

It could have been the real Selena, but she had denied that. Unanswered questions were in abundance.

"I don't know," the Zoesh said. "After the last trip

the Sky People made—and we must really stop calling them that; they are the *Youpaf*—after their last visit here, a young man arrived from the skies, calling himself a prophet. He gave the people this ridiculous story of your arrival, dropped off instructions for the people of Aquetzalli, and left."

"Who was this man?" I urged. "Was he a prophet? A time traveler?"

"A monk, from the library at Berbabsywell. He came and promptly left. Not of my doing."

"So this monk guy predicted the future, and you weren't interested?" I scoffed, mentally bookmarking this clue. The mystery was growing. "You might be a big creature, Zoesh, but you have the smallest mind of anyone I've ever met."

"The monks are fools. There *is* no such thing as prophecy. The future is constantly being formed, nothing is written in stone."

"Yet, here I am, just like that space monk foretold. And you don't seem surprised."

"It's a big universe."

"And you're hiding underground on a small planet. This tells me you're stuck. You don't seriously expect me to take a creature your size off-world, do you?"

"I am not always this large," the Zoesh replied. "This is the most comfortable shape for me."

"Right, so you'd shapeshift, somehow, then control me to take you with me. You'd evade capture and finally leave this world."

"Correct!"

"With those Sky People still coming around every five thousand years decimating the place."

"Not my problem."

"A government in shambles after you leave their leadership."

"Again, not my problem."

"Well, then, I guess we're at an impasse," I said, "because I'm not leaving this planet until you face justice, and you're not leaving here without me. So …"

"So."

"What are you going to do? Still trying to take over my brain?"

"And I will, quite easily."

"Except you won't," I replied. "You've been trying since I got down here, but you can't. And you know why? Because you love talking. And guess what, so do I! I've been talking, and I am still talking. The more you talk, the more I answer back. Haven't you noticed anything weird, friendo?"

I laughed, though at this point, no sound came out. It was all in his head.

"What a lovely chat," I said, mentally pushing back on the bridge between our two minds, "but I don't appreciate the intrusion. Nor the impersonation. Blayde will saw your head off when she finds out. Now, I'm going to leave you with this. I hope it stays in your head forever, asshole!"

And with that, I let out all my wrath, anger and hatred, my happiness, sadness, and love, letting him feel everything all at the same time. We humans could be small, but what we could do was *feel*. And we could feel so intensely it burned sometimes. And burn it would.

As I burned, I sang. An anthem to all songs that stay in your head longer than they're invited to, a song aggravates and stays stuck, like this creature before me.

*We're no strangers to love!* I sang with all my heart. Well, with all my head, actually. I had never felt so in love with Rick Astley as I did right then. Today, Rick Rolling was going to save lives.

The Zoesh screeched in my head, trying to drop the red-hot iron that was my mind, but I didn't let him. I grabbed onto its head tighter, forcing the words into its mind.

I was singing louder than I ever had now. Inside my head, outside, I didn't care. The creature shoved me out of its head—quite violently, in fact—as it lost a grip. Its hold on me evaporated just as fast, and I fell, landing right on the Zoesh's face.

It screamed as I smacked into its nose, trying to shake me off as it struggled with what I had left in his head. I would try shaking me off, too; it would be like having a tarantula on your nose. But I clung on for dear life, digging my hands into the leathery skin, begging it to stop.

Instead, it threw its head up, attempting to crush me against the ceiling. It was only then that I jumped, aiming for the neck, landing my ass painfully on bone, then sliding down the rest until I hit its back.

From there, I ran.

The so-called protector wasn't following me. He had fallen onto the platform and rolled around on his back, screaming. The mental link between the two must have been overwhelmingly powerful. I shuddered at the thought that that could have been me.

I felt cold, fresh air on my face as I ran, so there had to be an exit somewhere. The glowing walls pulsed blue and were somehow connected to the creature, flickering like strobes at times so that my head spun. It was enough to show me where I was going, down the back and further still.

The monster had given me everything for my escape, without even knowing it.

It had gathered its senses now and was searching for me, but I was literally on its tail, and the cavern did not allow it to turn around. But it could feel me there, a flea on its back. It gave the tail a great shake, and I went flying, hands held forward to protect my face.

I landed in the dirt, the stones cutting my arms. It stung like hell, but the adrenaline was pumping hard enough that it barely registered in my mind. I was almost free.

I pushed myself back to my feet as quickly as I could, avoiding the stampede of feet—this creature had way more than four. Not that I had time to count them, what with all the running for dear life and all.

There was a hole in the wall, barely enough space for me to fit, but I had to try. Light came through it, and I knew it was my only chance for an escape.

I threw myself in and started to climb, the glowing blue walls were enough for me to see my way up and out, the eternal climb was hard, but I had to do it, my need to get away edging me on. After what seemed like climbing Everest, my arms burning and skin aflame, I was out of the hole and into clear, breathable air.

My eyes stung as sunlight hit them for the first time in hours. But I was free—free.

The sun was setting, the sky red and orange and ... wait, sunset? I had climbed down at daybreak. And what was that sound?

With a recognizable hum, a shadow crossed over my head, an old rusty shuttle skimmed the treetops, its crackling hum filling the sky with electricity. It threw up dust and dirt, sending sand into my eyes.

The Sky People had arrived.

# CHAPTER TWENTY

## *THE DAY THE EARTH-LIKE-PLANET STOOD STILL*

Nothing like a close encounter with death and a dinosaur to set my heart racing. Add some aliens to the mix, and that made my entire week.

I took a breath registering the barren land before me. For the life of me I couldn't recognize where I was, not that I would know where I had ended up on this foreign planet without GPS. I couldn't have been that far from the pyramid, yet I couldn't find it anywhere on the horizon. Maybe the Zoesh was larger than I had thought—or maybe it was the smoke obstructing my view in every direction.

It was probably the smoke.

A shuttle flew over my head, the noise like the roar of the Zoesh. But its sound was the only impressive thing about it: The little ship was a trash can, its belly aged and rusted. The shock of seeing a ship in this place held me frozen for a minute. So, this was how it was going to be.

As the smoke cleared in the wake of the shuttle, I saw the golden pyramid in the distance—the craft was heading to the city, which was where I wanted to be. I started off in that direction, the ground hot beneath my feet, and I hissed with every step I took.

The grasses around me were reduced to a cinder. Whatever incineration the sky people were planning had already started, searching for their escaped prisoner exactly where the creature knew they would look. His hiding place was impeccable.

With a strengthened determination, I trudged on. There was only one way to save the people here, and that was to alert these Sky People to where the Zoesh was hiding and bring the monster to justice. Hopefully they could take him without causing too much harm elsewhere. It was the only way this mess could ever end.

Bringing the Sky People to justice for their crimes, however, would not be so easy.

I was in a difficult predicament here. On the one hand, to save the people of this planet, the Sky People had to be stopped, for good. The only way to do that was to give them the criminal they were chasing. On the other hand, the Sky People had tormented these people for millennia. Something more permanent had to be done.

If the Zoesh didn't stop me first. I was the only

person who knew its location, so it was sure to come after me. As the emperor, it could easily have me killed on sight. I would have to be careful.

I would ask Zander about it. He had experience with this sort of thing; he and Blayde had a working code of ethics that could be applied to this kind of situation.

Shit. A week ago I was thinking they should stay out of other people's problems. Now I'm trusting them to solve mine. To solve the issues of everyone on this world.

I guess I was starting to see things their way. Power was getting to my head. Hey, I was a goddess after all, right?

The tents I had seen earlier were gone. What of the people? Had they found shelter? Or had they burned? Seeing no ashes here, I assumed they were all right. Hopefully they had made it to the city. It wasn't far, after all. In a few minutes I would be back, I would find Zander, and we'd deal with the alien invasion together.

I counted my paces as I walked, taking in the size of the monster below my feet. It must have been at least a thousand feet long. A parasite, leeching off this planet, killing any effort to eradicate it. I was going to bring this fuckface to justice, one way or another.

The wind blew over the deserted land, sending sand into my skin. My body was torn from my escape from the cavern, and I howled along with the wind as the dirt brushed against my cuts. Every step forward was a new torture, and yet I could not stop. I had to press onward.

Step one: Find Zander, tell him what I know. Step two: Get rid of the emperor, the Zoesh's puppet. Step three: Contact the Sky People and turn in the Zoesh. Step four: Make sure the Sky People never come back, ever. That's it, right?

Except, a small voice at the back of my mind reminded me, there's a step five. My own death — according to the prophecy. Everything so far had been exactly as predicted, including, I realized, the talk with the dinosaur. Everything had played out just as the mysterious monk had predicted.

I was going to ride a bomb. And then, I was going to die. And, surprisingly, those two events were not related.

Not much to look forward to in my last hours. It was worth staying alive until the end, though. Maybe I could get something done with my life.

I shivered, though not from the cold. If this was going to be it, was I proud of what I had accomplished? Would I be all right with dying on a planet light-years away from home, from everyone I loved?

Or was I going to die on my home planet, so far into the future that no one I knew would ever care?

There were days when my mind welcomed death. When I would lie in bed, eyes forced shut, begging for my existence to end. To fall asleep and never wake up. But today was not one of those days. Today, I would be dying for a cause.

Like Matt. Kind, sweet Matt. He had given his life to save mine, to give Zander and Blayde time to save the Killians and our coworkers.

I missed him. My gosh, how I missed him. I would have given anything to see him again.

When I had first arrived in the city, the rows of tents

had made the place seem vast. Now, it looked more like an impenetrable fortress—yet their gate was wide open. I walked into the city without a single person trying to stop me.

Weird. I thought the Zoesh would have used the emperor to try and get rid of me. I considered trying to hide my features since I was the only one for miles who had a golden headpiece, or light skin for that matter. I was going to be a sore thumb no matter what.

I kept walking, unease growing in the pit of my stomach. Every house I passed seemed empty and deserted. It was as if the Sky People had taken everyone.

I was wrong, though. As I got closer to the pyramid, the sound of voices grew. It was only when I passed around the Monolith that I saw the throng of people huddled in a mass at the bottom of the stairs. Waiting.

And then they saw me.

"Selena!" The word passed through the crowd like a wave. I froze as they turned to look at their goddess, barefoot and covered in scratches, standing in the middle of the street.

I think it was the scratches that tipped them off to the truth. They turned silent, as if someone had flicked a switch and shut them off. Shoulders hung, eyes grew wide, and voices faded . The crowd parted around me as I limped forward slightly on my injured legs.

No one said a thing, but I knew what they were thinking. Their goddess wasn't a goddess. She was a mess. And she was bleeding.

Thanks, universe.

I made my way up the steps of the golden pyramid, the steps burning my feet as I went. Once this was over, if I lived to see the end of it, I was going to need a soft pair of slippers and an excuse not to get up for a few days.

The guards at the top looked shocked to see me but said nothing. They parted to let me through, in silence, and I limped back into the hallowed halls, past the pictures of the Zoesh's meat suit through the ages.

I reached up and ripped a tapestry down for good measure.

The grand hall I had been brought to earlier was no longer any kind of 'grand.' There was no dais and no throne. In its place, twenty men and women sat in a circle, chanting, praying.

The emperor was not one of them. But Zander was.

It was Nim who rushed me, letting out a squeak of surprise. He wrapped me in a bear hug, and I hugged him back, feeling my tears run hot onto his chest.

"You're alive," he whispered, honey dripping from his lips.

Hearing Nim say the words made it feel more real, and I hugged him tighter. I had survived.

There were murmurs in the group seated on the floor. As I pulled away from Nim, I realized they were no longer sitting, and that they were coming closer. Zander reached out to me, putting a hand on my shoulder.

"How was the cave?" he asked, trying to sound as casual as he could while being weighed down with an incredibly serious tone. I gave him a short shrug.

"Could have done with fewer ordeals," I said. "And, um, there's something we probably need to talk about, but what happened to the emperor?"

"He ..." Nim scratched the back of his head, in a very Zander way. "He keeled over and died. Just, well, just like that."

"He what, now?"

"The man was gripped with some kind of ... seizure. There wasn't anything that could be done for him. It was completely unexpected."

"Not too long after you climbed down the ladder, he started acting strange, like there were two of him," Nim said excitedly. "One second he was calm and composed; the next he acted like... well, you. He sounded like you."

"And then he had a seizure," Zander finished, "clutching his head like it was about to explode."

Had Rick Astley been enough to drive the creature mad? To break its psychic hold on people? Or was it that it was too weak to maintain three connections at once? Either way, I was glad to be free of its control. The thought of the strange beast playing freely in my mind made me want to retch.

"After he died, there was some noise underneath the temple, and the whole place shook," Nim contin-ued. "That's when the ship came into atmo'."

"They went straight for Aquetzalli," said Zander. "The earthquake it created brought massive tidal waves over the city. The entire continent sunk into the ocean."

"Aquetzalli ... is gone?" I stammered.

Gone, and with everyone on it. We had failed. I had failed.

I could not save them.

Ancha grieved while holding the hands of Bismuth, the great chiefs of a now-lost civilization, their faces cold as the grave. None of us had time for mourning. We'd count our losses while counting our victories. I held back the tears for the people of Aquetzalli and Atlanta. I would cry for them all when this was over.

"Okay, there's a lot I need to tell you," I said, feeling relief wash over me as I realized the Zoesh had no way of stopping me now. I took a deep breath, trying to clear my head of failure, clear it of all the death. "There was a lot more to the cave than anybody here knows. The Evil One is down there. If we act fast, we could save everyone on this planet."

"The Evil One is the only one capable of making a goddess bleed," said Zander, making a big wave of his arms to amaze the elders. "How outstanding."

I nodded quickly. I was too tired for the pretense, too overcome with the sense of grief and failure to want to even try to continue being Selena. But these men needed a leader. And, blood or no blood, I had survived the Cave of Ordeals, their divine test.

That had to count for something.

And, so, I told them everything about their Evil One and the Sky People and how it had evaded them by hiding underground. And they listened to me. Every single person in the room was silent. They nodded in time with my words. Slowly, I felt an energy grow inside my gut. An energy calling me to rally, to fight, to win.

"It's time to bring this creature to justice for the crimes it committed not only against these angered gods but also against you. You do not deserve to be dragged into this monster's mess. The people of Aquetzalli and Atlan deserve better than to be caught in the crossfire. We are going to bring him to justice."

"But how?" asked a Wise Man—one of the emperor's own. "They're assembling the children at the Monolith right now. We don't have much time."

"Then I will buy you some time. Nim, you and I are going to infiltrate that ship. You think you can handle that?"

"Yes," he said, more confident than I had ever seen him. "If you're there with me."

"Every step of the way, partner." I flashed him a smile. "Elders, Wise Men, And attendants, gather your people. Rally them all. If they have arms, they will be used. I need you to grab torches and draw a straight line out to the desert. Zander, you need to go into the Cave of Ordeals. Find the exit in the desert, so people can mark the location. The Zoesh must still be too disoriented to escape, and there's nowhere for it to run, anyway. We're going to light up its hiding place so brightly, it can be seen from space. Everybody got that?"

"The children!" A guard rushed into the former throne room, hair disheveled. "It's begun!"

"Nim, come with me!" I shouted, running before I even knew what I was doing. Adrenaline pulsed through my veins, fueling my insane plan.

I was out the door in seconds, my eyes burning as the sun hit them once again. Nim's footsteps were close behind me, hitting the gold with a resonating thwack with every step. *Thwack Thwack Thwack.* I threw myself down the stairs, pushing through the crowd at the bottom like they were thick honey.

They didn't part for me this time. They were too busy crying, screaming out to their children on the Monolith.

The guard had been right: It was beginning. A monstrous ship hovered above the crowd, its engines thrumming loudly. Massive doors on the belly of the ship slid open, the interior glowing with a light brighter than the sun.

I pushed out of the crowd and dashed up the Monolith on the rickety wooden staircase they had built there. I was too old for the crowd, but would the Sky People care? Would they notice or would it matter, so long as they got their fresh blood for their gene pool?

That's when the world around me glowed. It was like waking up at the bottom of a swimming pool, your body naturally wanting to float upward.

"Slacken your jaw," I said to Nim and to anyone who was listening. "Try to stay calm. This won't hurt a bit."

A baby wailed, and the girl holding it sobbed into its small belly. The ship dragged us upward, pulling us into its heart.

I closed my eyes. Nim gripped my hand and gave it a squeeze. I squeezed back, even though my palm was clammy and gross. Blood and dust coated it, and I hissed at the pain of someone touching my wounds.

Small cuts make the worst pain.

Soon, we were all inside the belly of the ship, floating in the bright light of whatever tractor-beam technology they were using. The great doors slid shut beneath us, blocking the Monolith and the people around it from view. If all went well, I would be back down there in a few.

The second the doors closed, however, the tractor beam shut down and off flicked the light. We were plunged into darkness, the mass of floating children crashing to the metal floor. My chin slammed into the deck, sending jolts of pain up my spine.

I had been wrong. Small cuts hurt, but there was worse pain than that. My chin throbbed hard as I pushed myself back up and felt nausea in my gut. Ugh.

I fought the urge to retch. I was getting better at that by the day.

"Children," said a voice, booming. "Rise; stand on your feet. Do not be afraid. You will not be harmed. Quite the opposite. Please, remain calm."

In that same second, things happened all at once. A gas was released, spraying us down and giving everyone in the room a coughing fit. Then came a torrent of water from the ceiling, followed by a heavy gust of wind in our faces. In an instant, we were dry.

A door slid open somewhere to my right, and I turned to see a woman in a tight-fitting blue uniform march in. On her own, which was surprising. The lone woman lifted her hands in peace.

She looked human, but she was evidently ... not. At least not entirely. Her skin was dark, a reddish purple much like the people of this planet, and her long, black hair was braided off the top of her head, looping down her back. But everything else was too sharp: She was tall and lanky, her ears pointed and pulled back like Spock's. Taller than any human I had ever met.

Oh, and her knees bent backward. That was probably why I wasn't getting the human vibe off her.

"My name is Lieutenant Korra." She smiled. "And I would like to formally welcome you all to the *Youpaff*. We're excited to have you. Now, let me show you your new home."

And in that moment, my eyes met a pair I recognized. My heart sank so low it fell off the ship. Because Angee was not supposed to be here.

# CHAPTER TWENTY-ONE

## *JUST ANOTHER STORY IN A LONG LINE OF ALIEN ABDUCTIONS*

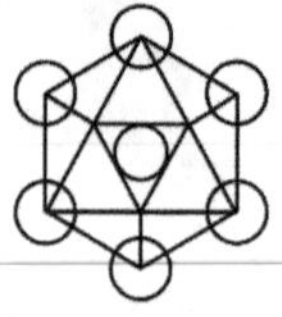

The lieutenant smiled a lip-less smile as she led us through the ship.

None of the children put up a fight. Other than Nim or I, no one here had ever seen a ship before. And just like my own experience, this drab old tub of a ship was not the best introduction to the worlds beyond our own. Even so, to them, this must have been the work of the gods. I know I would have believed it.

I at least had an inclination aliens existed: the children around me, however, only knew the Sky People from the nightmare stories they had been told. They were not alien to them, they were demons.

And yet, the children were silent. Even the baby had stopped crying. No one dared utter a noise, but they clutched to each other as life rafts.

"What do they want from us?" Nim hissed, keeping his lips taut. His eyes fixed on Angee's, and she returned the look with a solemn face of fear. "I assumed they would put us in cells."

"I think …" I replied, keeping an eye on Korra as she lead us down the corridor, "I think they're going to try to assimilate them into the general population. They need to refresh their gene pool, and apparently the easiest way to do this is to kidnap children from the planets they visit."

"So they've given up on finding the Zoesh here," said Nim, "if they're ready to move on. But hold on, I thought ships could travel faster than light? The *Traveler* could."

"This ship has been looping around this solar system for millennia," I said, "maybe millions of years. It's sure to be a little outdated."

"Why haven't they given up already?"

"Please, remain quiet," said Korra, turning to glare at us like disobedient school children. Her eyes faced forward once more, and she muttered under her breath. "Fuck me. How did I get babysitter duty? That asshole Tormen ..."

She led us into a large room with stalls on either side. It was only when she reached the end of them that she turned to face us.

"Right"—she indicated the stalls—"grab a uniform that looks like it might fit you. Then go in there and toss your old clothes down the chute. Change and come back out. Don't waste any time, now."

I took one off the table in the middle of the room, guesstimating my size. The thing was brown and scratchy, nothing like the beautiful uniform the lieutenant was wearing. It was second hand—maybe even third, fourth, or five hundred-hand—and when I stepped into the stall to unfold it, I realized the size was way off, too.

No matter. I put it on: the top was too tight, and the pants too loose, and the material itched all over. I threw my tunic down the shoot, into an incinerator, never to be seen again. The ipod, however, I slipped carefully into my pocket.

I turned, ready to leave the stall, when I was overcome with a sense of comfort I had never felt before. Like I knew that whatever happened outside that door, I could take it.

Maybe the cave of ordeals had done what it intended—it had tested me, and I had come through relatively unscathed. I had saved my mind from a creature that wanted to ride me off this planet. My own survival was fueling me to make it through whatever this new challenge was.

I could do this.

I had three plans in my head. One, if everything went well; another as a backup if shit hit the fan; and a last one, in case a giant dinosaur came crashing out of the earth and tried to eat me.

I wondered if this was how Zander felt; having plan after plan running through his head. If this was the confidence he felt. He must have had even more in his system, seeing as the immortality thing took a huge chunk of the danger out of the equation.

My own death didn't scare me. Nim's, however...

Yeah. This was probably how Zander felt most of the time.

I stepped out of the cubicle, surprised to see Nim fitting so well in his own uniform. His confidence wasn't shining like it usually did. Maybe his terror was just an act; I expected as much.

Nim had changed in the short time that I knew him from the obedient drone of a bubble society to a strong, courageous hero. A young man who could learn a language within minutes of hearing it. Who could stand up for himself in the face of false gods. Determined to help those he could with everything he had.

I was proud to call him my friend. And if Blayde didn't see it, then screw her. It's easy to stand up for people when you have nothing to lose. It's damn near incredible when you can stand up, knowing it's the last thing you ever do.

"And the tour continues this way," said Lieutenant Korra, evidently bored out of her mind. All around me, the children wore matching uniforms, each fitting more or less well, holding hands or carrying the smaller ones, silently sticking up for each other as we marched through the ship's haggard halls.

I needed to reach Angee, but she was behind me now, carrying a toddler and wiping its tears. The girl was stronger than I ever expected her to be.

We continued down a dingy corridor with a flickering light. Korra looked up at it, glared, and pushed on. If the *Traveler* was a delicate whale, then this ship was a crocodile, swampy and sharp.

Korra led us into a dorm with hundreds of cots as far as the eye could see. There were other children in this room, with different skin tones, different hair, sitting calmly on their beds, waiting. But Korra didn't stop here. She marched us down the main aisle of the room, past cot after cot after cot, past some other children, who brushed aside, looking at us sadly. We exchanged quick glances—we were not the only abductees.

The lieutenant threw open a large set of doors at the end of the room, and we were in a lecture hall, the same kind I had seen in my brief stint as a university student. A large screen was set up opposite a row of benches, and Korra made her way there first, making it clear she wanted us to sit.

So we did. Nim and I found seats together in the top left of the room, giving us an awful view of the screen. No one wanted to sit up front. Some of the older teens, Angee included, were hushing the younger ones, trying to keep an air of confidence to calm the others. Surprisingly, it seemed to work.

These children had probably been warned this would happen to them; their parents raising them with the knowledge that they would one day we taken by people from the beyond the stars. It was amazing to see how few babies there were, compared to the number there could have been. It was not the right time to bring children into the world, knowing they wouldn't stay long.

And then, the movie started. The lights dimmed, and the screen lit up, throwing the room into silence.

The video was probably as old as the ship itself.

There was a montage of people running—not just human people, the feathered and scaly kind as well—running up a mountain. The music was bold and uplifting, an anthem for the aged.

"BOLD!" the video exclaimed, focusing on the face of a young feathered person in a tight red uniform, turning slowly to face the camera.

"STRONG!" People in blue suits shot lasers at giant spiders, or something that looked like spiders.

"PROUD!" Those same people had removed their helmets, and waving a huge flag over their heads.

"These people make up the YOUPAF," said the narrator, his voice booming through the small room, "wouldn't you like to be one of them?"

The video cut to black for a minute, and then a face filled the screen once more: an old, tired face, of a dog-faced man stuffed into a uniform much too small for him. His sleeves had so many lines of color around them, it looked like he had shopped in a ribbon sale at Joann's fabric supply.

"You," he said, his voice filling the room with ease, "you have been selected to take part in one of the most important retrievals in the history of the Pyrinian force. This matter is completely confidential, and speaking of it with anyone outside of this room will result in your immediate execution. The prisoner known as the World Eater, escaped Novault Maximum Security Prison, after devouring the entire planet it was housed on. We probably should have seen that coming. However, this has severely weakened it: we have managed to track its movements to a small and insignificant solar system light years from here. Those of you selected for this mission will undergo cryogenic freezing to ensure you will not age during the two-hundred-year trip."

"Two hundred years?" Nim hissed, "They sent all these people out here to retrieve a creature who would outlive them all?"

"Shh," called the lieutenant, glaring at Nim, who shrunk back into his seat, his face going red.

"Once within the system," the man on the screen continued, "you will have to reduce your speed. We know the creature lives in this specific system, and we assume it is trapped there. However, we cannot be sure which of the planets and their hundreds of moons it will hide on. You must search every single one."

A picture of the Zoesh appeared on screen. The children in the audience gasped. Nim let out a low whistle.

"Evil One!" screamed one of the younger ones, and the others hushed them.

"That's what's living under the pyramid?" Nim asked. I nodded.

"It is capable of creating psychic bonds with weaker minds, controlling them for its own means, so caution must be engaged. The creature grows larger by the day, but it can release a burst of destructive power, returning it to a small form. The longer it goes unfound, the larger it will get. As it used its destructive abilities to escape its prison, it will be very small as you begin your journey. By the time you reach the solar system, it should be the size of a small shuttle. A maximum size has not yet been registered, but the creature is expected to keep growing until all resources are depleated, before moving on to another world.

"This mission," the camera cut to a close up of the man's face, showing every pore in his skin, "is of the utmost importance. You cannot return to command without the World Eater, or confirmation of its death. Killing the creature would be much commendable, but a near impossibility. But your mission does not end until death or capture of the creature. Long live the fleet."

"Long live the fleet," said Lieutenant Korra, "to hell and back again."

The lights turned back on, and we saw that Korra was not alone. There was a man beside her, taller and in a tight red uniform, leaning casually on his reversed knees. He eyed the crowd wearily. "You have been chosen," he said with a dignified voice, "to serve the *Youpaf*, as we have, and our fathers before us, and their forefathers. It is indeed a great honor.

"I am Admiral Cereko, the highest ranked officer of the UPAF *Scrimmage*. As you have seen in this brief informational video, we are in search of the prisoner who escaped to this system. If any of you know the creature of which we speak, please tell us now."

No one said a word—no one dared. He glared us all down. I didn't flinch, though his words terrified me: this was an Alliance ship. An extremely old Alliance ship.

"Do you love your parents?" he asked wearily, "Is that why you hide this creature from us? Did they let you in on their secret harboring of the criminal? What could the World Eater possibly have offered you, to make you hold your tongues?"

He waited, but again, there was no reply. He leaned forward, glaring down at us all with a fury in his eyes that was more than just determination.

"I asked you if you loved your parents," he said, "obviously, they do not give a damn about you. They let us take you, without a fight. They could have given the creature up, ended this all. But they didn't. They chose the creature over you. They gave you up."

"You should see what we did to the last planet," Cereko chided, "we left it a cinder. The air there is so toxic now that nothing will ever grow or live there again. We could do that to your world, too, if you don't give the creature up. Tell us where it is, and your families will be safe. Hand the creature over, and you will be spared."

He marched to the front row, and in one easy swoop grabbed a boy from the audience. The kid couldn't have been older than eight. In an instant, he had a gun to the child's head. Lieutenant Korra said nothing, standing at attention like she was in a trance.

"Maybe I'm being too lenient on you," continued the Admiral, "maybe you need a more material threat. Tell me where the World Eater is hiding, and this child will be spared. If not, he will be the first death on this ship today."

"No!" Nim pushed himself up on the seat. I grabbed his arm, trying to pull him back down, but he yanked it free. When had Nim gotten so strong?

The admiral looked up at Nim, smiling gleefully. "You have news of the creature?"

"Hell yes," he said, pushing past me. "I know exactly where it is, but I'm not telling you until you let that boy go."

"Fine." The admiral shoved the boy forward and

he toppled onto the floor. "Just know that if your information is false, you will be leaving this ship via the airlock."

Nim gulped audibly. It wasn't hard to hear in the silence of the theatre. In the bright phosphorescent light, his skin glowed whiter than anyone in the room, showing his bright red face off.

"The people of this planet didn't know who you were looking for," he said, "Or what you were looking for. You came here, burning and burning without asking those who are caught in the middle. I want your promise that when you find this creature, you will leave this solar system for good."

"If we find this creature, we will have no need of this place," said the Admiral.

"Exactly," Nim stepped towards the stage, "which means you could be careless. Leave them alone. I need your word."

"Fine, you have it."

"Then look outside," said Nim, "we found the creature. And they're showing you exactly where it is. It's hiding in a subterranean space underneath the pyramid and has grown large enough to stretch miles into the wastes."

A smile grew on the admiral's face: no, not a smile, something more powerful and extreme. The ultimate joy. Like he was coming in his pants.

"You see how easy that was?" he said, striding off the stage and marching towards Nim, "Come with me, boy, you are about to witness history."

"Sir?" asked Lieutenant Korra, "what do I do with the rest of them?"

"Skip orientation, it's possible they won't need it now." He chuckled, putting an arm around Nim. "You're a funny looking one, aren't you?"

Nim looked uncomfortable. He shot me a look, and I realized I had to do something to risk getting left behind. I stood up quickly, sliding past the benches in an attempt to reach my friend.

"Oy, you there!" the lieutenant called, "sit your ass back down! You've not been dismissed yet!"

"He's my brother?" I stammered. "I can't let him go alone!"

"You can, and you will," she spat, "now sit down and let the admiral leave in peace."

"Thank you, Korra," said the Admiral. "Now, what's your name, son?"

"Kereth Graham," Nim said, impressively fast, actually. "Son of Mahalus Graham, son of Talus Graham. Does this mean my family will be alright?"

"More than alright," the Admiral said, "they're going to be freed of the scourge that is the World Eater. And you're going to get promoted! Let's talk about your future on the *Scrimmage*..."

Nim turned back to me, mouthing the word '*help*' before being led out of the room. The door slammed heavily behind them.

"That goes for all of you," said Korra, trying to hide her own excitement, "Just because the mission might change, it doesn't mean you're not a part of this crew. And that means you have to obey certain rules."

It was at times like these I wished I could jump and go anywhere I wanted. Instead, I watched Nim being ushered out of the room, his eyes wide and terrified, without being able to do anything.

Impulsive Nim. If he had only waited. I could have handled this.

But I couldn't handle anything.

# CHAPTER TWENTY-TWO

## IT'S THE FINAL COUNTDOWN

"Who are you?"

I looked up at the little girl who had approached me. She sat down next to me on my cot, ignoring the signals I was giving that told everyone to back off. My foggy brain didn't want to think any more than it had to.

"I'm no one." I sighed. Crashing was always a painful experience. Not the best time or place for my mind to give up on me.

"You're new, aren't you?" she asked. "Are you a ... a grown-up?"

"I guess I am." I shrugged. "I don't really feel like one right now."

"I wish I was a grown-up, then I wouldn't be ... here."

I couldn't agree more. None of these children should have been here. I was an idiot to think I could save them all.

"I'm Teela. What's your name?"

"Sally."

"Did your brother find the thing they were looking for?"

Actually, I did, I wanted to say, but I only shrugged. "He must have."

"So"—the girl wavered from side to side—"so, can we go home now?"

I looked over at her sweet, innocent face and realized I didn't have the bedside manner to tell her she would live the rest of his life on this rust bucket.

"Why aren't you talking?" she asked. "Everyone else is. You think there's a way to run away?"

"I don't think so. If they're taking us to space, then there's nowhere to go."

"Space?"

"You know the stars you see at night? Well, this ... giant boat is going to see them up close. Space is the black stuff in between the stars."

"Woah," she said, her eyes sparkling, "so we can walk from star to star?"

"How long can you breathe underwater, Teela?"

"Long enough to catch three clams!"

"Well, you would need to hold your breath for ... five million clams if you wanted to get from one star to another, as fast as you can."

"Noooo," she said, excitedly. "You're so smart! Are

you a wise woman?"

"I thought I was—once."

"Wow, get a hold of yourself," said Angee, urging Teela away. I looked up and met her gaze, holding her soft brown eyes for what felt like an eternity. She held the toddler in her arms, still wrapped in a blanket, cooing softly.

"What are you doing here?" I asked.

"Kicking your ass. It's one thing for you to get yourself stuck in the middle of nowhere, but it's quite another to climb onto a sky-ship and then give up."

"I'm not giving up. I don't have any other course of action."

"Course you do. You stand up, and you fight."

"I can't fight."

"Then you lie through your teeth, but you don't give up. You're letting everyone down, Sally. You're letting me down. You're letting Selena down. So get up and fight!"

"I'm pretty sure Selena doesn't give a damn about me or any of us. She's got a bit of a mid-life crisis going on, and—"

She slapped me hard against the face. My cheek stung like a million bee stings. My trembling fingers rose to touch it as Angee looked down at me, seething. She readjusted the child on her hip. It didn't make a sound.

"What was that for?" I stammered.

"She was possessed!" Angee said to Teela, who was staring. "Mother said to always slap possessed people."

The girl ran off, but Angee stayed, one arm akimbo as the other held the child. In the brown jumpsuit, it was impossible to see her religious upbringing. She could have blended right in with any starship hand if it wasn't for the babe.

"We need to save Nimien," she said, tapping her foot against the cold metal floor. "And bring the Evil One to justice. Does Nim know where the hellbeast is, or was he vying for time?"

"I found it under the Emperor's pyramid," I replied, and her eyes widened. "Long story, but you're right,— we need to go."

I took a deep breath, focusing my thoughts. My brain was still foggy and cold, and thinking was as hard as walking in a straight line while drunk. I stared at my feet, breathing into my stomach as my therapist had taught me so long ago.

None of these children had any spaceship experience. I did, and the troops didn't expect that. Not from anyone they had picked up on this tiny, insignificant planet.

Step 1: Get out. Step 2: Find Nim. Step 3: If it's not already done, bring the Zoesh to justice for its crimes.

Not a difficult list. Now to make a plan out of it.

"Stay here," I said to Angee, rising to my feet. "I've got an idea."

"Fat chance," she snapped. "I'm coming with you."

"Have you ever been on a spaceship before?" She didn't answer. "Look, I might not be the goddess you wanted, but I'm the one you've got. And I think I'm here because I know how this stuff works. I can get you out, all of you. But you have to trust me."

She took a step forward, nodded, then sat down where I had been.

The door to the dorms looked like something you would find in a conference hall back on Earth, which I guess should be expected for a room this size. A guard, however, was posted before it.

"Integration is going well, I see," I said to the guard stationed there.

"Return to the others, please," he replied, coolly.

"Oh, come on, it's me. Didn't you get the memo?"

"The what now?"

"The admiral wanted me to stay with the kids," I said, "to help them adjust. Make sure we don't get any violent outbreaks, like on the last planet."

"The records don't indicate any violence on the last intake."

"Not the records you're allowed to see, no." I laughed. "Look, man, I thought you were briefed on this. I'm a counselor, and right now, I need to get back to the flight deck. All right?"

"I wouldn't do that." He stepped in between me and the door.

"Relax," I said. "It's not my fault the information didn't get passed down to you. Do I look like those kids? I'm a little too old, aren't I? And would any of them know about ships? I mean, come on."

"I don't know you."

"I had a bit of work done on my face. How would I gain their trust if I didn't look like them?"

The man eyed me suspiciously, then, with a heavy sigh, reached for the latch and opened the door. Success number one. I stepped outside and took a left.

"Flight deck is to the right." He squinted.

"Bathroom first," I replied. He shrugged and closed

the door behind him.

Finding Nim shouldn't be too difficult. I turned around, taking the direction the guard pointed out, and made my way down the empty expanse, trying to take everything in as I went. I needed to find my way to the command deck; Nim would be there if they were going after the Zoesh. My best assumption was to follow a hallway and look for stairs. The bridge was usually in the highest or most forward part of the ship, so it was quite literally onward and upward for me.

Ah, now this looked like stairs. I threw open the doors and was met with exactly what I was expecting: a thin flight of stairs that led up the ship. Hey, presto.

What I wasn't expecting were the soldiers vaping there.

There were three of them. Well, three of them remained after countless others had scattered. They stared at me like I had blown up their ship, their jaws dropping and smoke coming out of their ears. Quite literally, in this case. *Puff puff puff.*

"The fuck?" asked one of them, lifting his weapon so it pointed right at me.

I wanted to ask the same thing. So much for my daring rescue mission. I didn't have many options here: I could turn around and make a run for it, and most likely get shot down where I stood—no fun there—or I could try to talk my way out of this.

"Ah, this isn't the ladies' room," I said awkwardly. "Unless this is a gender-neutral thing? Ah. No. It looks like a stairwell. I apologize for the intrusion. I got separated from the other new recruits, and I—"

"You're no recruit," said the woman, her finger

shaky in the trigger. There was a dazed look in her eyes, one I recognized from early on in treating my mind. The gun wasn't exactly pointing at me, more like the space next to me where a fuzzy copy of me was probably standing. "I can understand you, but we haven't given the noobs any translators yet. So who the heck are you?"

"I'm sorry. I think there's been a mistake ..."

"Yo, this stuff really does open the mind!" the man beside her laughed. "I can hear colors!"

"Wow!" The woman laughed. I kept my hands raised. Her finger was way too close to the trigger for my liking. "Does this mean we can speak every language? Even the invisible ones?"

"Especially the invisible ones," said the second woman, and they all laughed in unison. I couldn't move. The trio stepped toward me, their guns at the ready, the barrels getting closer to my head with every passing second. I gulped, reaching behind me to grab the door handle, but it was no longer there. That, or my trembling hands couldn't find it.

"What's your name, color girl?" asked the man.

"Turquoise," I replied, stretching out the word so it sounded fancy and European. Not that I was trying to impress anyone. "Can you help me? I'm looking for a boy."

"Aren't we all?" replied the first woman. Finally, she lowered the gun, and her friends followed suit. "I'm Tipolinna, but you can call me Tippy. He's Vix and she's Falla. Are you from the moon?"

"Pardon?"

"There's a rumor about a woman who lives on the

moon," said Tippy. "Apparently she's got something to do with the World Eater. Is that you?"

"Oh, you mean Selena?" I regretted my words instantly. I was supposed to be Selena, dammit. Not that these people would notice. "Yeah, she's my fairy godmother. Emphasis on the god part, not the fairy."

They let out an ooh of awe in unison.

"No way!" said Falla. "Can you do tricks?"

"Sure," I said and faked pulling my thumb off, à la dad. They each did a double take.

"This girl's for real!" said Vix. "Shit!"

"Now, I need you to do something for me." I grinned. I had them eating out of the palm of my hand. Thanks, recreational drug use! "I'm still a godmother in training, and I *lost* my ward!"

"Oh, you poor thing!" said Tippy. "I would hug you, but then we'd all die."

I nodded, going along with this, whatever this was. "I think they took him to the bridge. His name is Kereth Graham, and he's with Admiral Cereko."

"Oh, the new lead?" Vix clapped excitedly. His gun swung wildly by his hip. "He's up on the bridge. I can show you! Unless you want to fly through walls?"

"No, thanks. That messes with my lunch. But please, lead the way!"

And lead the way they did. I had a full escort of high-out-of-their-minds trained soldiers surrounding me every step of the way. I was confused about who they thought I was, and they were confused about nearly everything else. So far, it seemed things were working.

Maybe things were finally coming up for once. It was better than trying to come up with a solid plan when my mind was stuck in another cycle of darkness and fog.

Tippy threw open the door of the stairwell, bringing us into a crowded hallway. A couple of people glanced our way, but their eyes didn't linger. To anyone else, I looked like a prisoner being escorted to the bridge. Nobody wanted to get in our way.

"Act casual!" Vix hissed, a little too loudly. A few strangers shot looks at us, but my little team looked so focused they probably knew not to interfere. We walked in unison down the corridor, me keeping my eyes on a point dead ahead, trying not to draw attention.

But this method didn't last long because, of course, my luck never lasts. If the universe wanted me here, it was probably for entertainment, seeing the list of obstacles it kept throwing my way. In this case, a rather large man who was suddenly obstructing the corridor.

"Tipolinna, where are you taking the new recruit?" he asked, his voice rough like the grating of rocks. The woman stood at attention, gun against her thigh.

"Sir! You can see her? Sir!"

The man let out a heavy sigh, looking past Tippy to scan me over. He rolled his eyes.

"Yes, I can see the recruit," he replied. "What have you been smoking this time?"

"Sir. I haven't smoken anything, sir!"

The man wasn't buying it, but he didn't need to say anything on that account. Instead, he locked eyes with me. And I wasn't one for locking eyes.

"What are you doing out of your quarters?" he asked, his pitch changing as he switched languages. "Did they hurt you?"

I didn't know what to answer; I couldn't think. The man waited for me to say something, anything, and I just... froze. I thought I was past this, the fear of the unknown situation. No one had a gun to my head, but the fuzziness in my brain simply would not recede.

I did the only thing I could do: I let out a scream, tapped Vix on the shoulder, which in turn made him scream, and made his friend scream too. And I, the brave and bold hero that I was, ran down the corridor and threw myself into the first broom cupboard I could find.

Illico Presto. I'm a badass hero.

"Shit," said the woman standing in the cupboard with me.

How Angee got out of the containment room, I did not know. She was standing there, a jar of cleaning solution in hand, staring at me as if she had just discovered I was a lizard.

"Angee!" I wanted to wrap my arms around her in relief. "What are you doing here?"

"I could ask you the same thing," she said, reaching for the shelf behind her to pick up the bundle of blankets there. The toddler she had been caring for cooed gently in her arms.

"I told you to stay in the room with the others," I said, catching my breath. "How did you get out? And why the hell did you bring a baby here? It's not safe!"

"I could say the same thing to you."

It was then that I caught her soft brown eyes and realized that when I had met her, they had been a vivid shade of blue.

It was also when I noticed that her baby had a green

tail.

"What the fuck?" I tore the blanket off the thing in her arms. The shock threw me back against the wall, and I stifled a scream. Not only was the toddler not a child, but it was a miniature dinosaur.

She was holding a miniature Zoesh in her arms.

"You just had to rip off the blanket, didn't you?" she scoffed. I felt a handle feeling for the edges of my mind, but it was so weak I slapped it away with nothing more than a stray thought. The little World Eater bared its teeth. Even after reducing its size almost a thousand times, those teeth still looked wicked big.

"Oh hell, Angee. Did this ... thing...did it breach your mind?"

She grinned. "We bonded, don't you see? We're going to stop the Sky People once and for all. It's what I've always wanted my entire life."

"No, Angee." I didn't know what the creature had planned, but it couldn't be good. You can't allow a thing that calls itself the World Eater to actually eat worlds.

"All those years I devoted to Selena, I should have been worshipping the Evil One," she said, stroking the head of the little beast. "Ironic, isn't it? That it took meeting you to see the truth about my goddess."

"That thing is trying to use you!" I reached for the creature. This small, it didn't look so imposing or dangerous. If I could grab its neck, I could... "Please, listen to me. You have to fight it. I know what it's like having it inside your head. You have to push back; you have to—"

"I found you!"

The door flew open, and there stood the man from

the corridor, followed by a whole slew of soldiers. I turned to leave, only to catch the tail end of Angee as she dashed up the wall and into a service tube at inhuman speed.

Shit.

"I need to get to the bridge," I said.

"Oh yeah?" the woman snarled. "What for?"

"I have information about the prisoner that your leader might want to hear." I glanced back at the wall Angee had scurried through, but she was long gone. I had to draw her out somehow, her and that miserable Zoesh. But to do so, I needed help from whoever was in charge of this ship.

And I needed Nim.

"Right," he said with a scoff. "What could you, of all people, know about the Zoesh?"

"I'm the Zoesh. You haven't seen a picture of me for so many generations now, but, hey, I'm turning myself in. Let the children go and arrest me." I snarled. I had to get into the head of the monster, which, luckily, was a place I had already been. "I am the World Eater, the Zoesh, the majestic, the last of my kind."

# CHAPTER TWENTY-THREE

## WO-OH, LIVING ON A PRAYER

You know when you have a great idea that seems amazing at the time, but then you quickly realize it was shit and have no idea why you thought it was good in the first place?

A few things I learned today: Impersonating a goddess will bring you face-to-face with a serial killer dinosaur, and impersonating said killer dinosaur would get you full access to the bridge of a spaceship.

Still not sure any of that is a good thing. I wished I were a planner, able to see the steps in advance rather than going with the flow and improvising. It worked great for Zander, but he had millennia of experience.

I had a random acting class as a high school sophomore.

I couldn't even conjure what had been going through my mind when I claimed to be the creature everyone on this ship was hell-bent on finding and destroying. I now had a dull feeling that it had made sense at the time, though the present me was completely angry at my past self.

Anyway, live and let live... or is it die or live? Never knew. And probably never would know judging by the state of things. I made my decisions, my mistakes, and I would have to live with them. If I lived, that was. Because I was being escorted to the bridge, to the head honcho of all head honchos, the commander's commander himself.

He was the first thing I saw when the doors slid open, revealing a bridge much like that of the *Traveler*'s, though lacking the beautiful gleam of the jewel of the Alliance. The commander stood with his back to us, staring out through the large windshield at the world outside. The planet was on fire. Everything I could see from here through to the horizon was burning. The golden pyramid was nowhere to be seen. I wondered where we were now, if we were even on the same continent.

"Lord Hokera," said my escort, and the imposing figure ripped his eyes from the view. I almost doubled backward. He looked right from the screen of a video game. This man had the purest white hair, like the summit of Everest, tumbling down like spider silk to the middle of his back. His face was covered in a crisscrossing of scars, the largest of which went right over his nose and ended just above his lip in a way that pulled up the corner and gave him an eternal sneer.

Wait a minute. Why would he have scars? If he had been on this ship his whole life, never having been to a planet, how could be possibly have gotten war scars? Unless … I shuddered at the thought. Unless he had gotten them on this ship.

I wondered what could be so dangerous here.

Around him, the men had gone silent. All wore the navy uniform of their fleet, some with gloves on their hands, others still with hats. They stood around the bridge, typing commands into heavy keys and keyboards, writing and typing, controlling and guiding. The ship sailed forward smoothly, barely moving over the bleak terrain.

The only man sitting was, surprisingly, Nim. He looked smart in his new uniform, a light navy blue to my scratchy brown. They had wasted no time in promoting him. He was safe—for now.

The weird thing was that he was flanked on both sides by men with batons; maybe he wasn't in such a great shape. I avoided meeting his gaze. I didn't want to make things worse for either of us.

"You lied," the one called Hokera said with a deep growl. For a second, I thought he had called me out, but he was glaring at Nim.

"No, I promise. I was—"

"You lied," the man repeated. "We turned the temple to dust. The cavern underneath was empty."

"No, I ..." All faces were on him: accusing, angry faces. I felt my hands tremble. Everyone we knew was in that pyramid. I hoped they had gotten out in time.

"Two weeks." The commander turned on his heels, wasting no further time on my young friend. "Solitary confinement. You're lucky I am a lenient man."

"No, sir, please. You've got to understand," Nim stammered. He looked up, and suddenly his eyes caught mine, lighting up like a beacon. I winked at him, though I didn't know why. This wasn't going to be a glamorous rescue.

"Who is this?" asked Lord Hokera, waving a gloved hand in my direction. "Why are you bringing a recruit to me? Haven't we had enough false alarms for one day?"

He shot daggers at Nim, who shrunk back in his chair. It was only then that I noticed that his hands were tied, quite literally, the cuffs digging into the already raw flesh of his wrists. The sleeves slid back down to cover them once again.

"This is different, My Lord," said the soldier. "This child doesn't have news about the Creature. They *are* the Creature."

"What?" The word flew from the Lord Commander like a bark from his tongue. He eyes dressed me down. "This ... this is the form the creature decided to take?"

Nim let out a squawking sound. The outburst earned him a baton to the gut. I forced myself to ignore him, no matter how much it hurt.

"That's what it claims, sire," said the soldier, slowly. The lord grunted, taking a step toward me. I held my ground, rolling old words in my head like a hymn.

*You have a power that can destroy them all*, I repeated to myself, over and over again, until my thoughts were fire. I forced Selena's haughty smile onto my face and glared at the man with a fire that could ignite a thousand suns.

I was starlight. I was plasma. I was a fucking ball of flame.

"And you..." Hokera edged closer with every heavy step. He was tall, and he glared down at me, his scars sharp in the artificial light. "You just ... you walk in here and give yourself up? After entire eras of searching, you, what, got tired of running?"

He wasn't convinced of my claim, of that I was certain. It didn't matter. All I needed was to call out Angee. But I still needed to prove my claim. And it was in times like these that I dared to dream that I had abilities like Zander and Blayde, that I could impress him with a jump, with a death-defying stunt. Instead, my only weapon was my mind.

"I ..." The words died on my lips as the punch came out of nowhere, his fist colliding with my jaw, sending pain up my skull. The commander's eyes widened, through with surprise or from being impressed, I did not know. I felt a sneer climb up my lips, an odd ferocity building inside my chest and forcing its way out.

"Generations have passed since your ancestors began their search for me, but you grow weaker with every iteration. You grow further away from me, rather than closer. And you know what? It's boring to always be right. It's boring to have you kill my toys every few centuries then leave without making any effort. I'm not giving up; I'm giving in. Bring me back to my prison. I'll only break out again, have a new batch of youth come after me. Maybe it'll make it fun again: a new solar system, a better ship, better men. You folk hardly even try."

He struck me again, harder this time, my blood

forming at the place of words.

"You fucking *asshole*," said the Lord Commander, pulling back his fist as I fell to the ground. "You dare insult us? You took our lives from us. We were born and bred to find you, and you think this is a game? You think this was fun?"

Before I could say a word—or try to, seeing the state of my jaw—he brought his foot into my stomach. I doubled over, my body winded. Everything burned.

"The rules are clear about hitting the female of the species," the commander said, placing his boot gently on my shoulder. "But then again, you're not truly female, are you? Or even human?" The foot came down in an instant, and pain flew through my socket. My arm fell limp at my side. "Not so strong now, are you, so-called World Eater?" He kicked harder. I tried to get up, but with my arm out of its socket, I couldn't press. I was out of breath, my heart racing, pain shooting through my face and stomach and arm.

My mouth tasted of iron and blood. The fire had blown out.

The man would not stop. He kicked my stomach again and again and again. He paused, his foot hovering on my knee, and I expected the pain to come. Hokera, however, wanted to make this last, to make it hurt. The foot only rested.

"You come to me," he said, panting, as if this was an effort for him. "You claim to be bored. You give yourself up to me and my crew, and you don't expect retribution for what you have done?"

Kick.

Blood trickled from my mouth. I was too weak to

spit it out.

"You gave up a stronger form to shrink down and speak to us," he taunted. "Your only power. You are weak now, weaker than us for the first time. Be happy I have my crew on a leash, or they would tear you apart right now."

I said nothing. I couldn't say anything. It was hard enough keeping my head above water—where had all this water come from anyway? It was like I was bobbing on a current, like I was floating, like I was ...

Drowning.

I couldn't breathe. I begged the air to come into my lungs, but it wasn't filling them enough. The commander chose that moment to bring his foot down on my knee. This time, I screamed.

The sound came out wrong. The cry was shrill and sharp, but somewhere between my windpipe and crushed jaw it had been turned into a jagged, whale-like sound, as if someone had smashed it with a rubber mallet. I could not believe it was my cry, my pain, yet, my body was filled with flame.

And it was receding.

"Tell us, how did you evade the prison?" the commander asked. "You're not so strong when you are small. Not even that small, really. They say you're a multiform. Doesn't seem like that to me, sticking to a form so bland." He kicked me again, and I desperately tried to hold back tears. "Whimpering. Like a child. Not like a killer at all. Is that how you escaped? Tried to instill pity? It won't work this time, you son of a Veshnurk."

Adrenaline pumped fast and hot through my veins,

an icy hot that burned at a level above the flame. And, yet, the pain held back. Somehow, with every kick, I cared less about the blows. Was I losing myself, or was he losing the will to hurt me? I assumed that being kicked repeatedly would feel worse than this, but maybe I was finally repressing the pain.

Maybe it was because the thought was so clear in my head, the knowledge right before me, resistant and true, the knowledge that I was going to die.

"You," said the commander, not at me, for once. "The smart one. What's your name again?"

"Lars, sir," a voice answered proudly. The man who had found me in the hallway?

"Well, Lars, I'm feeling generous today. You're promoted."

"Fantastic, My Lord! Today is truly a day for celebration!"

"That it is, Lars; that it is."

I now felt more ill listening to their conversation than from the pain in my gut. Where was the pain, anyway? Why couldn't I feel anything? I didn't want to move or even try for fear that it would bring back the pain.

And where would I go? I couldn't run like this. So much for my brilliant plan. The one thing I did feel was the tears running down my cheeks, far too hot for my skin. Everything was hot now.

The Youpaff had to go and leave this planet. If they took me away, right now, the real Zoesh would be stuck on the ship. They would find him, and this planet would be free of them both. Forever.

"Would you care to ..." the lord trailed off, but it

wasn't hard to imagine where he was going with that.

"It would be my pleasure, sure," said Sergeant—newly promoted Lieutenant—Lars. I heard the steps approach and prepared myself for another kick.

But it didn't come. Instead, the world fell into silence.

The pain was gone now. Even the flaming tears were just water. I turned my head and found that it followed my orders quite well. It had no problem lifting off the ground to have a quick look around.

"Hush, my child," said a voice, a beautiful voice. I blinked. So, this was death then. It didn't look much different from life; maybe a little greener, just a smidge. Were we green-shifted when we died?

The afterlife. Having been brought up in a WASPy household, I thought it was going to be heaven or hell for me, but there were no pearly gates before me. I felt my heart fall—if it even was my heart, at this point. I must be in hell.

But no fire and brimstone. That was a relief. Purgatory, then? Is this where you get sent for believing in aliens?

"You have not passed," said the voice again.

"Who are you?" I stammered. "Show yourself!"

She stepped forward, and I recognized her instantly: Selena. Only this version wasn't scowling or bored or angry. She radiated beauty and calm, a halo of peace. I gaped at her.

"Selena?" I stammered. "But you—"

"I apologize for how my other-self treated you in the temple," she said, touching my face with a warm hand. The touch sent electrical tingles up my cheek. "She was young and confused. I have moved past her now."

"You ...Where ... where are we?"

"Look around. What do you see?" she asked, kindly.

I cast a glance. It was the ship, the same place I had been mere seconds ago. Only it was greener. And the people had stopped moving, which was odd. Lars was caught in the moment of lifting his foot for a kick, his tongue stuck comically between his teeth, excitement in his eyes, a bright twinkling light.

I let out a snort. This weird-ass creep would have kicked me, if it hadn't been for Selena stopping time.

"Well, I didn't stop it, exactly," she said, responding to my thoughts. "I dragged you out of it. I didn't know if you would make it, but, hey, humans can handle one or two dimensions, so long as you don't mess with their minds too much."

And here I was thinking I was strong enough to resist the Zoesh's mind while Selena read mine like a book. I hadn't felt her at all.

"I exist out of time, dear. I know what you're going to say. It's how the higher dimensions work."

"I'm in the..."

"Fifth dimension," said Selena, "sort of. Maybe dimension four-point-five, right between them. It's not like anyone can bother us here."

"And you dragged me out of the third dimension

... because ..."

"I wanted a chat." She smiled, somehow more radiant than before. "Would you like to take a seat? We can sit on the floor together. Try not to make any large movements. You might end up at the wrong end of the universe."

"Oh ... kay." I sat on the floor as she requested. It felt like nothing, and I wondered if it was even there, if anything was truly here.

"I know you have many questions," she said as she took to the floor before me, "and I will try to answer them. We are in no hurry; time can wait for us to return." I shuddered, and Selena frowned. "Are you cold? Are you tired? Am I scaring you? I'm sorry. I haven't spoken to humans in so long. I forget. I—"

"No, I'm just ..." What was it, exactly? Scared didn't even begin to cover it. The one thing I wasn't was in pain, and for that, I was incredibly relieved.

"I had nothing to do with that."

"You didn't heal me?"

"No." She shook her head. "I guess I'm not the only one looking out for you."

"And why are you looking out for me, exactly? Why do I deserve a guardian goddess? If this version of you has been here the whole time, why didn't you show yourself? Why didn't you help me earlier?"

"It's a long story, one I'm not proud of. But I couldn't stand by and do nothing."

"But you have been," I snorted. "I've been impersonating you. You could have shown yourself at any time!"

She smiled gently. "I know I shouldn't have brought

you here against your will. But you were so close! I ...
drew you in. You were always destined to be here, after
all. Your intervention on this planet is a fixed point in
time. That nice boy knew so, too. He had all the facts."

I sat up straighter. "The nice boy?"

"The monk, a few millennia ago," she said, seeing
very well that she had my attention. "He showed up
one day with these beautiful stories and a promise that
you would come. He didn't stay long, but we had a chat
and he told me everything."

"Let me get this straight. Some guy, a few thousand
years ago, knew I would show up here? This prophecy
shit is legit?"

"He came from a collective of monks who docu-
ment all information in the universe. I hadn't heard of
them until that moment. But he was, as you say, legit.
I had, after all, lived this moment before, and I will live
it again, thus is the nature of time. I knew his story was
true and finally saw the strings of time weaving together."

"How can you have lived this moment before? I
don't think I have—"

She put up a hand to stop me. "Don't try to
understand it. This is beyond what your mind is built
for."

"But you knew this was going to happen?" I
stammered. "You knew you were going to die and what
the Zoesh would do? I thought you said no one could
see it coming."

"It's complicated." She sighed. "Look around you.
Look at me!"

Her body morphed through a series of complex
shapes and fractals, like an invisible hand giving putty

a squeeze. She smiled as she took on my form once again.

"You can only see, can only comprehend, what is a tiny fraction of the whole," Selena said. "Think how weak your eyes are, how many wavelengths you can see out of all the possible waves out there. How your senses are limited to a handful, how your dimensions can be counted and calculated with the fingers on your tiny hand. Can you possibly believe you could understand something so complex with the tools you have? Over half the things I want to tell you have no words in your language and do not even exist as a concept. So, please, be calm and listen. I want to help you."

I was calm. I listened and tried to not let my eyes wander over the room or at the woman who looked so much like me.

"What ... what am I supposed to do now?" I stammered. My eyes fell on the form of the young soldier who was so intent on kicking me while I was already down. The look in his eyes was something I could not place my finger on: a look of ferocity, of eagerness, and, above all else, of peace.

"Well, I have to send you back. As lovely as this chat has been, I can't keep you here forever. Well, I could, but then nothing would really happen, would it?"

"And what's supposed to happen? I've already failed on most points. Look at where we are now. These people think I'm the Zoesh, and your so-called ex isn't in his cave."

"That fucker shifted," she muttered, crossing her arms across her chest. "Dammit. He's made himself small again. That's not going to be easy to find."

"We know he's on the ship," I replied, crossing my own arms. For a goddess who was supposed to know all and see all, she didn't seem that aware of anything. "He's taken over Angee. My friend. Can you help me? I mean, you can see time way better than I can. Don't you already know what's going to happen? Where he's going to be or how this all ends?"

"Yes and no, in a way, but it doesn't work like that."

"Then what good are you?" I snapped, pushing myself up on my feet. The world around me wasn't moving the way it should have, which was unsettling to say the least. "You brought me here to, what, give me a pep talk? Give me your blessing?"

"Yes."

"And that's it? You told me a story about your shitty life and told me I have to stop the Zoesh from going back into hiding? You haven't told me anything that can help. This has been an enormous waste of non-time."

"No." She flew forward and was upon me in a second. "You don't get to muck about in my name and then turn around with such insolence. You're supposed to be in my name. You're supposed to help these people."

"Why do you think I'm still here?" I laughed. "I stayed because I can help them, not because I enjoy pretending to be a celestial being!"

"And a fat lot of help you've given them so far!"

"I am getting my ass kicked because I told them I was the Zoesh. I am going to die on this floor so these starship troopers go away without burning this place to ash. I am putting my life on the line for them. I don't see you doing that."

She said nothing, but her face turned red, although

it was almost brown with the greenish filter in my vision, and I could practically see steam wafting from her ears. And then without a word, I was flung back onto the ground, the wind knocked out of my chest. I had been kicked back into time without a goddess to watch my back.

# CHAPTER TWENTY-FOUR

## IT'S THE END OF THE WORLD AS WE KNOW IT

I gasped, suddenly feeling every throbbing pain in my body. Lars was still coming at me and would bring a final blow to my weak, low-dimensional being, the cheap knockoff of the closest thing to a goddess I would actually meet.

At least the cheap knockoff was doing something. Even if that something was dying for people she did not know, on a planet she couldn't even name.

A planet with her moon.

I took a deep breath, preparing for the blow that would end it all.

It didn't come.

Lars crumpled to the floor beside me, wheezing. Standing above him was a woman with brilliant madness in her eyes reaching for my arm and pulling me up before I could take in who she was.

"Blayde?"

She turned to face the commander. "Don't you fucking dare touch a hair on her head," she spat, standing taller and stronger than the real goddess I had just met. "If you mess with her, I will end you!"

Hokera took a step toward her but didn't go far. Blayde was more fearsome than what had given him those scars, and he shied away from her, a terrified puppy.

"Now, are you going to find the Zoesh, or do I have to do everything around here? Friends don't beat up friends for trying to help them save the world, you know. It's not a competition; it's a fucking rescue mission. And don't just stand there!"

Hokera stared at me over Blayde's shoulder, whimpering. Probably my cue to say something.

"I kinda told them I was the Zoesh to get on the bridge," I said, "but it's on the ship, yeah."

"It's lying," hissed Hokera, lifting a trembling finger to point at me. "Don't you see? It's healed all its wounds. This thing is just the Zoesh in disguise! Your friend is gone, and ..."

He stopped talking, staring at me in wide-eyed awe. Blayde spun on her heels, her own jaw dropping. I didn't need to ask them what they were looking at because I saw it too. My skin glowed—a pure white light that reeked of onions. Was this a dream? If so, I was dreaming the looks on everybody's faces, the utter shock that wiped away smirks into oblivion.

The great goddess Selena had risen, and she was fucking pissed.

"Keep looking, dumbasses!" I shouted in a voice so heavenly, angels would have wept. I couldn't tell who was in control of my mouth, Selena or me, but I had a feeling we wanted to say the same thing in the end. "He's on your fucking ship! You're not leaving until you take him!"

I pointed a hand at Hokera—or my body did; I wasn't really controlling my limbs all that much—and the man flew backward, hitting the door to the bridge with a whelp. He crumpled in a heap on the floor.

They began shooting at me, rifles spitting fire toward my body, but they passed through me like I wasn't even here. The bullets were like bee stings and nothing more. I felt myself smiling, excitement rising in my heart as I took in the full realization of what was happening to me.

I was Selena. Powerful and mighty and true. I was ready to go medieval on these assholes.

Not like that, though.

"You all right?" Blayde asked, awestruck as the firestorm ended.

"Yeah, I met Selena again."

"I can see that." She nodded slowly. "Are you ..."

I looked down at my hands, still radiating that odd white glow. I felt in control now. I just wasn't the only one in here. Power coursed through my veins. Like the fire from before, but this time, it wasn't imagined by a girl trying to cope with the possibility of death. This time, Prometheus had given her a flaming torch and left her free to do as she wished with it. I could do anything I wanted. I could blow up the ship if I chose to. I could drop everyone here. But the Zoesh eluded me. Even as I concentrated on finding Angee, he wasn't making himself known.

"What the hell is going on here?" shouted Zander, rushing to my side.

"How did you get here?" I met his eyes and felt relief wash over me. He was here; he would know what to do. He got close, then stepped back, my energy too strong for even him to handle.

"Snuck into a shuttle," he explained. "Nimien?"

Nim crawled out from under a console, smiling nervously.

"Sally's got powers now?" he said, more excited than someone who had just faced death ever had the right to be. "Cool!"

"*Countdown commencing,*" said a voice over the intercom, shaking me from my concentration. "*Fifteen minutes until launch.*"

"What the heck?" I shouted, turning to face the control console. Every screen displayed numbers, counting down to who knew what. I looked up at Zander, but he shook his head.

*He's shrunken himself,* said the real Selena, bold and clear in my head, angry even. *He probably blew up a nice chunk of this world in the process.*

"So how do I find it? If it's still with Angee, we have to find her!" I asked, ignoring the chorus of angels that sang every time I opened my mouth. "And what's that countdown for?"

*You don't,* she replied. *You'll never be able to, but we need to save this planet. The commander has initiated the launch sequence for a large, destructive bomb. It would raze the entire continent. Get this ship away from here and destroy the bomb.*

"But how?" I asked. But this time, Selena was gone.

The energy pulsing through me was beginning to burn. It grew hotter by the second, scorching me from within. I yelped, letting out a blast through my hands, casting a man backward. But there was too much for me to hold onto.

"She's wrong," I said, not that anyone outside my head could follow my conversation. "What do we do?"

No one answered, but all eyes were on me: unstable, confused, little old me. I did have the power of a higher dimensional being coursing through my veins, but it didn't mean I knew how to use it. But they were looking to me to find a solution.

"There's a bomb," I said, trying to stop my voice from sounding supremely ethereal. "We need to defuse it. Get the ship away. Save Nim. Save the children, and end the Zoesh."

Blayde pointed to what looked like a small photo booth in the corner. No one else stirred. Apparently, between the three of us, the entire bridge was out of commission. Nim was the only other one still conscious, and he was staggering from his hiding place.

"Listen carefully," Blayde said. "We're getting on that teleport. But someone needs to stop that bomb."

"*Twelve minutes until launch,*" the voice added for dramatic effect. I nodded, strangely aware of how panic wasn't rising. Was this how it felt to live without anxiety? Or was it the goddess taking over my skin?

"On it," said Zander, trying to type in commands on the console.

"You ... uh ... stop!" A soldier appeared in the hallway, flanked by another dozen men and women in uniform, pointing a gun at us. "In the name of the law, I order you not to use that teleporter!" He obviously never had to use that phrase in practice, having been raised on this ship and away from any real confrontation, just the edge Blayde needed.

"Technically it's a tele-*trans*-porter ... poor use of grammar, man," Blayde said, her love of defiance filling her whole. "And I thought we made it very clear: We don't follow the rules." She whispered to me. "Attack formation B. Go."

"But I ..." I started. It didn't matter. In seconds, she had jumped around the room, and the men were on the ground, knocked out cold. Zander, however, looked frustrated at the panel before him.

"What are you doing?" I asked, perplexed.

"Auto command. I set in coordinates, they fly, we'll teleport out of here. They won't know what hit them; no military training whatsoever. Sure, they follow the rules, but they've never faced real combat. They'll just go to the next planet. They're predictable. Now come on; we're going."

"*Ten minutes until launch*," said the voice.

"But what about the bomb?" said Nim. Only he wasn't terrified; he was stoic. I was projecting my own terror on top of his lack of emotion.

Nim wasn't scared at all.

"It's going to destroy everything on this continent," said Zander, reading the console for himself, "but I can't stop it. We have to ..."

And suddenly, it became clear.

"Take it all in," I said, grinning. I felt the energy flowing through my body and knew what had to be done.

"What now?" asked Zander.

"Go," I begged. "Get the kids, get into the teleport. I'm going to save the world."

*Take a great leap of faith, jump, and take it all in.*

The words of a man, a monk, thousands of years ago, entrusted to a forest to pass on to me—to Selena. And right now, we were one and the same.

I ran to the back of the ship as the countdown raced in my ears. Only the countdown slowed as Selena pulled me through the dimensions, keeping the timer from running down.

"Is this going to work?" I asked her.

No response. But my skin went hot for a second, a single pulse, and I took that as a yes. Selena was with me on this. After all, she was me.

The ship was in a panic, but I was only a breeze. I was the wing, and I stopped for no one, running through the monstrosity of a space bucket, lower and lower and lower through the levels, pushing people out of my way with only my mind. The two people guarding the weapons were blasted to the side as I slid into the room.

"It's all or nothing," I said, taking a deep breath, though I no longer needed to breathe. I looked down at the floor, staring at the huge warning sign below the bomb.

Oh, yeah, and I stared at the bomb too. It was massive, a hunk of rounded metal larger than a car. I shuddered, sensing its destructive power through the huge casing.

And then I saw the rest of the room. The stack of

this same bomb rising all the way up the ship. Hundreds of bombs, maybe thousands. Or maybe my eyes were playing tricks on me. It was hard to see with the light pulsating off my skin.

"You!" said Angee, rushing at me. Unlike the others, I couldn't feel her presence, and her body came out of nowhere, tackling me to the ground.

"Yes, me," I said, but the voice that growled was Selena's. "Hey, honey. Fancy seeing you here."

Angee swiped a punch at me and I dodged it, ducking out of the way and taking a swipe at her head. Missed her by a hair.

"*Five minutes until detonation,*" said the computer.

Angee pushed herself back up, poised to attack once more. The Zoesh was tied to her back like a baby, glancing over her shoulder and glaring at me. The part of my mind that was being borrowed by Selena filled with fury at the sight of him.

It was all up to me now. It was time for me to end the secret reign of the Zoesh, bring him down and take the old Alliance ship with it. They both had to pay for what they did, for the lives that were lost getting caught in between the two. I had to make up for the lives Selena had refused to help.

But to do so, I would have to kill Angee.

"Worthless human," she laughed, showing all her teeth. "Even with the power of a hundred thousand suns beneath your skin, you cannot lift a finger against me."

I swung a punch, but I was a poor fighter. Angee dodged my move easily, her hands behind her back, not even trying to fight back. She didn't need to. All she had to do was run out the clock, let the bomb drop, make the ship believe she was dead for good while nuking an entire world to cover the Zoesh's tracks. I was the last line of defense against the end of a world, and I couldn't even land a punch.

"*Three minutes until detonation,*" the computer reminded me, digging the knife a little deeper.

"You stole my friend's mind," I snapped, circling Angee as best I could. She laughed again, the dinosaur on her shoulder laughing in tandem.

"She gave it to me easily," he replied, hands twitching. "She didn't put up a fight like you did."

"You are a demon to her," I said. "She lived her life for Selena. She was going to jump into a volcano for her. You living in her mind goes against everything she believes in."

The creature grinned with Angee's smile. "Which makes this victory all the more ... satisfying. I mean, look at you. You have a goddess riding shotgun, and you haven't even managed to touch me. Go die on the planet with the rest of them, where you belong."

Angee's hands twitched again. I knew this woman was a fighter. Even after living her entire life in a temple, she was smart enough to know her goddess didn't want her sacrifice. She had fought at the top of the volcano, and today she would fight again.

"Angee," I begged, staring right into her eyes and ignoring the dinosaur behind her. "Angee, listen to me—"

"*One minute until detonation.*"

The floor shook and trembled, a square pulling away to reveal sky below. Clouds rushed beneath us, wind whistling through the hangar and filling the room with sound. My hair whipped around my face as I struggled to stand. The first of the bombs slid down a rail to align itself with its only means of escape.

"Angee," I repeated, my voice steady through this terror. I would not look down. Heights were my enemy, but right now, the Zoesh was a million times worse. "Fight him. I kept him out, and I know you can too. You're strong. Stronger than anyone I have ever met. You have stood your own without flinching even before the Sky People arrived. You've fought the Evil One all your life. Just fight a little more now."

"*Thirty seconds.*"

Angee screamed, launching herself at me. I grabbed her around the waist, making the Zoesh's tiny body squeal. A hand went around its neck, while the other fought Angee's grip. She was stronger now, but so was I.

"You have to fight it!"

"*Twenty seconds.*"

"Your people are down there, and they need you! More than anyone's ever needed Selena, more than anyone's needed the idea of Selena, they need you to stop the bombs. You need to save your people, Angee."

"*Ten ... nine ...*"

She shoved me off her, growling, leaping away and putting the hole in the floor between us. Her stance was wide and furious.

"I know you can fight the Evil One. It's your worst enemy. It wants your people dead. And you're the only one who can stop it."

"*Three ... two ... one ...*"

"Please"

In that last instant, she turned to me. Her eyes glowed for a second, just a moment, and she smiled. A courageous smile, a forced smile, a smile just for me.

"I was born to jump from high places," she said, time waiting for her move. "I just didn't know how high."

"*Disengage.*"

With a horrifying scream, she leapt. Angee roared as she pushed herself out of the hangar, taking the tiny Zoesh with her. I didn't think. I knew what I had come to do even before I had reached the room; the words of the ancient monk were strong in my mind. I leapt into the clouds, chasing the bomb and Angee with the wind.

She searched for my eyes and found them, and in that moment, I saw her free of the burden of a master in her mind. She had won. She was sacrificing the beast on her back, taking the dinosaur down with her.

"Angee!" I screamed, but my voice was whipped away by the wind.

Before me, falling even faster, was the bomb. The metal monster was a rock through a pond, plunging toward the earth. I dove headfirst after it, the wind racing past my face, burning my cheeks as I plummeted out of the sky. And, yet, I felt no fear. No hesitation. The void no longer sent me reeling.

I was falling.

I was flying.

And now, just as the prophecy predicted, I was stradeling a bomb. Yeehaw, motherfuckers.

"What now?" I asked the sky, asked the voice in my

head. The metal was cold through the rough uniform, yet I couldn't shiver even if I wanted to.

*Be calm,* the voice urged, finally responding. It sounded like it came from deep underwater. *Lean in. I will protect you.*

I closed my eyes, grabbed the bomb tightly, and leaned in.

The blast rippled through my being. I was the void, I was a ghost, yet the energy was exploding outward as the bomb shattered, sending its destructive force far and wide.

But it wasn't going far and wide. Because it had to go through me first.

As it burst, it burned the energy rolling off me, destroying the excess of power Selena had jammed into my body. It was contained, pushed back, walled in by Selena herself.

I screamed as the two forces faced each other, burning where they touched. I felt Selena crying out as well, a war cry like no other. It filled my mind and the sky around me.

Then, all at once, the energy was gone. Like a switch being turned off. And now, I was straddling a pool noodle, falling from the sky and plummeting toward the earth as any good stone would when faced with gravity.

# CHAPTER TWENTY-FIVE

## THE SKY IS FALLING, SALLY WEBBER!

"Ah! Fuck, fuck, fuck, fuck!" I screamed, clutching the foam uselessly. Gone was the energy. Gone was the bomb, gone was Selena. Gone was Angee, her life given for her people to survive.

Gone was my chill. Welcome back, vertigo!

The ground rushed toward me, and I knew in my heart I was going to die.

Die again? I wasn't too sure what had happened back on the ship, if anything that happened with Selena counted as reality. I clutched the pool noddle for support, wondering how and why that stupid thing would be the last thing I would hold in this world.

I closed my eyes and screamed. The wind tore that

scream right out of my mouth and gave it to someone else. The clouds, maybe.

And then, out of the deep blue of the sky, I heard sound again. I heard my voice, and it sounded stupid. I shut my mouth, realizing I was on the ground—on the ground and not dead.

My arms tightened around my savior. I didn't care whose arms they were, but they held me tight, and their hold was gentler than the wind's. I dug my head into their chest, somehow knowing from scent alone who had come to my rescue.

My space-jumping alien friend, Zander.

And I sobbed into his chest, relishing in what it was to be alive. He had saved me. Like my knight in shining armor, he had taken my momentum away, sending it to who knows where. And I was alive.

"Is she going to be okay?" asked a voice, from far behind us. Nim.

"She'll be fine," Blayde replied. "She just fell out of a sky while detonating a bomb. Also, I think she was possessed for a little bit back there. I think she's allowed a good cry."

"She saved this entire planet," said Zander, cradling me. His voice was soft and reassuring. "She's allowed more than a good cry. She's allowed an excellent cry."

Fuck yeah, I was.

I needed a burger right about now. And some fries and a good soda.

I needed to go home.

I pulled away from Zander's chest, realizing I was probably squashing his legs. He didn't seem to care. My cries turned to soft hiccups, and my tears had almost dried up. I was exhausted from crying, exhausted from this whole awful ordeal.

I stood on shaky feet, grasping my noodle for balance with one hand and Zander for support on the other. Why the pool noodle? I'm convinced it was once the bomb, but I didn't really care. I guess it was better than a whale or a bowl of petunias.

"Selena?" I asked, and the group shook their heads. But I wasn't asking them; I was addressing the woman who had been in my body just a few minutes ago. I got no reply.

Except a slight breeze—maybe that was her. Had she survived the explosion? Or had the bomb devoured her? She hadn't hesitated when I had realized what I had to do. Now, I wondered if she knew how it would end.

If this was the death she had been expecting.

"Angee?" I asked them, which got me looks of confusion.

A cool breeze ran through my hair, and I let out a heavy breath. It was an eerie sight, the sky red with clouds of gray, the planet silent except for the wind. It was like when I had found my way out of the Zoesh's cave. Only this time, I felt fine. All my cuts and bruises were gone. All I felt was the lingering burn of pure energy in my veins and the lack of heat on my face.

This was the planet I had saved—Angee had saved, with her sacrifice. A dusty, beautiful place. A place now without Atlanta or Aquetzalli. Places and people I had failed to save—twice, in the case of Aquetzalli. Although this was a victory, it felt weak. I felt undeserving.

I was no hero. I wasn't even a goddess. In the end, I had only been there to help Selena and Angee do the heavy lifting.

The golden pyramid was no more, having been destroyed by the Sky People. There was nothing on the horizon but a cluster of strange buildings: small pyramids organized around two larger ones, none of them with buildings on top. Just flat, as if cut off, or someone had forgotten to finish them.

But we were not alone. Wandering around us were dozens, maybe hundreds, of children in scratchy uniforms. Many were too dazed to say anything, let alone cry. They stood in the desert, staring at the sky in silence, watching the ship leave. The kids were all right. At least, that was a victory we could add to the list. We had gotten them back to the earth, safe and sound. What happened now, I could not even begin to guess.

And there was Zander, skin golden in the setting sun. Sometimes I forgot he was eternally a man with a weapon. His hair reached for the sky, shimmers of golden rays playing through the streaks. He wasn't smiling until he turned and saw me, and in that instant his face burst into life, sunshine beamed from his smile. In that moment, I could not imagine a sight more beautiful than him standing there, looking at me the same way I was looking at him.

"Where are we?" I asked. "Is everyone ...?"

Before I could finish the thought, he pushed a finger against my lips, holding them shut. Joy turned quickly to confusion.

"Wandjd?"

"Shhhh."

I pushed his hand away, taking the finger along with it. "Are you shushing me?"

"This is how they do it in films, right?"

I laughed. There. That was the Zander I had missed. The moments I thought I was going to lose, the moments I thought I had lost forever. This was the man who radiated like the sun and couldn't get movie tropes out of his head. We had saved this world, and we were alive, and even he didn't know how this scene should play out.

"The teleport took us straight down to the surface," he explained, trying to smile through the worry. "We got everyone we could. They didn't need to be asked twice."

"We saw you falling, and Zander went after you, like, *pow*!" Nim laughed ecstatically. "It was the coolest thing I've ever seen!"

I grinned as I looked up at Zander, my friend, giving his hand a tight squeeze. "Thank you for saving my life, again."

"Anytime." He winked, then caught himself. "Don't do this again, all right?"

I laughed. "I really hope I won't have to absorb any more bombs anytime soon." I gave him a playful punch on the shoulder. "So, what now? Are the Sky People gone for good?"

"They didn't find the Zoesh," Blayde said sadly, "so they'll be back. But we just saved an entire generation from that ship. When they return in five thousand years, who knows what they'll be like. But these kids here? They're going to tell their kids the truth, and their kids will know the truth. The next time the ship comes back, the entire planet will be ready to give them the Zoesh. It'll be over, once and for all."

"But Angee ..." I looked at Nim. No, I couldn't tell him that's how she died. "But the Zoesh died in that explosion. They won't have anyone to give."

We wandered through the children, searching for anyone who might be injured. For the most part, everyone had survived their brief excursion to the alien ship. The worst of it all was cuts and burns from mishandling things on the ship itself.

We wandered around the small pyramids, the small structures oddly familiar to the pyramid we had left in Atlanta. They lined a wide road, ending at a larger building, one with steep steps but no doors. Or maybe the doors were invisible.

Avenue of the Dead, I thought with a shiver.

In a central square area, surrounded by the unfinished pyramids, was a statue. A shrine to Selena, it seemed. I made my way up it carefully. Before I knew it, I was on my knees in front of her, fighting to hold back tears. I dropped the pool noodle at her feet, in guise of offering. It probably meant nothing to the golden idol.

"Thank you," I said, staring up at the sky. To my amazement, the moon was in full view above the tall pyramid, as if to tell me she was all right.

Imagine my surprise when the noodle disappeared and my duffel bag took its place. If I wasn't crying before, I sure was now. My face drained like a faucet as I took the bag into my hands, my only tether to my home planet.

At some point, the sound of whistling wind started

to rise and become louder until it sounded like actual voices. There were people coming from every direction, spilling onto the pyramids and shouting. There were locals—Atlans and Aquetzallians. The people who had been in the golden city before all this shit had gone down.

And they were singing.

It was a joyful song. No matter where these people came from, they were singing together, raising their weapons high in triumph. They beamed down at us, excited, jubilant, their children by their sides. Hugging, laughing, surviving.

"Are they ...?" Nim began to ask, but we stood frozen. Something was wrong.

Ancha walked up the alley, clutching Bismuth's hand, to the cheers of the natives. Bismuth held her spear high above her head in victory. I didn't know what to do, how to react. I had thought we could make a quick exit without going through the hassle of celebrations and thanks. I hadn't even considered they would want to celebrate with us.

We had to go, though. There was a tension rising, a stagnancy in the air:. The wind had stopped. It was troubling, and I felt my heart racing in my chest.

I slung my bag over my shoulder, just in case this paranoia had some essence to it.

Some of the people on the pyramids were still in their bird costumes, though they were off their stilts. They looked even more ominous without them.

Ancha raised her arms, and the people around her went silent. I had been right: The wind died, and its absence was more marked in this silence.

"My friends," she said, "today is a great day. Behold, before you, the saviors of our world: the great goddess Selena and her attendants!"

Cheers erupted from the crowd once more, and I blushed. Maybe it was all the eyes on me that made me so uneasy; I didn't know. All I knew was that I needed to get away.

"You saved us from the fire from the skies," Bismuth boasted. "You brought back our children!" That was followed by a great whoop of cheering. But my friends and I still weren't convinced. Nim edged closer, trying not to disturb the horde.

"The Sky People have left us, and we have survived," she proclaimed. "All thanks to you! You deserve all the riches we could ever give you. We will reward you greatly!"

"No, thank you!" I responded as loudly as I could. The world was silent as I spoke. "We did not help for riches or reward. We helped because it was the right thing to do. The best gift you can give us is to allow us to leave in peace. Please, listen to your children. Prepare yourselves for the Sky People to return. But right now, we must ascend to the heavens, so please let us go."

"That is our duty," said Ancha, lifting her hands high. I saw electricity spark up and down the shaft. "We are here to obey, to help. Let us free you from your earthly bonds."

The spear flew out of Bismuth's hand before I could react. Nim's feet lifted off the ground as he flew backward. A large golden shaft stuck out from his chest, pinning him to the pyramid beyond. His body engulfed in flame as he wailed and screamed, as his flesh burned.

"Nimien!" I cried, rushing toward him, but a spear flew past my face, blocking my way as it narrowly missed my nose. The earth jolted as it smacked into it, sending electricity through the ground.

"Sally!" shouted Zander as fire burst from the ground around us. The flames ran up my legs, charring them as I ran.

Selena's statue was engulfed in sparks. Flames danced up her shrine. I watched in terror as her face melted from her body. I couldn't see where I was going. There was smoke now, flames rising all around me.

I heard coughing and saw Nim through the fire. He coughed up blood, spewing it out of his mouth before he stopped moving altogether. Even from this far away, I saw the light leave his eyes.

Nim was dead.

I ran at him, screaming, crying, but Zander grabbed me around the midriff and dragged me away.

"The other way, Sally!" he shouted. "Up the pyramid, come on! We need to find Blayde."

"No. No, we have to save Nim!" I sobbed. "He can't die! He can't! We saved him once; we have to—"

"We have to go. Now!" He grabbed me so harshly he cut the breath from my lungs.

"Let me go!"

"Do you want to survive?" he screamed into my ear. "Do you? We need to find Blayde!"

"No, we need to save Nim!" Even over the crackling flames, I heard the people chanting, saying their goodbyes oh-so-pleasantly as we burned.

"We release you from your earthly bonds!" cried Ancha. "We free you! We free you!"

"Stop!" I shouted, tears streaming down my face. "Please stop!"

But they didn't stop.

"Sally, come *on*!" Zander stopped waiting for my compliance and picked me up off the ground, effortlessly pulling me away from Nim's corpse. The flames were glad of his sacrifice, eating him up with relish. I screamed as they engulfed his face.

"Save him, Zander, please!" I begged.

"I can't!"

"What good are you if you help everyone but the people you claim to care about?" I screamed.

I tried to break free of his grip to save Nim, but Zander was too strong as he carried me over his shoulder. I kicked and screamed, my eyes filling with tears. I was only vaguely aware of Blayde grabbing his hand before we jumped away from this place of fire, away from the burning ruins of this planet.

Away from the burning frame of Nim.

# CHAPTER TWENTY-SIX

## *THIS CHAPTER HEADER WILL NOT MAKE YOU SMILE*

At first glance, the sky above me was green.

At second glance—or many hundredth or thousandth glance—the green was just leaves. A forest shielded me from the sun, the gentle light sifting through the branches of tall trees. The blue sky was barely visible between them, and the colors filled me with a quiet peace, reminding me of home.

It wasn't home, though. I was pretty sure the trees back home didn't have metal branches.

I sighed, closing my eyes to block out the sight of yet another alien planet. My hands ran through the grass, gently combing the blades through my trembling fingers, a soothing sensation I had missed for such a long time.

My hands became fists. I ripped grass from the ground as every muscle tensed.

Fire. Flames. Spears. Spaceships. Nim, his body aflame, burning just out of reach. His screams filled my head until I couldn't hear anything else.

Until I was the one screaming.

I couldn't breathe. Even with my eyes closed, I felt the world spinning around me, the ground coming out from under my back, retracting all support. I was falling into the void, and I plunged my fists into the earth to stop myself from crashing further.

Tears streaked out of my eyes, burning my skin as they fled my body. It hurt; it hurt so much. My heart pounded so hard I was afraid it was going to explode, that I was going to explode, that this was going to be the end of Sally Webber.

And, I thought in that moment, maybe an end was what was best. I didn't want to exist in this universe anymore. In this fucking cruel place that killed off my friends with impunity. First, it took my brother. Then, my boyfriend. Now, my protégé, a brilliant boy who was destined for greatness, not to be released in a stupid sacrifice under an alien sun.

It took the best from us. It would always take the best from us. Death leaves no one behind.

I wish it would take me now.

My body remembered the pain of the repeated kicks from the commander, his anger and hatred only a fraction of what I felt toward myself right now. I remembered how it felt to have liquid fire running through my veins, the emptiness of it going out. My heart pounded more now than it did then.

End this, end this, end this.

My lungs were empty of air, yet I felt like I could scream forever. I failed at everything. I failed to keep the people of that planet safe. I failed to bring the Zoesh to justice. I failed to stop the Sky People from returning. My ears rang as I shouted at the universe and at myself. How could I live in silent guilt when I felt it all? When I was responsible for so many deaths?

I was no goddess. Fuck destiny; it obviously had poor taste in defenders. It made me believe I could make a difference, only to find out I was as insignificant as anyone else.

So many deaths, so much pain, so much hatred and fear—

It was only then that I felt the arms around me—the cool skin against mine, wrapping around me from behind, holding me as I screamed. Small arms, but strong like tree trunks, firm enough to hold me down without causing me pain. They cradled me as I sobbed, my skin still as hot to me as if it were on fire. A voice trying to soothe me as I whimpered for my mom, for my dad, my home. My planet.

My home.

Breath returned to me as my body ran out of energy to continue to panic.

Like coming off a high, there was an awakening. I opened my eyes, which ached with exhaustion from the tears they had released. There was a dull ache all around, my muscles feeling spent, my mouth dry, my voice probably hoarse from the screaming. I was drained, but

I was breathing.

And then I noticed the arms. Not the arms I had expected. Actually, damn near the last ones I anticipated coming to my aid.

Blayde.

For the first time since I had met her, Blayde wasn't a warrior. She whispered soothing sounds in my ear, brushing my hair back with her fingers, prying strands from my sweaty brow. *You're safe now*, she whispered, a promise from the most reliable of sources.

I whimpered slightly, out of shame. There was no point in holding anything back from her anymore, not after she had seen me at my worst.

Holy shit, Blayde was hugging me.

Even odder, Blayde was trying to help me, not reprimand me for having a loud mental break. It was Blayde, but not the Blayde I had come to know. This was the Blayde the world was not allowed to see.

There was something deeply unsettling about this.

"Where ... where are we?" I managed to ask. Ah, yes, my voice was hoarse, as expected. Nice.

"Not Earth," she replied. "Not yet. A place with no name, but we're safe here."

Her voice was light and reassuring. Her fingers deftly pulled my hair back, forming a ponytail that she fastened in place. It was only then that she slipped away, turning to face me.

She had been crying. The great, unbreakable Blayde had been crying.

"Where's Zander?"

"He's trying to find us water and food. He needs to ... clear his mind."

My eyes met hers, holding her gaze, words traveling between us that needed not be said aloud. She put her hand gently on my knee, warm and reassuring. And I—I must still have had that death wish—put my hand on hers. I didn't dare smile. There was nothing to smile about.

"Nim?" I said.

"He's gone, Sally." Blayde's usually impassible face slipped for a second—just a second—but in that moment, I saw a woman I didn't recognize. She was scared, sad, hurting, an old and tired Blayde.

She could not feel physical pain, but she could feel the deepest pain of all.

"We have to go back," I stammered, hopping to my feet. My brain shot endorphins left, and right now the panic had passed as I tried to balance the abundance of adrenaline it had given me for no reason. I was antsy, energized, borderline manic. I had to go. I had to act. I had to do something.

Blayde shook her head.

"We have to," I said, more determined than ever. I opened my fists, feeling the muscles clench. My palms were sweaty. I missed mom's spaghetti. "We have to get him out of there. We can give him your blood again. Bring him back."

"It's too late, Sally." She rose and brushed the dirt from her leggings. She had changed out of the rough-spun tunic back into her usual wear, all indication that she had ever been to Aquetzalli now gone.

"It's Nim," I snapped. "We have to make time."

"It's too late!" she said, harsher now, though without raising her voice. "Sally, you've been asleep for days. We've been waiting for you to wake up before discussing ... what happens next."

"Days?" I stammered. Impossible. We had jumped, and I had ...

How had I gotten to that forest floor? I realized now I had no memory of anything between screaming and the sight of Nim.

I shuddered. The last memory I had was of his body going up in flames—and me failing to protect him.

"No, I couldn't have been out of it for days. You're lying. You just don't want to go back. You never cared for Nim. You didn't want him along in the first place! He was always a burden and you—"

"He was a human being!" Her eyes burned holes in my forehead. "Did I want him around? No! Because I knew something like this would happen. Exactly this! To him. To you. One day, you'll be the one I'll be mourning. Whether it's my fault or old age taking you, you will die, and I'll keep going. Because I can't fucking die. It never ends for me. Nim was not the first person to die under our care. What? You thought you were the first to travel with us? Fact of life, Sally: Everything will die on you. You have to learn to accept it and move on."

"He was my friend!"

"Why do you think he wasn't mine?" she snapped. "You think I wanted him to die? I just knew he would, sooner or later. And so. Will. You."

I took a step back. "Is that a threat?"

"No," she replied, shaking her head. "It's a fact of life. Everything in the universe will die. Except for me. And my brother. No exceptions."

"But he was my friend," I said, tears streaming down my face once more.

"And it hurts. It's the only thing that hurts anymore."

I stared at her, unable to say a word. And she just ... smiled. Not a cruel smile. Just a weird, creepy smile, so forced I could practically see the strings holding up the corners of her lips.

"Nim is dead," she said, again. "Accept it. Perhaps now you see why I didn't want you along. It's nothing personal. It's just the only thing that hurts anymore."

I said nothing, clarity washing over me like a torrent. Her spite of me. Her cold acceptance of me. Her cold acceptance of Nim.

I did the only thing I could think of: I reached out and hugged her.

And she hugged me back.

We clung to each other awkwardly, not saying a word for the longest time. I would have cried, but I had no tears left. And with Blayde pulled up close against me, strong enough to snap me like a twig if she wanted, I felt the safest that I had in days.

"Oh, I have your bag here, with your—" She pulled away, avoiding eye contact as she did. "Zander thought getting rid of it might help with the pain, but I think it was meant for you to keep. A perfect Cinderella ball gown, just for you."

"Cinderella never had a ... never mind. She, at least, got a happier ending," I said. "The slipper was hers all along, so the prince knew it was her he danced with at the ball and married her."

"In my experience, stories are just that: stories," she said. "No one gets a happy ending. Just an ending."

She handed me the dress, and I clutched it, weighing the cold silk in my fists. Selena had somehow thought it worth putting back in my duffel when she returned that to me. This stupid thing had fared better than a living, breathing person.

"They killed Nim."

"Yes, they did."

"In cold blood."

"They didn't think twice."

"Because of me. I pretended to be goddess. They wouldn't have tried to free us from our *earthly bonds* if I had admitted I was human."

"They wouldn't have, true. But that's not the point. Those people are safe now. The Sky People never finished roasting the planet or abducting the kids. There are other cities on that planet, other continents, full of people who will build a life there because they missed this culling. They're better off for the next time they come. They will no longer be led and controlled by the Evil One. A lot can happen in five thousand years; they'll be ready for the next time."

"But what if they're not?"

"They'll be ready."

"We have to hope, right? That all this was for something?" I sighed. "The Youpaf can turn temples to dust, Blayde. And the prisoner is still loose. Five thousand years may be a long time, but it's not enough."

"The World Eater may be loose, but it's weak. Multiforms, polyshapes, polymorphs, shapeshifters, or whatever you prefer, they take a lot of energy to compress a size like that into a shape small enough to hide. Trust me; it'll be weak for a very long time."

"So, they'll be okay?"

"Definitely." She paused, wetting her lips with her tongue. I realized then, maybe not for the first time, that she was a very convincing liar. "We did good back there, Sally. It might not feel like it, but we did. Angee and Nim did not die in vain."

"They did not," said Zander. He dropped a bag full of berries at his feet, staring at me with wide, questioning eyes. "You're awake."

"Yeah," I said. Duh. That's what it means to be walking and talking, right? It's the definition of not being asleep.

"Are you all right?"

"Yeah."

"You sure?"

I shrugged, nodded, and shook my head all at once. From the outside, it probably looked like a spasm. Zander didn't laugh. He just looked at me as intently as ever.

"Are you going to be?"

Here, I nodded. I was going to have to be. It's what Nim would have wanted.

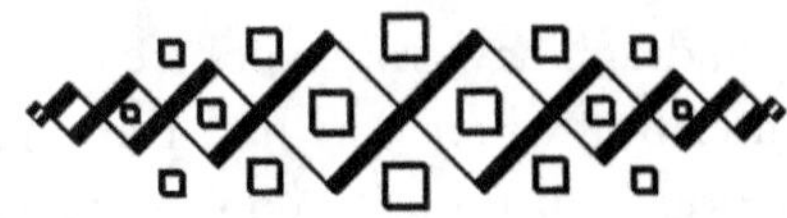

We held a small memorial for him in the forest.

He had never even set foot in a forest. Not one like this. Nim had only seen trees for the first time a few days ago. He would have loved it here. There was so much for him to see.

There was so much Nim would never get to see.

Blayde used her pointer to engrave a stone. None of us knew what to write or say. We hadn't known him for very long, after all. In that time, we had exiled him from his friends and family, everything he had ever known; we had saved him from a life of indentured servitude; we had dragged him through an ill-fated adventure on a planet none of us knew the name of.

He had died there. He would forever remain there. We didn't even have a body to bury.

In the end, we had written his name and his planet of birth. Nimien, from Aria, the fourth human colony. *The boy with stars in his eyes and fire in his veins.*

"We should each say something, shouldn't we?" suggested Zander, his voice almost a mumble. "Blayde?"

She nodded slowly, propping the stone against the base of the tree we had chosen together as Nim's symbolic resting place. She rose, blasting her hands in front of her, staring at the ground. I had never seen her more vulnerable, and I had seen her naked.

"Nimien," she said, her voice heavy, "you should have been with us much longer than you were. You were smart. You were quick. You showed so much potential. You didn't have much choice in what you did with your life, but when you had the chance to do something good, you took it. You impressed me. I'm sorry I'll never get to see what you could accomplish. I'm sorry, kiddo."

She stepped back and glanced up at Zander, a silent signal for him to begin. He cleared his throat, his voice breaking like a pubescent teenager.

Like Nim, when he was scared.

"I'm not sorry for what happened with your people," he said, staring at the stone. "We could have met anyone in your city. Instead, we ran into the only boy who was up after hours. Who pretended to be scared, when, in fact, he had found a way to circumvent the system. Who put on an act the entire time we were there, just so that we had no choice to take you with us."

"What?" I stared at Zander. Blayde did not seem surprised at his words. If anything, it appeared she had known this about Nim, too. I, however, could not believe it. Zander shot me a glance—a glare, even—not to interrupt.

I didn't, but I was shaking.

"You were way smarter than we could ever give you credit for," he continued, "and smarter still than we will ever know. You were a clever boy; you were a partial war. The universe is not going to recover from your loss. You were an integral part of it. While I cannot bring you back, I will keep you alive in my thoughts and memory. The brightest stars burn the shortest amount of time, but they go out with a bang and leave beauty behind. Sleep well, my brother."

And then it was my turn. I hadn't had much time to think about what I was going to say, and after hearing Zander's words, I still wasn't sure if I knew what to say. I stepped forward, staring at the stone, at Nimien's name spelled out before me.

"Nim," I said, letting out a heavy breath, "I didn't have enough time to get to know you. But you were my friend. And no matter who you were or weren't, I'm going to miss you. I'm going to miss you so much. I'm sorry ... for everything."

And I stepped back.

Who was he, really? Had he really manipulated us into taking him from that city? No, he couldn't have. He hadn't wanted to leave. He fought Zander the entire way. He was electrocuted for just being in our presence. How any of that could have been manipulation, I would never know.

Nim wasn't exactly around for me to ask him.

We left the stone at the base of the tree, just as we were going to leave Nim: in the past. Our small camp was packed up and then we jumped. We jumped to a planet with orange skies and milky white lakes. It was not Earth.

Jump.

We fought giant racist beavers on a planet with no stars while they yelled obscenities at each other. It was not Earth.

Jump.

We ate lunch with the king of a small island nation, his castle a ship so large everyone on Earth could have lived on it.

Jump.

Planet of the grapes.

Jump.

Telepathic crystals.

Jump.

Not Earth.

Jump.

Still not Earth.

Jump. Jump. Jump.

The landscapes flickered past my eyes faster than changing channels. I hadn't slept in days. I hadn't said a word in just as long. Jumping no longer hurt; it no longer felt like anything. I couldn't tell if we were the ones moving or if the universe was changing around us.

Maybe Earth had gone by now. Maybe we passed it years ago. I didn't know how long it had been. I didn't know if it would ever stop.

And then, the ice beneath my feet broke, and I let go of the hands that had been holding mine for so long.

# CHAPTER TWENTY-SEVEN

## *I GET MY SOMEWHAT HAPPY ENDING*

I was drowning.

Quickly, I found the light, forcing my hands to dig the water away from me and to claw my way to the surface. I was lucky; it wasn't far.

"Holy fuck, this is freezing!" My teeth chattered like the wheels of a train rushing over a track, as I pulled myself shakily from the pond I had inadvertently crash landed into. Ice lay in clumps above the surface, and I swatted them away as I headed for the bank, my drenched body climbing from the cold water.

It felt even colder stepping out. The wind hit me, and it was like reliving the Ice Bucket Challenge all over again. Even so, I felt chilled to the core; my very bones turned to icicles. Worse than the cold, however, was the terror of being alone.

"Guys?" I shouted into the night, my head snapping around fast enough to give me whiplash. Relief flooded over me as I found them: Zander, pulling himself from the pond and shaking the water from his hair like he were a swimsuit model; and Blayde, sitting casually on a rock near the shore, watching this all.

I let out a sigh, falling backward on the cold snowy bank. The ground was frozen solid, and I instantly regretted this decision.

"Okay," I panted, catching my breath. "Who was steering that time?"

Zander pointed at Blayde. Blayde pointed at Zander. At this point, I wasn't sure either of them cared enough about the destination to even try taking control. They didn't even look at each other as they dropped their hands, going back to their respective activities as if they were on a mission: Blayde, checking her pointer for water damage; Zander, inspecting the trees for something familiar.

I sat up, my shaky hands undoing the waterproof lining of my duffel bag in search of warmer clothes. I found better: my towel. I smiled as I pulled it out, thankful that I lived in the same universe as Douglas Adams.

"So, does anyone know where we are?" I asked as I patted my hair dry, trying to take the ice off of my body and stop my teeth from rattling. But it was going to take a lot more than that to warm me up.

"Deep, lush forest; snow, " Zander said, mechanically pointing out anything that could help us deduce our location. "Water in the pond, nothing dangerous. An oxygen and nitrogen-rich atmosphere, the good stuff. There's too much light pollution to tell what the sky is like, but there are definitely stars above us. We might need to wait for daylight to get more information."

"Any chance this could be Earth?" I asked, hopeful. The trees looked familiar. Heck, even the pond looked familiar. But at this point, it could have been wishful thinking.

"Maybe." Blayde was the one to respond this time. Her voice was harsh as usual, but she was paying more attention to our surroundings than me, so her tone was more deductive than judgmental. "Light pollution means there's a town or city nearby, so let's start there. That would be better than sticking around here in the ass chilling cold."

She was already marching away, her voice dying as she walked deeper into the forest. I stuffed my towel into the bag and slung it over my shoulder, scared to lose my guide. Zander said nothing, pinching and letting go of a tree branch he was analyzing.

I followed Blayde into the thicket, the trees swimming in closer around me than I would have liked. And then—they were gone. I had stepped onto a wide, asphalt street lined with street lamps and sidewalks.

"So much for a lush forest, Zander. More like a park or something of the likes. Come on; let's get the mortal someplace warm before she freezes. We can't lose another—"

She snapped her mouth closed, not finishing the thought. But I knew. We all knew what she meant, who she meant. I took a deep breath, trying to calm myself and center my thoughts.

Zander pushed through the thicket, blinking as the light hit his eyes. He was still frowning as he scanned the street from left to right, trying to taking in the dull, gray buildings and snow-covered street.

Blayde took a single step to cross it, checked both ways, then turned back to us, a weak smile on her face as she waved us forward. As if jinxed, a car raced toward her through the gloom, its headlights piercing the semi-darkness. The brakes screamed as it halted, the driver laying heavily on the horn as he came to a stop only a foot in front of her silver legs. Blayde threw up a hand sign that came off as crude on any planet, but Zander and I could only stand frozen in the middle of the road, staring in awe at the car.

The driver threw his door open, flying out onto the street as if his seat were on fire. He was an older man; his head leant forward slightly; dressed in a thick, wooly sweater that hugged him from the neck to the seat of his pants. As he strode toward Blayde, he shouted, his voice carrying over the silent street.

"Oy, you!" he shouted, his voice thick with an extremely heavy accent. "What the hell is your problem? What are you doing standing in the middle of the fucking road? It's dangerous! The roads are icy as it is. I could have skidded; I might have run you over—"

Blayde stared at him, hands outstretched, as if she were unsure what to do with them.

Joy surged through my body, and I rushed onto the road, ignoring the warnings he had shouted, ignoring the ice below my feet, grabbing the man around the neck and hugging him tight; he hugged me awkwardly back, confused.

"What's that for, Ms. Webber?" he asked, astonished. "Is this your friend? You should tell her—"

"Oh, Arthur, I've never been happier to see you. Ever." I looked up at the stars, the recognizable sky. My sky, my stars, my trees, my snow, my road, my street—my planet.

"I'm home!" I shouted to the heavens, lifting my arms high above my head. The world around me was just as I had left it. Then turning back to Arthur, who was still glaring at Blayde, all I could do was grin.

"Oh, don't mind her," I said cheerfully. "She's just never seen snow before."

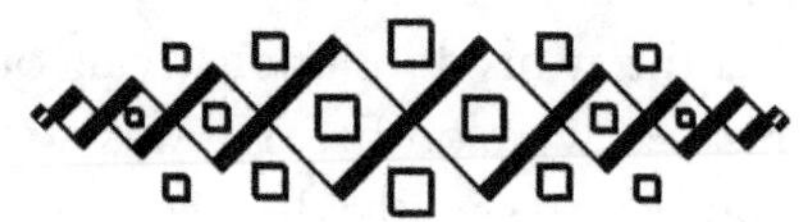

Arthur kindly drove us back to my house, despite the fact we were all soaking wet.

You see? Arthur was a good friend.

He asked no questions as he dropped us off in front of my apartment, and here we were again. This was my door, to my building, on my own planet. There was a part of me that still did not believe we had made it this far, that somehow, through all of this, the universe had brought me back home.

But it had. Thanks, Universe. I guess you can be kinda cool sometimes.

Once he was out of sight, it was time for one last jump; this time into my living room. Having left from within the room itself, I hadn't exactly thought to bring along the keys. Like an idiot, I had also forgotten to turn off the lights. But then again, when you're offered a chance to visit another planet, your lights are the least of your concern.

Just the smell of my apartment was a sufficient welcome back. The potpourri in the corner, the worn leather of the sofa, the mere warmth of the room: It smelled like home. It smelled like a hug.

I dropped my duffel bag next to the armchair and threw myself down on it. This, of course, squashed my nose, but I didn't care at this point. I inhaled the smells of home like I was drowning and this was air.

When I finally pulled myself away, I was happy to see that Zander had gone back to fitting in as well. He sat in his favorite chair, one of the only things I hadn't changed in the living room in the time he had been gone. His eyes closed as he relaxed.

"You want something to drink?" I asked, breaking the silence. Blayde looked up from where she sprawled on the couch, her feet draped over the armrest like she was some kind of big cat. But if she was content, she sure didn't show it.

"Not really," she grumbled, her own eyes closed. The water from her hair was making a small puddle under her head, and I remembered then how wet I was.

"Towel?"

"Nah."

I probably should have imposed on her, but you try telling one of the most powerful women in the universe she needed to dry off. I wasn't going to let anything get in the way of my happy return.

Only, it wasn't happy. I was excited to be home, sure, but there was something missing. Someone who should have been here, alive and happy and free.

I shook the thought of Nim out of my head. There would be a time to mourn him later. As I said, I wasn't going to let anything get in the way of my happiness.

"I'll take a towel," said Zander, prying his eyes open and offering  a weak smile. I heard relief in his voice, glad to be back in this familiar place. "And if the offer still stands, I'll have some water, too, thanks."

"I don't mind brewing us some tea," I suggested. "I think we need it."

"That sounds fantastic," he said, his smile growing wider. "Can you make enough for the three of us? Blayde needs some too. No, you shut it. She does. I'll get the towels if they're still in the same place!"

"They are!" I said, making my way to the kitchen and pulling out the kettle. A glance over my shoulder showed me my note was still firmly in place on the countertop. I guess Taylor had meant it when she said she wasn't coming back.

That's something I was going to have to mourn later, too.

I put some water in the pot to boil, pulling out mugs from the cabinet, expecting Blayde to refuse his offer, but she remained silent so I made sure to get one out for her. With that done, I returned to the living room, booted up my computer, pulled my iPod out of the duffel bag, and plugged it in for a good charge.

"So?" Zander asked absentmindedly, as he stuffed a towel under Blayde's head and gave it a good rub. She said nothing as he dried her hair. "We've got the right where, but dare I ask?"

My eyes lingered on the numbers at the bottom of the screen. I blinked, hardly believing it—how could they be true? They were more improbable than impossible, but, still, the odds of seeing those small numbers were unbelievably high.

"Is everything all right?"

Zander was suddenly behind me, glancing over my shoulder. I pointed a shaking finger at the screen, where the source of my shock sat, unaware of how much they meant.

"It's February 4th," I replied. "1:23 a.m."

"Is that good?" he asked, obviously worried.

"Zander, we left at ten last night," I replied, a wave of relief washing over me. "We were gone for all of five and a half hours. Not even long enough to be missed."

"That's it? Wooo hooo! Woo hoo! Yeah! Yeah!" he cheered, his feet slamming onto the floor hard enough to wake the neighbors, dancing and waving his arms. If we got a noise complaint, it would be his fault. "We did it. We did it!"

"Doesn't the theory of relativity say this is supposed to work the other way around?" I asked, my hands shaking as I put my computer to sleep. "We age slower if we travel near the speed of light than those stuck on the planet, not the other way around. Right?"

"Someone's been doing her homework," Blayde snickered from the couch.

I shrugged. "I had time to brush up on some basic physics while you two were gone."

"But five hours?" Zander interjected, unable to calm his excitement. "That's awesome!"

"But it makes no sense!" I said. "We've been away for weeks, months. The only way we can be back here now is if we traveled back in time, and that's not possible. You said it yourself."

"Oh, shut up," Blayde begged from the sofa, her mood growing increasingly worse as time went by. "Cool, we got you back to your time, to your space. Nice and comfy, cozy. Now, one of us needs a shower, and I think it's evident who I mean." She picked up a pillow, which she threw blindly at Zander. It sailed across the room and crashed into his face, bouncing off and falling into his hands. He rolled his eyes, but his grin didn't waver for an instant.

"Manly odors are *not* pleasant," she continued, smiling only slightly. "And they're more muddy smelling right now than manly—even worse. Hit the shower."

Zander froze, raised his hand to his head to salute, muttered a quick and reproachful "Yes, ma'am," and left the room.

The second the bathroom door was shut and the shower was running, Blayde fixed her gaze on me.

"Did all your stuff arrive in one piece?"

I zipped open my murky, smelly, damp, and slightly singed bag. Its contents were jumbled inside, but nothing seemed broken. Blayde's tools, however, were gone. Sometime between Aquetzalli and now, she had extracted them and had hidden them on her person. Why she did, I would never know.

"No worries here," I replied as I stood and grabbed the bag to walk it to my room, where I placed it delicately on the dresser.

"Which bed do ya want, Blayde?" I asked on my

way back through the kitchen. "You get first choice since Zander's out of earshot."

"I'll take the couch again," she replied, a lack of interest obvious in her tone. "It was nice."

"It's not the same couch, though. My parents stayed here while I was in the hospital after the accident. They didn't dare touch Zander's bed, or mine for that matter, and the couch was put away ... Well, to make a long story short, they had no idea how to refold the bed."

Blayde snorted something that sounded awfully close to a laugh. I was starting to warm to her. How couldn't I? She had saved my life more than a few times, and though she didn't care for me much, she was an incredible person once you got to know her.

I took the armchair Zander had been sitting in and leaned back for the first time since my return home. The comfort I felt was overwhelming. It was such a small thing to come home and sit in your favorite chair, yet it was everything to me.

"I can't believe I'm home." I sighed.

"You didn't think we'd get you back?" asked Blayde, looking up from the couch.

"Sure," I said. "I trusted you to get me home, but I thought I would die before actually getting here."

"I seriously doubt you would have, what with Zander protecting you at every move."

"And you. You're amazing."

She sighed, that familiar tone of annoyance still present in her voice.

"I don't feel that amazing; not right now." She returned her stare to the ceiling. "It used to be me and Zander, traveling the universe, doing what good we could, helping those when we were able, but it's changed now. And then there's you, Sally."

"What about me?"

"You're a natural at this. I mean, the *Traveler*? You solved it. You. And then in Aquetzalli, when they thought you were a goddess? You improvised her character from scratch. You did that all by yourself. And now, I'm going to tell you a secret even Zander doesn't know."

"Blayde," I said, shaking my head. "You don't need—"

"I have to get it off my chest," she snapped. "Because, Sally, back in Aquetzalli, I felt useless. For the first time that I can remember, in hundreds of years of memory, I've never felt useless before."

"Oh, Blayde, don't say that." How else could I reply? "You've saved civilizations. You've saved me. You're not useless."

The shower shut off, and the door to the bathroom opened a minute later. Blayde fell into silence. Zander waltzed back in the room, drying his hair with a towel, clean but wearing the same disgusting clothes he had arrived in: his leather coat covering a muddy brown tee-shirt (was it supposed to be that color?) and a worn, dingy pair of jeans. Unlike her brother, Blayde's shiny, red coat seemed like she had bought it yesterday, though I knew she never left a planet without it.

"Tomorrow morning, we're getting you guys a lot of clothes." The whistling kettle called me back to the kitchen to finish the tea. "I mean it. I'm not too bad off after the incident at the plant. I got a lot of money from the court case, and after everything—"

I turned around. The room was empty. The sofas, now smudged with dirt, were without occupants, the towel Zander had been using in a heap on the floor. Not a warning, not a sound, nor a sign.

They were gone.

They had left me.

# CELESTIAL

If you liked this book, please consider leaving a
review on Amazon and Goodreads.

# ACKNOWLEDGEMENTS

You know, I thought these books would get easier to write over time. The only reason I haven't yet ripped my hair out is because of the people who have screamed some sense into me along the way.

Anna, you helped me take this holey draft and stitch it together into something readable and loveable. Your tough love made Celestial my favorite book yet. Your endless insightful pointers helped shape this book and I really couldn't have done it without you.

Michelle, as always you're the voice of reason and the power that drives me forward. You see directions in my books I didn't think possible. You catch me when I go too deep into some weird delirious sidetrack. I love learning from you and I'm excited to see how far we can go.

Cayleigh, not only do you make this novel sparkle and shine, your notes always bring a smile to my face. I totally got distracted reading an article about poorly written children's books because of you. Thanks for everything.

Apryl, my mom, the best mom in the world and no one can tell me differently, who read Celestial before anyone else and wrote the most encouraging notes I had ever received. You taught me how to read, helped me write my silly stories, shared with me your love of books: I just hope that I can write books that you will love, too, and I'm so excited to keep writing more.

Now the girls to which this book is dedicated. I've been beginning to realize just how many amazing women are part of my team. Having friends like you make me feel like nothing can stand in our way. You fuel me, encourage me, push me to be my best. This book couldn't have happened without you.

Alix, who flew a thousand kilometers to surprise me at my book signing. I keep getting teared up at the memory. Friends like you are so hard to find, and I hope I can be worthy of your friendship for the rest of my life.

Valentine, who challenges me with incredible books, who reminds me to strive harder, that the impossible is something to strive to break. I'm entirely on board for that bookstore. If I ever become a bestseller, you know where my money's going.

Cora, you are incredible. I can't believe we met thanks to Starstruck, and you're the best thing that's come from me writing these books. It's hard to think if I had never published, I wouldn't know you, heck, that's terrifying! You have helped me become a better writer, and I can't wait to write with you, too.

Finally, to Hugo, who's sitting on the couch right now and has no idea I'm writing this. You have no idea how helpful you are. Thanks for letting me anxious-cry on you. Thanks for supporting me even as I spiral into all night writing binges. Thanks for being my voice of reason when my inner voice is busy telling mad space stories.

And as always, to Joanna. Always to Joanna. I love you!

# ABOUT THE AUTHOR

S.E. Anderson can't ever tell you where she's from. Not because she doesn't want to, but because it inevitably leads to a confusing conversation where she goes over where she was born (England) where she grew up (France) and where her family is from (USA) and it tends to make things very complicated.

She's lived pretty much her entire life in the South of France, except for a brief stint where she moved to Washington DC, or the eighty years she spent as a queen of Narnia before coming back home five minutes after she had left. Currently, she goes to university in Marseille, where she's starting her masters of Astrophysics.

When she's not writing, or trying to science, she's either reading, designing, crafting, or attempting to speak with various woodland creatures in an attempt to get them to do household chores for her. She could also be gaming, or pretending she's not watching anything on Netflix.

seandersonauthor.com
www.facebook.com/seandersonauthor
@sea_author